A PLACE OF FOG AND MURDER

A
LOU
TANNER
P.I.
MYSTERY

T.E. MACARTHUR

To the San Franciscan

LOU
TANNER
P.I.

MYSTERY
NUMBER ONE

T. McCul

Also by T.E. MacArthur

Paranormal Thriller Series
The Skin Thief
Pillar of Flesh (working title – coming soon)

Lou Tanner, P.I.
A Place of Fog & Murder
Requiem for the Tin Man (working title –coming soon)

The Volcano Lady Series:
A Fearful Storm Gathering
To the Ending of the World
The Great Earthquake Machine
The Lidenbrock Manifesto
The Doomsday Relic

The Gaslight Adventures of Tom Turner
The Yankee Must Die: Huaka'I Po
Death and the Barbary Coast
Terror in a Wild Weird West
The Omnibus Collection of Tom Turner

Anthologies (Participant):
Twelve Hours Later: 24 Tales of Myth
& Mystery
Thirty Days Later: Steaming Forward
Some Time Later
Next Stop on the #13

A Place of Fog and Murder by © T.E. MacArthur.
Published by Indies United Publishing House, LLC

First Edition — First Printing, 2019
Second Edition, 2023

Book format by T.E. MacArthur
Cover design by S.N. Jacobson and T.E. MacArthur

ISBN: 978-1-64456-645-9 [Paperback]
ISBN: 978-1-64456-646-6 [Mobi]
ISBN: 978-1-64456-647-3 [ePub]
ISBN: 978-1-64456-644-2 [Hardcover]
Library of Congress Control Number: 2023943628

Attributions:
Veteran Typewriter font by Koczman Balint.
Port of San Francisco, Ferry Building: ID 37248306@Celso Diniz
— dreamstime.com

INDIES UNITED PUBLISHING HOUSE, LLC
P.O. BOX 3071
QUINCY, IL 62305-3071

Acknowledgements

To **Lisa Orban** of <u>Indies United Publishing House</u> for all the help and encouragement – and patience. Lots of patience.

To my Street Team: **Lisa Towles, Dover Whitecliff, BJ & AJ Sikes, Bill Christianson, Jeff Cathcart** and **Sharon E. Cathcart** for the amazing support for which I can never say thank you enough.

A tremendous thank you to fellow Indies United author and brilliant editor, **Ana Manwaring**, for Alpha Reading this second edition.

And much gratitude to **Stephen Jacobson** for once again creating a fabulous cover background, one even better than the first cover. I didn't know that was possible.

In memory of Tay McArthur, Mary-Margaret Gridley McArthur, and Patrick James Lacy. You are deeply missed.

Author's Note

Welcome to a strange and wonderful Science Fiction 1930s America. Dieselpunk meets Raymond Chandler. Break out your copies of "The Big Sleep" and "The Thin Man" when you're done here. Pull up a bottle of Old Forester Bourbon and a pack of Chesterfields (actually, you can skip the later – please,) and put on some Billy Holiday. Let go of everything you thought you knew about the time between the world wars, femme fatales, hardboiled detectives, and technology. In short – have a good time – my treat!

Lady Shamus,
damn right that's me.
Flatfoot in heels.

THE CITY AS PROLOGUE

There are different types of danger out in the Big, Bad World. Of them, crime is the biggest. Every crime comes down to greed and fear. And every criminal is either a coward, a blackmailer, or a bully — sometimes they're all of those at the same damn time. And sometimes, they're the good guys.
I speak from experience.

-Lou Tanner, P.I., Notes for female Pemberton Graduates, 1935

The City was a haunting specter tonight. Eerie lights seeped through fingers of thick fog, revealing high-set rainclouds — when you could see them — in the color of dried blood and decomposing yellow. With the late fall comes all the dying. The trees, the leaves, the long days of summer, and the patience of one's fellow man to remember his manners and to keep his homicidal desires to himself.

It was that sort of evening, too. Wet as an overworked cafe dishwasher and colder than a corpse's embrace. *That* sort of evening.

I shoulda' stayed inside with a snoot full of bourbon and a Guy Lombardo concert on the radio. *"Shoulda"* being the operative word.

Look, every city has its tales of wasted youth, unapologetic greed, and emboldened desperation. The deep wounds of history are nothing more than slashes between those who have and those who have not. I've been both of those, up and down, rich and poor, always riding on the hills in life's little cable car.

Such things make people hate big cities.

Me? I like the City.

I guess I do belong here, if only in the shadows.

But, San Francisco, *my city*, brightens all its dark and dingy alleys with unique charms I can't always put my finger on.

Sure, we have old fashioned cable cars left over from the last century. The Ferry Building and the Palace of Fine Arts, still standing after the 1915 Panama Pacific Exposition. The Fisherman's Wharf Amusement Park. Chinatown and its exotic clubs. The Zakheim Murals on the Union Pacific rail aqueducts. The Trolleys and Nightcrawlers. The Montgomery Street Aero & Rail Station. All the architecture of allure.

And all of it a façade cloaking a city hanging on by a thread. Nuthin' but pretty dressing, like a prostitute robed in a hand-me-down Adrian gown she found tossed in the trash by some respectable person who wouldn't be caught dead in anything so out of date.

Any nostalgic, wistful thoughts passed right through my brain and vanished into the bleak fog.

Nostalgia is fine, so long as you are remembering only the good ole' times.

And in this business, my business, and in this city, my city, good ole' times are damn rare and precious.

When one looks for the dirty and the ugly underside of civilization, one can't clutch their pearls when it shows up on a dead body.

CHAPTER ONE

Nobody warns you that the universe is out to get you. Nobody.
In fact, everyone will flat out lie to you, fibbing gleefully about how everything's going to be just fine. If you ask a dead woman, robbed of her future by a murderer, she probably won't lean on the side of optimism.

-Lou Tanner, P.I., Notes for female Pemberton Graduates, 1935

I was hearing things, like desperate cries in the night, the shuffle of predatory feet, and ghosts of murderers past sneering at the dumb dame all alone in the fog and rain.

Me. I'm that dumb dame.

My mother called me Lillian Lucille.
My friends? They call me Lou.
I call myself Private Investigator.

And there I was, the lone woman on a dark, empty street. No excuses — I accepted that job, never mind the blackmail that made me do it. Screw it. If I had to do this, then I had to do it right.
Right?

Anxiety kept rapping on my head, like a drunk trying to get back into the gin joint that had just thrown him out. That rasping, demanding voice kept crying wolf in my ears. I wasn't getting paid for that job. I was alone and wearing the equivalent of a neon sign over me saying, "Come get me."

I shook it off. This was neither the time nor the place.

As I glanced around at the worn neighborhood, with its former glory dwindling away in flaked paint chips, broken windows, and shattered wine bottles, I couldn't help but take stock of my own deteriorating situation, starting with the fact that I was in the Bayview section of town, within spitting distance of *the Pointe*.

Yeah, that place.

Nobody honest ever wants to go to *the Pointe*.

But there I was. It was the last place I wanted to be.

All those depressed rows of buildings could easily be my reality, at a second's notice.

This, or prison.

Uncle Joe would be mortified.

I lit up a Lucky Strike and felt the soothing balm of nicotine fill my lungs. My nerves loosened their death grip on my heart.

It rained for a moment, then returned to heavy, spitting fog. Be nice if it would make up its mind.

Was I nervous? Damn right I was — being human after all. Who wouldn't be, under the circumstances? But I'm no fainting lily. I'm also no Automaton or Robot. 'Tons and 'Bots aren't allowed to do what I do anyway.

An occasional sedan or coupe rolled by with those new-fangled darkened windows, blacking out the driver, and headlamps useless after six feet — a secretive hiding place on wheels. Their tires sucked up the water oozing down from the skies and splattered it in a wider pattern along the road, hissing as they went. Empty corpses of metal? Ghost cars continuing into the night?

I've also got one hell of an imagination.

Then, my heart leapt. There was a Nightcrawler coming down the hill. About time. The sleek, white, bullet-shaped vehicle was

4

headed down the single track that ran past me and the sight of it let some air out of my over-filled anxiety balloon.

Well, damn it. The Available Sign was off. It already had a passenger. It streaked past, splashing some water on the cab stand, and me.

I was alone again. There wasn't enough good light at the cab stand to let me finish reading the magazine getting soggy in my satchel. Not precisely a good night.

I had one last errand to run for the biggest jerk on planet Earth, Agent Jim Mason. This wasn't the worst one of his many unpaid jobs, but it was the last one, or so he'd said. All I wanted was for him to release my license and badge. He promised to shred his false report to the War Department, the one that could and would land me in the slammer for the rest of my days. Lousy blackmailer. I tried not to spit and cuss. Not a pretty behavior for a lady, or so my mother was always reminding me.

The *Pemberton Correspondence School of Private Investigation's* essential course book and manual had nothing on what to do when the Shamus is the victim. I had memorized every chapter, and that topic didn't make the cut. I walked into this with my eyes open and my brain asleep.

I let a long exhale empty my lungs into a spectral billow in front of me.

My disguise, the one Agent Mason ordered me not to use, itched. I don't take orders from anyone. Not my style. Sure, I could leave off the disguise, sure, if I wanted everyone to know what I was up to and exactly who I was. Which I don't. Expose my identity during one of his jobs? Not a chance.

Normally, I pass for Myrna Loy, the actress. Dark hair, dark eyes, wicked jaw. Not tonight. I did everything necessary to look plain, dull, and invisible.

And it had worked. So far.

Now, "*plain, dull, and invisible*" was sopping and exhausted from running errands for an ungrateful former-client turned first-rate blackmailer. And, I was tired of knowing things — mostly things I didn't want to know.

Twenty minutes since I pushed the 'Crawler signal. So tempting to hammer that button again and again, cathartic in fact, but it wouldn't help — the eye-burning beacon lighting up the sky above me blazed as it was supposed to.

Damn, it's quiet. Like a ghoul is creeping up on you quiet.

Nothing but the low, mechanized rumble from the Hunter's Pointe Militia Base. I was far too close to that place for my comfort.

In this silence, every twitch and shake of a leaf might as well be a clap of thunder. My ears strained for fog horns, arguing couples, stumbling drunks — anything. Hell, the latest Fats Waller tune on a badly-tuned radio somewhere would be perfect. My ride showing up would be the best of all.

I could hear my own heartbeat.

Hairs on my neck, those not stuck there by the damp, stood on end.

Smell. More like, stench. I was acutely aware of every scent in the air, like a predator being stalked by something much, much bigger than itself. Sharp. Decaying. Filthy. Moist.

I held my cigarette up to take another drag and saw my hand was trembling. Must be the chill in the air. I don't scare easily – that was my story and I planned on sticking to it.

And it was too quiet.

San Francisco is a damn big city, despite its small real estate footprint. Damn big cities make damn big noises.

It was deathly quiet.

Then the Golden Gate fog horn moaned, calling out like a prognosticator of doom beyond the horizon.

My shoulders relaxed. Hey, it was sound. That creepy horn worked fine for me.

Footsteps.

Short stride. Fast. Cloppy — maybe a hollow heel. A woman's shoes. Like my mother used to wear. Scuffing. Sliding. Irregular rhythm. My guess? She was moving fast but looking back to see what was behind her. It tripped up her pace.

My hand dropped to my hidden gun. Fingers slid hopefully to the .41 Remington Double Derringer holstered in a stocking holster, clipped on my leg. The cab stand was partially shadowed by an awning that covered it and the open space between it and a dilapidated phone booth that hadn't been serviced in years. I just fit in that small gap and it was a good place to stay low. Unseen.

Those footsteps were close. I'd lay a bet they were coming from that alley one door up from the stand.

A trickle of water poured from the corner of the awning and splashed on the asphalt below, spitting droplets in all directions.

I'd looked down that alley before calling my hack. Its dark outline was only pronounced by the remnants of a neon sign that once read, "Open 24 Hrs." The windows on the building, a former Mom-n-Pop, were boarded up. Only the "O" and "N" still blinked and glowed. This had been a neighborhood with hope — once upon a time. Before the Pointe.

Footsteps. Slowing. Coming closer.

I braced and pushed harder into the shadows between the stand and the phone booth. I could be wrong, but I didn't think the alley went through to another street. At the end was a cigarette advertisement, painted on the back of a brick building from the next street over, lit by one phosphorescent lamp.

I pushed harder into my shadows.

A gal rounded the corner from the alleyway, rushed past me, splashed my feet with puddle juice, and hurried along without slowing down to say sorry. She didn't see me. She was covered head to foot in expensive looking clothes. She hugged the shadows and moved without a steady gait. I got the feeling she'd melt into the building's brickwork if she could. Her every move said she wanted to be somewhere else, fast, like death was right on her heels and she owed it a gambling debt.

Was it the weather she was dodging? Yeah, right. Any gal who willingly runs in those heels must be afraid of something, and it isn't a light rain shower.

At the end of the block, she stopped and looked both ways. Turning slightly, she noticed the cab signal shooting the company's emblem onto the clouds above. Her hands released their death-grip on her coat and fell to her sides, still knotted up into fists.

She wasn't just afraid, she was terrified.

Then, that was when I heard the other steps — following her route down the alley.

So did she.

The gal froze and gripped the collar of her coat tightly to her throat. The shadow from her hat covered most of her face. I could see that her lips were parted, panting, waiting to scream.

Heavy footsteps echoed from the alley. Flat-footed. Thudding. Regular, like a trained athlete sprinting to the end.

Masculine.

Call it my *Women's Intuition*, but it was obvious to me, the gal needed help. I got into this business to help.

I dropped my cigarette into the puddle at my feet, crushed it with my toe, and walked out from the shadows, getting drenched in the process. The scuff of my shoes on the sidewalk and my sudden appearance made her jump. She stifled the scream she'd almost released.

"You look lost," I said, a little loudly. Not the wittiest thing to say, but I waved like an idiot, trying to appear to be Jane Average.

"No. I ... ah ... need to find someone. I mean, I'm looking for ..." She walked a few steps toward me. I still couldn't see her face for the hat brim pulled low and the coat collar pulled high, but she was thin, had a fashionable silhouette, and a voice that was a little high pitched. Fear was gripping her. "Actually, I am all turned around," she admitted too quickly and sickeningly-sweet for my comfort. "I need to get over to ... another neighborhood."

Thought you were looking for someone or someone looking for you?

Her story was adjusting to the circumstances. I knew the type — truth was just a tool of the moment. Okay, so, she was still in some sort of trouble, and I didn't let go of my *Galahad* response just because she was struggling to keep her story straight. I kept smiling for her and listening for those other footsteps.

Now? Nothing.

Not even a cousin, twice removed, of an echo.

The masculine footsteps had stopped. Maybe, he was waiting to see what I'd do, or what she'd do now that I was in the picture. More gut instinct here, but it wasn't hard to put this scenario into clear scope.

She approached me, and her voice had a little throb in it, right where she'd put it on purpose. "Your 'Crawler is coming. May I take it?"

And leave me here in the rain, with someone tailing you? Mere blocks from the creepy, secretive goings-on over at the Pointe?

Hell no.

"It's very important I get where I'm going fast," she pleaded.

Glancing up the street, and over toward the alleyway, I couldn't see anyone. I hadn't imagined those footsteps, had I? "We can share. That'd be fine by me. I'd like to get out of the …" I let my gesturing at the clouds finish my sentence.

"Oh, yes, of course. Of course, we can share, that would be great, these cabs take so long, you know, and it would be better to share the cost anyway, don't you think, two gals off to the races ought to share a cab, are you heading over to Union Street? Everyone's always going over there." she quivered, thinking her babbling made her sound confident.

"That's us, two gals who shouldn't be out alone, on a day like this. You sure you don't need more than just a cab? Maybe a policeman or —"

"No, no! Just a ride. It's all I need."

"It's none of my business but you look to be in trouble."

She opened her mouth. Something told me that she wanted to talk. "I'm … I'm … wait, here's the cab," she pointed.

Boy-howdy, you can bank on 'Crawlers having good timing, especially when you don't need them to. The mechanized cab was heading down the hill in our direction.

Okay, we'd get in the cab and I'd get her to start talking again. Not that I really had time for this, but I sometimes just can't help myself. Shamus to the rescue.

"Look at me, all discombobulated. I'm just running terribly late, I'm all confused, silly me." She had that affected, Mid-Atlantic accent I knew all too well. "I hope you haven't been waiting too long, I mean, the weather is dreadful, don't you think so, it's just dreadful and I didn't expect to be out, I would have packed an umbrella …" We were back to the babbling.

The 'Crawler's locks popped for us. The passenger section slid out and she slid partially into the seats, not leaving enough room for me to get in. Nice. I'll need to get pushy. I'll need to get a good look at her too, once we were underway.

Her hands were shaking. She grabbed off her gloves before sliding a little further in. Still not enough room for me … oh Wow-wee, she had a rock on her finger worth twenty-G's if a dime. It found light in this darkness to sparkle.

"Latin Quarter, Broadway at Columbus," she said to the brass speaker-horn. 'Crawler, driver-less cabs were operated by dispatchers down by the wharf.

Honey, weren't you going to Union Street? Ah Truth, the ever-flexible Demon.

Her head was covered first by a patterned scarf of roses and leaves, silk to be sure, and then a grey Fedora pulled way down. Gloves were now sitting in her lap. Overcoat, it still taking up too much of the seat. I'd needed to get closer to gander a look at her, while she faked a giggle and a fussed over making room for me. Finally. I could play along for a while longer.

Perky nose, in silhouette, plus pouty lips. Young, I thought, but couldn't confirm it until I had a chance to look at her skin and eyes. Her jawline hadn't started its slow descent into antiquity, as mine had.

A kicked-bottle made a startling racket in the dark. A man stopped where the neon light pierced into the alley, and faced me, knife in hand. That was definitely a knife. No imagining that. While it gleamed in the street light, he drew back so his face remained shadowed.

"Hey, you, hold it right there!" I shouted. Oh yeah, Lulu, that move was genius. Pure genius.

He retreated further back on seeing me point at him and turned on his heel to flee the scene.

"Stay here," I commanded the scared gal.

I had my heater out from under my skirts in less than two seconds. An old-fashioned weapon, but damn if it didn't do the job.

Pushing away from the cab, I braced against the brick building and checked down the alley. A figure, in silhouette, down by the lit cigarette ad, ran away, stumbling, and trying to not be there in a big hurry. His confidence level had changed; he wasn't running as surely as before. I moved quickly into the alley, gun held up with both hands.

He stopped only long enough to get a look me over; not that I got anything better than a crappy eye-balling of him. His silhouette gave me bits to mark him by, not much else. Overcoat. Narrow brimmed hat. Compared with the trash bin he ran past, I decided he was tall. His coat could conceal virtually any body size, but my quick impression was one of athletic health. Not much to go on, but better than nothing.

"Miss," I called back toward the 'Crawler, "if that guy was following you, I think you can relax now. We should take you to the police, so you can —"

The cab door slammed shut and the 'Crawler sped away.

She left me here.

Alone.

Knowing someone had been chasing down the alley.

Damn it.

The rain started coming down in much bigger drops and I swear I thought I saw a flash of lightning.

The fog horn cried out and I detected a slight snicker in it.

Abyssinia, doll, as they say. Be seein' ya.

Whatever trouble you're in, Sweetheart, isn't my business anymore. I sure hope no one leaves you stranded in the rain.

Grabbing up my damp skirt to put away my heater, I cursed her a couple more times.

It got quiet again and I felt conspicuously alone. Again. After listening for anything normal, the wailing trumpet of Louis Armstrong started floating down from one of the apartments to challenge the foghorns to a duel.

Wet, or cold, or both, I still had a job to do. One way or another, I was getting soaked.

Did I mention I could be a real sap sometimes?

Chapter TWO

Fear does several things. It pours ice down your spine.
It makes your legs fail you. Your senses telescope
down to a pin-point and you forget the feeling in your
hands. It's not just in your mind — it's physical and
visceral. But we humans were built to respond by
either fleeing or freezing. A P.I. has to fight such
responses or die trying.
If only it were that easy.

-Lou Tanner, P.I., Notes for female Pemberton
Graduates, 1935

I made my way back to my office, taking odd routes
where I could see if someone was tailing me. Uncle Joe taught
me that, and it's my habit now.

Tanner Private Investigations greeted me on my office
door.

Tarps still protected my recently acquired, previously
misused furniture. Drying paint fumes filled my nose. The
walls and the window sign weren't done yet. Oh well. The
painters said it would be another day. My satchel fell over on
the secretarial desk. I righted it, cautiously, then seeing nothing
exploded, I backed away. The pins coming out of my wig set
loose waves of relief on my scalp and freed the monster
headache waiting in the dark. My feet hurt, my hair hurt, and I

was damp through and through. But — I was alive. And there awaited something decidedly alcoholic in my desk, in the next room.

Sauntering over to my desk, the clunk of my shoes kicked off provided some satisfaction, countered by my tugging on one particularly disagreeable hairpin.

The door slammed closed behind me.

I spun to face it, a heavy paperweight giving my knuckles extra gravitas.

Agent Mason, jerk Bruno, G-man, and tasteless dresser stood with his hands buried deep in his overcoat pockets. I saw that slight lump under his arm, no doubt his shoulder-holster complete with government issued rod.

I felt my sass rising in my chest, wrestling for room with my pride. Walking out to him, I decided the sooner I got this over with, the better.

He stuck out his hand, demanding without actually asking. I looked at his hand and tossed the wig into it. "I told you not to go in a disguise. They can see right through that sort of …"

"Relax. They didn't."

"I told you not to."

"And I assessed the situation and decided to ignore you." I gave him my back to stare at. I had a bottle of something medicinal in my desk, like every good detective should, and I wasn't offering him any. Not a drop.

"Where is it?" Mason was the kind of guy who makes your skin crawl when he talks. His sentences tended to end with a squeak, as if he wasn't sure if he would stop yacking.

"Didn't your mother ever tell you, you get more with honey than vinegar?" I turned and pointed down at the satchel and glowered. "Help yourself, or do you need me to serve it up on a tray, with a sprig of mint?"

Mason didn't like it when I talked back to him. He hadn't since the first time I'd sassed him. Too damn bad.

He scrounged around in my satchel to find the file. Once he opened it, he ignored me, so I poured myself a shot of Bourbon from the bottle I retrieved from my desk. Glass in hand, I strolled back into the front office.

"I was guessing you were more of a Rye girl, being from upstate New York." He didn't bother looking me in the eye.

"You need to do better homework. I lived on both coasts and one-time overseas. I drink what I like." I sarcastically saluted him. Resting my sore backside on the edge of the front-office desk, drinking deeply, observed him. Not that I really wanted to. I wanted to go to bed.

His hazel eyes raced across each page inside the file. "You know what's in here?"

"Nope. Nor do I want to." I continued to sip.

He finally looked up at me with a disingenuous smile. "You should. Turns out we have —"

"Stop!"

"I thought you were curious about —"

"What part of S.T.O.P escapes your understanding? I don't want to know. I didn't want to know about the goings-on at Hunter's Pointe either, but you set me up for that one. Happily, I know nothing about your current hustle. Call it 'willful ignorance.' Any honest sleuth wants nothing to do with dangerous, paramilitary nutjob nonsense. I'm done. Got it? Done. Do I need to spell it for you too?"

At first, he seemed annoyed, then amused. "I didn't ask you earlier, did you see anything interesting at the Pointe, when you were there?"

"No! I met your contact outside the security perimeter."

"Liar. Oh well, it doesn't matter. We got what we needed tonight. And they ain't the wiser, or so you tell me."

"Sure, they are." I drank deeply, letting him see the gorgeous amber contents of my glass. "Maybe your current mark followed me here." Now I was the one lying, but I needed to gauge his reaction. As much as he acted like one, Jim Mason wasn't a fool.

"You don't need to worry." He needed to convince himself more than me.

"Just like that. I don't need to worry." Oh Sarcasm, my best friend.

"I wouldn't worry about it. I told you, you were only getting a file for me. They ain't the sort to get too upset. Now, the boys at the Pointe? Those militia boys enthusiastically play soldier. Still … maybe you don't need to worry about them either."

"You should. Don't blackmailers get their comeuppance in the end?" I asked, allowing the alcohol to end my sentence for me. "You got what you want, how about you ante-up with my license and badge, and that damn fake report to the War Department."

Laughing, he waved me off. "I didn't bring those out tonight. I wasn't sure you'd be successful. Besides, I might need another favor."

Another?

Damn him … another!

I didn't want to be right about this, but I was. The blackmail never ends. He'd never stop, because men like him never do. He forced me to do his bidding at the cost of my career and my livelihood. Probably my life. That was how it worked.

Rage can be a funny thing. I don't remember too much between his gregarious comment and my planting my heater right between his shocked and terrified eyes. He raised his hands in a warding gesture.

When it comes to rage, I can be ambidextrous.

I switched that sweet derringer to the left hand and prodded his coat with my right. Out came his rod, and he swallowed either a curse or a protest.

"Hold on, Lou, I'll bring them by tomorrow. I promise." He coughed and raised his hands as if to ward off any attack.

When this angry, I become a whole other person — someone you don't ever want to meet. "No," I spit through my teeth, "you'll meet me tomorrow morning at Crabtree's Signal Tower, at Kearny and Market, eight a.m. You'll have my documents, a signed declaration stating you've decided you haven't any complaint about me, your so-called report to the War Department, and my badge." Each word came out with force.

"Lou, I —"

"You wrote up that little piece of garbage putting my life in danger. You set me up to take the fall for you. They shoot traitors, you know, if they don't hang them."

"No, no, you got me all wrong, Lou." His tone was desperate, and I took so much satisfaction in that. He took a tiny step back. "I was just kidding about favors. Sure — I'll give you everything you asked for. You got my word."

Liar. Coward. I thought it so hard, it came out of my mouth.

"Miss Tanner, do you understand how many laws you're breaking right now?" Oh, he tried to sound tough, but I'd shaken him up too hard. "I gave you my word. I'll give you back your badge, license, the report, everything. Scout's honor."

"I should take the word of an agent of the government who interfered with the proper conduct of the City and County of San Francisco and tampered with the U.S. Mail by intercepting legally issued licenses, then blackmailed a civilian with a false accusation? It's a damn wonder the War Department isn't here trying to arrest me."

"I never gave the report to them. My word of honor."

"Take your word of honor? What honor? Interfering with the mail is a Federal offense. Think your bosses like your dirty laundry showing up in the papers? Don't fool yourself, I'll do it — no, no — shut your yap — I don't want to hear it."

Mason went white as a sheet, maybe even a little green.

He opened his mouth, but nothing came out.

My little .41 confidence maker was doing its job on both of us. "Eight o'clock, tomorrow morning. Got it, Mason?"

"So, what if I give you your little badge — what then? You think you'll hop right into business and start makin' a load? You're a dame. No one will ever take you seriously. I'm the only one who giving jobs to you. Me. And I own your ass, Honey. I don't have to give you nothin'." The words caught in his throat in places, but he was planting his feet.

My heartbeat was pounding inside and outside my head. Everything shrank down to the point where I was keeping my rod pressed on his skull. "Crabtree Signal Tower — Kearny and Market," I repeated slowly.

"Why should I? I'm a government agent. To you, I am the government. I can do whatever I deem —"

My answer was a right hook.

I broke his nose and when he tried to recover, I pounded him again.

Most girls don't know they can do that.

I'm not most girls.

I left him on the floor, dazed and bleeding, and I unabashedly took possession of the all-important file. He crawled away from me, clutching his bleeding schnoz. The file he desperately wanted fit perfectly back in the satchel next to my copy of *The Black Mask* and *D&S Detective* magazines.

I wondered briefly if he had any idea an average dame could do that to a full-grown man? Apparently not, and besides, I've never been an average dame. I strolled out as if nothing happened.

After such a performance, my only logical next stop? Stan's Bar on Franklin. I didn't care how wet I'd get hoofing it over. I wanted another drink and a chance to smoke the rest of the pack if I wanted to. All the way there, I fumed and replayed the incident over and over in my head, along with a variety of responses I was too sleepy to think of. Damn the consequences.

Drinking and smoking. The perfect combination.

I didn't used to be like this — all anger and gun pointing. In fact, it's bad form to go waving one's gun around, but as a PI, I sometimes need the motivator.

I needed to remain a class act, damn it.

I thumped on through the door of Stan's, looking like a wet sheepdog, took a booth, and settled in.

The place was fairly empty. I guess the weather kept the regulars at home. A man arrived after me and took a spot at the bar. Now, there were two of us. He looked like the average down-on-his luck fellow trying his best to keep up his dignity. He took off his cheap but decent hat and ran his fingers through thick salt and pepper hair, leaving some of it sticking out in odd directions.

Stan himself walked up to me. In his late fifties and as wide as he was tall, Stan looked at me cock-eyed. "Bad day, Lou?"

"I've only been coming here for a couple of weeks. What makes you think —"

"I'm a bartender. Ya think I don' know dat look? I know dat look. Bourbon? Neat?" I love his Big Apple accent. Reminds me of home.

"Yeah, you know me alright. Thanks. Oh, and Stan, put that fellow's drink on my tab."

He looked over at the man at the bar. "Want an intro? I ain't acquainted with 'em. Doesn't come in here regular like."

"No." I held up my hand, with a cigarette already balanced between my fingers. "No, I just — sometimes it's good to do something nice. No credit to me, just tell him to leave his coin in his pocket and enjoy his drink."

For a moment, Stan shook his head. "If yer gonna' be in the Big Boy's business, ya gotta' stop bein' nice. *Nice* don't get ya nowheres."

I lit up.

Nice should get you somewhere, shouldn't it?

The man at the bar looked confused when Stan refused his money. The down-on-his luck fellow was a nice-looking guy. Heavily lined features: what I call an interesting face. Maybe I should let Stan introduce me, but honestly, the last thing I needed was a fling.

Stan's always right — nice should get you somewhere, but it doesn't. I pushed the half empty cigarette case out in front of me and accepted my drink from Stan.

Drinking and smoking.

Reminded me of when I was last in the Big Apple. My pal and famous detective, Nick Charles, went through a pack and a half of cigarettes, not to mention a bottle of Scotch, in the time we were waiting for his wife to finish up at the Salon. My hero, Mrs. Charles. Most folks would expect I'd prefer Nick. He's swell and all, and a damn fine P.I., when working, but it's the Missus who had the bulk of my admiration. Nora Charles was as sharp as a razor and twice as smart as her spouse. But like the rest of us dames, the credit doesn't come her way. I still like her plenty. Heck, she even looks more like the actress who plays her in the picture-shows than I do. I look like Myrna Loy or so everyone tells me.

I didn't need to smoke them all tonight, so I grabbed the case and shoved it back in my bag.

I missed them — the Charles. I missed my old friends in New York, but it was the price I had to pay for restarting my life.

My friends out here were few and I was happiest that way. I preferred the controlled solitude of managed loneliness.

I sat down in a back booth. The cushion under me was loose. Surreptitiously, I slipped the file underneath. Just in case Mason's embarrassment wasn't enough to stop him from trying something stupid before eight tomorrow morning. I could drop by Stan's in the morning when he was restocking and cleaning, and I could retrieve it before my meeting.

Drinking and smoking. Until my eyes wouldn't stay open. After a while, it puts loneliness on the back burner.

The man at the bar kept peeking over at me. It was the booze talking, but his eyes looked me over as if trying to be amused. As if he knew me.

Paranoia all over again.

In that moment, I decided I'd had enough to drink.

I sobered right up and headed home using every indirect route I knew. At least this time, I worried for nothing.

Stan the bartender was more than a little surprised when I asked to come in around seven forty-five. I was more than a little surprised to find him awake and supervising the deliveries. Did Stan ever sleep?

The expression on his face told me he wasn't happy I'd used his bar as a safety deposit box. Sure, I apologized, as I retrieved the file. He was due that much.

"Ya remember dat mug, dat one you bought a drink for last night?"

Sort of. "Sure," I said, shoving the file into my bag. "What of it."

"Left right after you did. Watched you walkin' up the hill."

"Didn't sit well with your gut," I asked, trusting in my bartender's intuition.

"Yup. He didn't follow you, but he did watch where you got off to."

"Good thing I never take direct routes home." I patted Stan on the shoulder. "Thanks, Stan. I appreciate you watching my back."

"If yer Uncle Joe was here, he'd powder my brains if I let some mug pester you. Ya keep yer peepers open — I ain't always gonna be dere."

The mention of Uncle Joe made my chest tighten. I guess some hurts don't ever go away.

I love it when I'm right.

At eight a.m. sharp, Mason met me at the Signal Tower, all by himself, looking more than a little sheepish. A bandage covered the bridge of his nose and a little dried blood still lingered around the edge of his nostrils.

I picked that time of the morning just to be a rat — it was too early for the likes of Mason, and he probably hadn't slept very well — not that I had either, but a broken nose was about as uncomfortable as it gets. The bruise on his temple guaranteed that he'd slept on his right side. Personally, I hoped he had nightmares about being caught as a blackmailer or getting the stuffing pounded out of him by me. Both carried a promise of shame, which I found satisfying.

Me? I'd dressed up a bit — why not? My togs were a little out of date, but then, when does a hounds-tooth wool suit ever go out of style? It was a single-breasted, hip-length jacket with matching skirt and overcoat. Blue silk scarf knotted into a bow at the collar, black oxfords, heels, this time, gloves and beret completed a fashionable appearance.

My little derringer was in my purse for the moment. I felt ready for anything Agent Mason might dish out.

Out, in front of God-n-everyone, I made him hand over my license and badge and one life-ending false report.

Dejected and embarrassed, not to mention bluing under both eyes and swollen from his broken nose, Mason pulled his hat down and his collar up.

Me, I felt like the weight of the world was coming off my shoulders. Watching him try to dodge all the automobiles and Trolleys and Nightcrawlers, while crossing Market at Third Street, was funny. A 'Crawler almost got him too. Ha! I was counting on never seeing his mug again, yet, deep inside, I was sure I would. Men like Mason were Users, and Users always come back like a bad penny.

Well, I wouldn't see him for a little while. Certainly not until his nose healed. And, while he'd never let me pull that move on him again. I'm not out of options. I'd think of something else.

The morning was cloudy and still foggy, but some streams of sunlight worked their way out and to the ground. Maybe we're in for some finer weather?

I really did feel lighter. Not that I was surprised, with everything taken into consideration, but my sense of doubt about ever escaping Mason's clutches had been heavier than a locomotive. And I know my locomotives.

I took a moment to light up a cigarette and admire the Lotta Crabtree Signal Tower Fountain. The Signal Tower was a handsome bit of public art. Bronze cast and glowing, despite the fog still milking on penthouses like a kitten. Lion's heads, griffins, etched-glass images of sailing ships, rose above the ornate base. Victorian aesthetic decoration wrapped the tower with its bright lamp, one hundred and fifty feet above the street. At the top was a speaker for public emergency announcements and a red light, all part of the City's warning system. In theory, we would be directed on where to go and what to do in case of an invasion or an earthquake. Presuming anything broadcast over the City speakers could be heard and understood. The monthly tests sounded like muffled screams, hardly intelligible.

The actual water fountain stopped working in '06, when the Big Quake mangled the pipes below it. It was dizzying in its outrageousness, but then, so was Lotta.

Wind whipped down Market, making me pull my coat collar tighter. None of the trees had much left in their branches to blow away but plenty of leaves still covered the sidewalk, plastered in place by the damp.

Swaying with each bump in the sidewalk, a Delivery 'Ton, with a basket of milk bottles in each hand, worked its way down the sidewalk. Its human-esque form looked completely non-threatening. Big wheels replaced legs and it moved slowly enough to avoid colliding with pedestrians. The name of the dairy farm decorated its tin chest. It was sweet in some ways.

Two down-on-their-luckers changed their path to close in on it. One shouted at it about 'Tons taking jobs from humans, while the other knocked one of the baskets of milk bottles to the ground. The 'Ton stopped to try to pick up the basket, and the two men were on it — kicking and yelling, slamming dents into its semi-hollow sides.

I yelled.

I don't know why. The 'Ton didn't feel anything. I just couldn't stop myself. I was witnessing bullies at work. I learned the hard way, there were few things more loathsome than a bully.

Others on the street were of a similar mind.

The Ne'er-do-wells ran away, laughing. The cops won't do anything. They hardly lifted an eyebrow for humans when harassed on the street, they certainly weren't interested in helping mechanical gizmos.

We had trouble getting it back up onto its wheels. After a moment, it took its one remaining set of bottles, reconnected with its delivery signal, and rolled away.

Was it the human-style form that made me sympathize with it? Or just that I despise bullies so much I would defend a rock from one? Was I a so-called underdog; maybe I just projected myself onto the mechanism, like a reel at the picture shows. I am human, even when I don't want to be.

Humans aren't the "be all, end all of intelligent life," despite what we tell ourselves constantly. In fact, we had the habit of being pretty damn lousy. I guess my optimism hadn't woken up this morning.

First, we used and abused the Negroes. Then the Irish. The Jews had always been someone's scapegoat, which certainly didn't make it right. Now, we had technology we never imagined before, and instead embracing the convenience, we feared being displaced by them. Same damn fear just focused on a new target. Fear made bullies and fear made good people do stupid things. I was proud for a moment I wasn't only person rescuing that 'Ton. My philosophy was simple: no bully can be tolerated, even if he was haranguing non-sentient things like 'Tons and 'Bots. It was wrong. Period!

At my feet were puddles of milk — wasted. Hungry mouths waited in the shadows and alleys of the City, and waste was inexcusable.

What I could do about it, I did.

What I couldn't, well, I'd accept it. For now.

With my diploma from the *Pemberton Correspondence School of Private Investigation*, and an operating license from the City and County of San Francisco, all in hand, I was armed and ready for my new life.

Breathtaking client?

Desperate evil gangster?

That was how it always started in the pulp novels, wasn't it?

I was happy with the reality of investigation work. What happened in the pulps was great to read but nowhere near realistic.

I'd be busy ordering basic, take-me-serious stationary, and acquiring a couple of necessary items, eating lunch while I had the chance, and otherwise setting up shop.

I even managed to barter a couple of extra office chairs, leftover from the previous tenant, for a pair of opener tickets for the Seals. Sure, they'd sold off Joe DiMaggio, but he wouldn't be gone for another year. That meant this year could offer some of the best ball played at Seal Stadium. Too bad they'd traded a star like DiMaggio, not a smart move, and I'd thought better of Lefty O'Doul's management.

All those errands for me included picking up the evening paper, and to see if the latest copies of the Black Mask and the Diesel & Steam Detective magazines were in yet.

A man bumped into me. Tall. Moving too fast. Hidden under layers of winter attire. He mumbled something. I didn't catch it.

I stopped for a moment.

The sidewalk was nearly empty. Why had he —?

My hand dropped down into my purse. A wave of relief cooled my skin — my badge and coin purse were still there. Everything was still there.

Staring down the street as I double checked the purse, I couldn't find him. He vanished. But I remembered that he'd been like Alley-man from the night before, yet not so solid or wide. I didn't have the same sense of size from him. But, damn my senses, I needed facts.

He was nowhere to be seen.

Then I found it.

The note he'd left me.

CHAPTER THREE

Every case has a beautiful client — that someone to
fill the role of Damsel in Distress — and a horde of
lowlifes to complicate matters. I learned right away
that you can't assume what actors are coming to your
stage or what roles they'll play when they get there.

-Lou Tanner, P.I., Notes for female Pemberton
Graduates, 1935

I gaped at it, knowing perfectly well it wasn't something I'd
forgotten in my purse. A flat, crisply folded piece of paper. I read it,
twice, three times, then crushed it in my hand. My fingers froze. I
turned around a dozen times, to check who was where and doing what.
As they say, "just 'cause you're paranoid doesn't mean someone isn't
out to get you."

I hate it when I'm right. I hate it when they're right.

The street tunneled down to a pinpoint of sound and threat.
Every movement rattled my attention and twisted my core. Didn't take
detective school training to know — the man who'd bumped into me
had dropped it in my purse.

A note.

Three words.

Sprinting to the office, in the Fox Theater Building at 1352
Market Street, Suite 333-A, I was greeted by the completed sign on the

far window. The painters had done a good job. And for a moment, I chose to ignore the crumpled note in my hand.

My office was on the third floor, overlooking Market Street, a couple of blocks from City Hall, out in front of the Civic Auditorium. Situated on the southwest wing of the building, I had a great view of the street. The decorated arch above the Fox Theater marquee was as iconic a frontage as any building had the right to. The building offices had separate entrances to each wing and the occasional difficulty of having to claw your way through a line of unyielding ticket-holders.

My fingers began to warm from the exertion alone.

The more I thought about it, the more I dismissed the note as nothing more than a creeper writing out his sickness rather than whispering it in my ear. Or, shouting it at the world.

I wondered if the guy might be one of Mason's cronies — a notion heating me up faster than anything else today. I wouldn't put it past Mason to be petty. Mason's embarrassment changed the situation — he was acting on impulse driven by his wounded manhood. He wouldn't call in official help after he'd been pummeled by a woman he'd blackmailed. Especially because he'd taken a beating from a woman.

Then, of course, my original premise still held up under scrutiny; the man from the alley, with the knife, was responsible for the note.

No. I was wrong. It wasn't Alley-man. I'd been in disguise, and it had been dark and raining, and my sense of Alley-man was his bulky overall presence. The note-leaver left me with the impression of being thin. But no. It wasn't Alley-man.

It was just a creep trying to play me.

I let my breath flow out with all the tension. I had more important things to do than to pay attention to the note I shoved back in my purse. Much better things.

My office. My sign.

I love the window now. It didn't only welcome me, it declared me, Lou Tanner, heart, mind, and soul — a flatfoot — a Private Eye.

It looked good.

My heart settled into a satisfied rhythm.

My insides warmed at the sight.

There are plenty of barriers for a gal like me to overcome. And I need to get past them right quick. Rent was due soon enough.

Hell, since Investigations is the chosen title, as opposed to "Investigator," it suggested a whole company full of employees, and one might go so far as to mistake me for the secretary.

That reminded me — I needed a secretary. Maybe I should hire a man for the job — to be a wiseacre and throw this man's world for a loop.

The letters were in blue on a cream-colored rectangle. They were also painted on the reverse, so everyone in the building across the street could read them. My neighbors were no doubt thrilled. Thrilled if they can see it past the bright red and white "Fox" sign for the theater downstairs.

I stooped to pick up the mail dropped through the mail slot. The paper slipped from my arm, and I scrabbled to catch most of the sheets before they hit the floor. I dumped the whole mess onto the desk and tried to make it look purposefully arranged.

Scrounging it out of my purse, I looked at the note one last time. I'd invented a couple of explanations, but I had proof of none of them. Still, a creep or Mason made the most sense.

Clean handwriting. Male. No flourishes.

You're being watched

I wadded it up and threw it into the waste basket with some energy. I'd stay alert in the here and now, because that's what real detectives do, but I was done with the past.

I shook off those pesky thoughts. I wasn't wasting any more time on the nonsense of those men. I had a business to run. Today or tonight was the first step on a trail only I would blaze for myself.

The whole block lit up again before a distant rumble rolled down the street.

Unusual weather for the City.

Standard San Francisco weather normally only consists of two weather patterns, fog and not-fog. One or the other. Never both. Of course, four seasons exist, but they're not seasons, not the way I remember seasons while growing up in upstate New York. Out east, one has spring, summer, fall, and winter. Here, we have Rainy, Hot, Foggy, and Earthquake. Oh yeah, Earthquake Season. A little ham-fisted temblor gave us a shake down only a few days ago.

I'd slept through it. One becomes jaded over time spent here.

Look, if it doesn't knock over the bookshelves or rearranges my furniture, it's not something too exciting. Certainly not at 4:30 am. Nothing is exciting at 4:30 am. Almost nothing.

Thunder and lightning, though, aren't usual around here. Rain? We have rain. We have fog that thinks its rain too, tries really hard, then retreats back out to sea.

Lou Tanner.

New Shamus in town.

Short, specific name, with no fluff or stuff.

Just get 'em in the door and I'd convince them they needed me. A twenty-five-dollars-a-day-plus-expenses kind of need.

And of course, who could ignore the damn cat? Curled up on the radiator. Black as midnight. A little extra fluffy – he had been wet and then groomed himself into a show piece. One pink toe on the left, rear paw.

I don't know whose cat he was. A street cat or stray? He decided to take advantage of the painters and movers going in and out of my office, to make himself at home. Under normal circumstances, I'd send him on his way with a big scrap of lunch meat, but with the squalling weather outside, I couldn't bring myself to abandon him to the rain. Thus, the little sneak gets a pass for the night.

Desk, arranged in front of the window, like the boss's desk should be. Check! Name plate. Check! Telephone. Check! Tidy stack of files – though, with nothing in them yet. Yeah – okay – check! Picture of Mom and Dad. Sam Spade didn't put a picture of the folks on his desk, but he doesn't have my family, and I was proud of my family. Big check!

And, the last known photo of Uncle Joe Parnaski.

My chest tightened again.

I'd taken the photo.

He was in Gumshoe Heaven now. And if I didn't do anything too stupid, I'd join him there some day. The Investigator's Valhalla. That dear old mug will be waiting for me with a hug, a cup of Java, and plenty of stories.

Uncle Joe would be proud of me.

His photo had a place of honor on my desk.

Pemberton's - Chapter 40: Setting Up Shop. The *Pemberton's* manual had a nice list of items all investigators should start with. A gun was first amongst them.

Mission achieved, if you ask me.

I didn't need more. I'm a P.I. That's it. Nothing more or less. It's all I've ever wanted to be and looking at that painted window, I know I'm where I need to be. The thought warmed me even more.

I hooked my wet overcoat on the hat rack along with my hat. Tossing the rest of the mail down on the unoccupied secretary's desk, I limped through the separating doorway and over to my desk.

My gams were killing me. My dogs were barking, though the cat didn't care. I slipped my high-heels off and let my calf muscles stretch. I dropped my purse into a drawer with one hand while shaking out my brunette curls with the other. With all the walking I'd done today, I was sure I'd worn a hole in the toe of my stockings. I knew how to mend it if I had. I wasn't sure where I'd left my needles and darning egg.

Sitting in my Boss's Chair caressed my ego. Cushy leather and sculpted back support. Me and my ego could reside in that chair for a long, long time. Turn off the big, overhead light. Let the Fox sign warm the room with a glow of red. Lock the door – lock out the whole world. Pull the bottle of bourbon out of the drawer and to hell with a glass. I'm the lady my mother raised me to be, but in private, I'm only little ole me and I'm willing to swill. No need to dirty a glass.

I'd left my copy of this week's pulp magazine collection in my coat. I hoped they weren't creased. It's a weakness I embrace — I love reading about the exciting lives of detectives, fictional and otherwise. It was also a good resource for learning about potential players in the Crime Game. A who's-who of gangsters, grifters, and ne'er do wells.

The weather cleansed my troubles and the events of the past few days faded into the hinterlands of time and shadow. Out of sight, out of mind.

The rain was hammering the window now, which didn't bother the cat in the least – he knew he was safe and dry. The occasional light show broke up the sedating rhythm. I stretched my legs out and clutched the bottle to my stomach. Old Forester Bourbon suits my tastes. I blame Philip Marlowe. He gave me my first bottle of that amber nectar.

I gripped the bottle top, ready to give it a hard twist and pull.

My door squeaked.

My hand reached to the derringer on my leg.

CHAPTER FOUR

Hate and Revenge. Each moves the world more than any other emotion. You risk getting short changed with love every time.

-Lou Tanner, P.I., Notes for female Pemberton Graduates, 1935

The grip of the derringer felt good. Too good.

A little, polite knock followed.

"Miss Tanner?"

His voice was smooth, with enough baritone in it to make my shoulders feel all tingly. Not to mention, weak. When it comes to beautiful men, all my smarts go hiking.

I never knew if I was disappointing or otherwise surprising a client when they encounter me for the first time. I stood up on my sore feet, hiding my gun in the same moment, and indicated the client chair to him. "That's me. How can I help you?"

He thanked me and acted as if seeing a woman detective wasn't such a big deal. Notable. He took off his crisp, new Homburg hat and ran his fingers through his hair.

What a looker.

I shouldn't think such things about a potential client, but I was a human, last time I checked, and I appreciate a fine-looking man.

Swells like this fellow inhabited my underutilized youth, especially after Daddy got money. This man — he was no common

Swell — had everything it would take to make any of those rich, entitled boys jealous. I could imagine him strolling down Market and turning heads as often as Jean Harlow or James Cagney might.

Rich man's confidence in every step, he strolled up to me and handed me his card. Heavy, textured paper, in cream, with clean, modern lettering. I drew my thumb across the raised detail. I had cards too, but not quite the quality of the one in my fingers. This man had dough to spend.

Elliott Noel Lockwood, President
Yerba Buena Import Company
San Francisco and Long Beach

"Mr. Lockwood, please be seated." I indicated the comfy, client chair.

He didn't take a seat at first, instead poking around his hat. He was trying not to make eye contact. It was that, or the hatband inside his Homburg was coming loose, which I doubted. Interesting.

I put him at around forty years old, six feet tall, lean in the body, with long, slender fingers. Dark blue eyes that, when they deigned to look at me, were like holes in the ocean floor — equal parts allure and unknown, and maybe just as deadly. Shiny black hair dappled with grey and white at the temples only. A straight, narrow, wicked jaw, with thin well-formed lips, and a strong nose. A few smile lines lingered near those lips, reminding me that some men's lips just needed to be kissed. A touch of five-o'clock shadow dared to darken his chin and begged my fingers to discover how rough it was.

There were, however, dark patches under his eyes. Those peepers didn't look so bright and clear. He wasn't sleeping well. Something was stealing those nighttime winks and I'd bet a nickel he was about to tell me why.

He dressed the way you'd expect a company president to dress. Brown suit cut to perfection. Rust colored tie, with dark socks and handkerchief square. Dark brown Homburg, the fifty-dollars-on-Park-Avenue kind, now sprinkled with rain water — maybe the rain knew better than to make him look sloppy. His overcoat, of top-quality wool, he kept slung over his arm. The epitome of well-heeled, masculine charm.

"Thank you for seeing me without an appointment. And, rather late." He looked back at the empty outer office. "I didn't mean to intrude. No one was there to check in with. Your lights were on and I probably shouldn't ..."

I couldn't help thinking, and you were cruising around the third floor of an office building, at this hour, hoping to find me in? You had some astounding luck.

"Please don't be concerned, Mr. Lockwood," I said, falling into my old Mid-Atlantic voice; the one I use when I want to impress and to build trust. "Your timing is fine. Would you like to hang up your coat?"

He shook his head and held onto his overcoat like a child's safety blanket.

I decided to start things light — make him relax. "And, there isn't anyone to check in with. I'm looking for a secretary who's just the right fit. The cat doesn't belong here and has lousy handwriting anyway."

A grudging grin appeared and disappeared from his face. "Lack of thumbs," a nice match to my humor. "What do you call him?"

"'Not My Cat.' 'Fuzzy Freeloader,' on occasion."

His shoulders relaxed, and he looked over at Not My Cat, whose ears swiveled and twitched while nothing else moved.

"May I ask what it is you do at your company? Import and Export are a bit vague. I'd like to know more."

Lockwood puffed up a bit. "Raw and finished metal for later machining. Recently, we've started working with large scale mechanisms, such as those in your average automaton. They are getting more popular by the day. It's a bit risky but has enormous payoff potential."

"Running on those big batteries we're all hearing about?"

"Yes," he added. "Clockwork winding mechanisms are a thing of the past. Batteries and self-winding are the wave of the future."

I liked the sound of his pride in his work. A client should be given a chance to brag about their daily lives, but now I needed to get down to business.

"Now, Mr. Lockwood, you're here with specific questions and you are interested in straight answers. I'm happy to oblige." This was a man who didn't waste time or resources. "Would you like tell me why you're here and tell me about whatever it is keeping you up at night?"

Lockwood didn't strike me as someone who impressed easily. He took in my gender and insight with little to no reaction. He wasn't even surprised by the feline, who stood up on cue, stretched, and curled down on the other side of his body.

The delicious Mr. Lockwood wasn't looking me in the eyes yet. Very disconcerting and telling. I like to watch people's eyes as they provide uncensored reactions. A man's eyes — you can read chapters on him before he ever says a word. Not looking me in the eyes was a sign he knew this too and was afraid of what I might learn.

Then, all of a sudden, he was staring straight into my soul.

A bit of the storm outside threw a bolt at me and it rode up and down my spine like a getaway car at a robbery. Such a good-looking masculine face yet with such desperate eyes.

"This is very embarrassing for me. I hope you'll appreciate that. What I need — what I'd like — I'd like to hire you to find someone for me, Miss Tanner."

"Who?"

"My daughter — stepdaughter." He reached into his jacket pocket and handed me a nice photograph.

If only I had a dime for every father looking for his wayward daughter. Or wife. Being an uppity female was a fad these days. I guess it comes with giving us gals the vote; we were turning into a rowdy gender. Maybe we'll shock all and sundry and run for President next.

The girl in the carefully-staged photograph was in her early twenties, if that old. And she was a beauty. The kind of beauty who learns fast that she can wrap men around her little finger. There was a frightening sense of intensity and manipulation in the gaze she gave the photographer. And, she had a look of something familiar about her.

35

"Her name is Francis Coventry. Frannie. She's ..." He hesitated, looking for the right word. "Missing."

"Run off," I asked.

"Oh, she does it all the time. No, she's missing. Her mother and I don't know where she is. She isn't at any of her usual clubs or with friends we have contact with."

"When was the last time you saw her?"

"A while ago. Let's say, a long time."

"And you want me to find her. What then?"

"Talk to her," he looked at me again, eyes making his sincerity apparent.

"About?"

"Whatever women like to talk about. Maybe tell her she has someone in her family who's worried. Or, we know she's making some wrong choices. She's never listened to me, and I prefer she doesn't listen to her mother. That's half the problem."

Ah, he was divorced or would be soon.

I set the photograph down on my desk. "And that's why you came to see a woman P.I?"

"Yes. It's an obvious choice if one is looking for discretion."

I laughed a little. So did he.

"I own a home in the City but I'm staying at the Stanford Hotel, for the moment. I can't send some fellow after her. He'd scare her."

"And?" Come on, out with it.

He gathered his words again. I was about to offer him a wheelbarrow to carry them in when he blurted out, "and she might do something ... regrettable."

"Because he's a 'he' and she is good at manipulating that angle?"

Mr. Lockwood didn't answer in words. He lowered his head a bit and stared at the floor. When he looked up at me, he appeared like a man stuck in a hole and out of rope. "Frannie came into my life when I met her mother. That was only six years ago. Needless to say, I didn't influence her upbringing. But when I married the family, I married into the responsibilities coming with family. What I thought was the start of an exciting marriage turned into an exercise in wrangling two wild women, including the one who isn't quite a woman yet. Her mother and I filed for divorce."

"But, you are still looking after Frannie? How old is she?"

"According to her birth record, twenty. Maturity wise, fifteen." He nodded with some inner thought. "She lives at home still, with her mother."

So, Mommy had possession of the house and Step-Daddy lived in a hotel. The Stepdaughter was wild and likely ungrateful. There was a recipe for resentment. "Do you like Frannie?"

"Why do you ask?" His clipped voice cut through our discussion.

"I like to understand the relationships in the situation." *Pemberton's* manual didn't cover this particular mode of interrogation. I learned it from my mother. "Do you like her?" A bad notion was planting itself in my fertile bean. Were he and Frannie having an affair, causing the divorce? It wasn't unheard of, though I sure hoped it wasn't the case for Mr. Lockwood. I may be vaguely attracted to him, but, as a professional, I couldn't write off any unpleasant ideas if they might lead to the truth. Did he want me to find her so he could renew or attempt a relationship with the attractive stepdaughter?

For a moment, he frowned and really rolled my question around in his head. "No. She's pretty much her mother, Irenie. Pleasant until they get what they want. Or don't. Her mother's real name is Irene Margaret Coventry, but she goes by Irenie."

I considered what it was Frannie wanted and didn't like the options.

"Unfortunately, Frannie's not of age yet, and her mother keeps egging her on with the bad behavior. So, I am trying to do one last good thing for her. Maybe I'm hopeful she'll make some better choices in friends, in life — in everything."

I watched him take the photograph to look at it. His expression wasn't one of a shamed-filled, secret lover or a man caught with his pants down. It was disappointment. After a moment, he pushed the image back to me. "Miss Tanner, I've never regretted decisions in my life, except for two. Bringing Irenie Coventry into my life is number two."

I didn't ask about regretful decision number one. If he wanted to tell me, he'd say something. To play my cards right, I needed to keep an open option to ask him. After all, regrets often overlap out of habit. "I need this photograph. And a list of places she frequents, names of family, friends, and acquaintances. Anything you can give me."

He nodded again and pulled another piece of paper from his jacket. "I gathered you would. This is the best list I can come up with. Some of her friends ... well, let's just say I'm connected to their social circles."

That much I could believe. Lockwood moved in the upper-to-mid middle-class circles of bridge clubs and restaurants, political hopefuls, and successful people holding out against the economic climate.

Some of those names were men of a certain caliber. I recognized a couple from the news section of *D&S Detective Magazine*: *Dopers, Hatchet Men, and Mob Bosses.* The rest, by the look of their names, appeared to be the swell crowd. All manners and no brains was my experience.

I was suddenly reminded of the fact I wasn't wearing my shoes. I pushed my feet further under my desk and scooched the chair closer.

"Are you wanting me to bring her home, one way or another?"

He was off to thinking-land again, as if he hadn't really considered all the possibilities. Ten-to-one odds said he was doing this as a favor — perhaps for her mother?

"I don't think so. I certainly don't want her forced to come home. She'd always resent it and never forgive me. I can't explain why that's important, I don't know why myself, but it is. I only want to know she's okay and to tell her mother, putting an end to this whole mess."

"Washing your hands of it?"

"That's part of it. And, maybe, I'd like for her to have a smart woman tell her a few facts about life she hasn't heard before?"

Smart woman, sure. But how did he know?

"Well, Mr. Lockwood, Babysitting, Counseling, or Detecting, any of the above, I charge twenty-five dollars a day, plus reasonable expenses."

"In advance," he asked, taking out his wallet too quickly.

"One hundred dollars on retainer, non-refundable, for the first four days. That covers everything immediate and allow me to tap resources. Later I'll send a detailed invoice for you —"

"If you ever find an assistant? Ever thought of hiring a young fellow?"

He got me to smile with that one. "It's only a simple invoice, with all the breakdown, nice and neat. I can do my own typing for now."

Like a well-bred man, he stood up and offered me his hand. It was warm from gripping his hands together, under his coat. He had been anxious about our meeting, but now I could sense his relief.

No shoes on, I didn't step out from behind my desk.

There was that spine-tingle again as my fingers touched his.

"I can reach you at your office?" I pointed at his card with my chin, while handing him mine.

"It's the best way, but I wrote my hotel number on the back, too. Just in case." He handed me five crisp twenties, fresh from the bank. He came prepped and organized, but I expected it from the president of a company. He turned to leave, started to put on his overcoat, and stopped. Without looking at me, perhaps out of shame, he added, "Please be careful. Some of my stepdaughter's friends are not the nicest people." He finished putting his coat on and did me the favor of glaring at me. "If things become dangerous, I can always hire —"

I cut him off with a wave of my hand, and a nonplussed dismissal. "You needn't be concerned. I've dealt with far worse than those on your list," I over stated. Sure, I had a run in with a couple of crazy, kraut scientists last year – thank you Agent Mason — but I hadn't looked his list over and maybe I was too quick to answer, to keep him from thinking he might need to hire a man.

And, based on experience, he was lying to me, either purposely or by omission. I wondered who would be more of a problem — the handsome stepfather too worried about appearances or the gorgeous stepdaughter looking trouble.

Finally, he mumbled, while putting his hat on. "It's not worth getting killed over."

CHAPTER FIVE

They tell us gals that Women's Intuition is a bunch of
nonsense, yet, in the same breath, they tell you a man's
Gut Feelings are trustworthy and accurate, an
extension of his superior primitive survival instincts.
Yeah, buddy, I got your superior instincts right here.
Here's some news for them: no one survives like a woman
who knows she's in danger. I'll bet my intuition over
some mug's gut every time.

-Lou Tanner, P.I., Notes to female Pemberton Graduates,
1935

My first case.

Not a family friend whose thirteen-year-old son stole candy and
change from his mother's purse. Not one of Mason's freebies. Not a
tag along with Uncle Joe.

A real case of my own.

So why didn't I feel like celebrating?

I didn't like that Lockwood avoided looking at me at times.
People have the habit of looking away when they lie to you. I ran my
encounter with him through at least three chapters in the *Pemberton*
manual on client evaluation. If the *Pemberton* folks had been in my
office, they would be as unsettled as I was. A top businessman and he
doesn't look people in the eye? You call that negotiation? The eye-

contact thing was still bugging me. And, he whipped out his wallet too fast. There were too many the holes in his story. Big holes.

Who spends big moolah on a kid he doesn't like, on the kin to a woman he's divorcing, and listed the whole brutal mess as his number two regret in life? Number one must be a doozy. The whole thing wasn't cricket and I was too tired to make sense of it. I needed to sleep then regroup.

Didn't need *Pemberton's* manual to explain it.

My first real case, and it wasn't small. And, one hundred clams in my pocket. I ought to stick that in the bank — as if I trust banks these days. But …

I do need a secretary. No, I need an assistant. I need someone who can do small jobs, research, and can be trusted to make solid decisions. Good with clients. Ballsy. Tough enough.

And, I hated to admit, able to go without pay every once in a while. This business only guarantees danger and annoyance, never income.

The rain was relentless now. My best guess, and hope, Mr. Lockwood had a cab or a car waiting for him downstairs. He didn't strike me as the Nightcrawler type. He'd go back to the Stanford and wait for the news. Maybe he would sleep well again.

I can see the street below my window — a bonus for someone practical and paranoid like me. Sure enough, Lockwood, I recognized the hat, rushed forward to a fancy, hired-car, the kind you spend cash on if you want to impress while not employing a full-time chauffeur.

A figure strolled out of the shadows to watch Lockwood's car. Overcoat, maybe a Fogger like Agent Mason likes to wear, or a cheaper imitation coat. Dark hat. The Fox Theater sign coated him in surreal, dark red neon.

Was he the same man, the creeper, who put the note in my pocket? No, I'd decided he was some creeper not right in his head.

The sign shut off. The Theater closed. Looking at my wristwatch, it was eight p.m.

The figure appeared smaller, now he — or she — wasn't radiating with reflected light. Not tall enough to be the man from the alley, yesterday. I was guessing. Alley-man had been closer, on level ground with me, and next to a standard-sized dumpster. Well, that was a good thing. I'd hate to think Alley-man followed me. No, this guy, or gal, was not looking at me. If anything, he had been interested in Lockwood. Maybe I'd go and have a four-letter word with him? I went so far as to ask Not My Cat what he thought I should do. He pushed his fuzzy head against my fingers before taking a half-hearted nip at them.

I could be overreacting. My inner klaxon wasn't going off. Still, it didn't make me happy seeing someone taking too much of an interest in my client.

You're being watched

Then, the figure seemed to engage in a private conversation with himself. Gesticulations and all. Maybe it was the crazy guy who gave me the note? Plenty of touched individuals around. More than one of them a veteran of the War. So many came back, "not right." Shell shocked. Beyond seeing my Uncle killed by a gunman, seeing a dead Nazi last year, and later helping to identify my own parents' bodies after their automobile accident, I had limited perspective with death and dying. It was always "over there."

The figure looked at my building and disappeared back into the shadows, jogging a bit, as if starting to run away. If he was a veteran, I sent a silent wish he finds peace.

It took me a half hour to write up the encounter in my notebook. Everything goes in there. My memory was fine but *Chapter 34: Proper Record Keeping*, or as I liked to call it, *Cover Your Ass*, wisely tells every detective to write it all down — it could be evidence to save you or the difference between life and death for a client.

The sky was still lighting up outside and the staccato of the rain fit the latest jump-jive-song. I had a feeling Mother Nature took off her gloves and was trying to tell me something. Yeah, I've been a lifelong optimist, so I ignored the warning signs and let her drum my window until I nodded off.

Around midnight, I woke up, forced my feet back into my shoes, told Not My Cat to stay until the storm passed, and caught a 'Crawler to home. No human cabbie was out driving in this mess, at this hour, either because he had good sense, or his Union shop told him not to.

The white, bullet shaped vehicle, splashed with a little mud, pulled up to my piercing, two-fingered whistle. Learned that one in the Big Apple. The two-person vehicle ran on a single track, with two wheels on either side to balance it. Dependence on only one track allowed the system to build about anywhere at half the cost, to make turns and hills better than a two-track trolley, and to squeeze into tight areas. Perfect for the terrain of San Francisco.

The side of the driverless cab slid out toward me and I stepped around to the front, then backed into the seat. With a jerk, the seat and I slid into the vehicle. It wiggled a little, unsteady at first on the track, it stabilized itself with the wheels.

The pre-fabricated voice recorded on a brass cylinder. I heard a tang in the sound you don't get with a wax recording; asked me where I was going. After my new client, I was glad for the lack of a driver as the last thing I needed now was someone interrupting my thoughts. I was reviewing the marvelous Mr. Lockwood's story and behavior, over and over.

Out, over near the wharf, the 'Crawler dispatcher was waiting for my response. Home. That was the only place I truly slept these days. I leaned toward the microphone in front of me and enunciated my address. With so many driverless cabs out, I wasn't sure my 'Crawler's radio signal would reach the far-away dispatcher. I had quite a shouting match the other week when the signal was fuzzy and the frequency overcrowded.

Gears whirled, and the vehicle shook a bit as it clicked and adjusted. Rolling forward, it stopped while one of the tracks moved to allow it to connect to the appropriate line. We sped off.

No problem with the signals tonight. Let's be serious; who was out on a night like this? Only a dumb dame who needed winks.

The 'Crawler had no trouble winding its way over to 10th Avenue. Where hadn't they put 'Crawler tracks? We passed one of the late-night trolleys rumbling down Judah.

In front of my building, the 'Crawler stopped and offered its brassy gratitude. I tossed coins into the meter box, and it released me from its innards to run under my awning. No pay – no release — the Nightcrawler's unofficial motto.

It's a good building, and new enough not to be falling apart. A woman's boarding house. I couldn't help but think it was a half-way house for dames caught committing the crime of being single.

The front door and lobby lights both lit up with my arrival. Damn alert motion sensors — I don't know who invented them, but they never worked to my advantage. Now Mrs. McCarthy might get up to see what her newest tenant was up to at this hour.

A big sign greeted my fumbling keys, "No men after 9 P.M. No overnight guests." It wasn't a set of rules to Mrs. McCarthy, it was part of the Ten Commandments brought down the mountain by Moses. And she was willing to defend it with the fury of Joshua.

Luck was with me and I stole away, up the flight of stairs to the first residential floor before my landlady toddled out to the lobby. I opened my door to the dark apartment, managing not to shriek when lightning flashed and illuminated the whole place.

My coat, gloves, and hat all ended up in a damp puddle near my entry. I'd deal with those in the morning. Automatically, I looked to make sure my peace keeper was in its usual, handy location. A Louisville Slugger — thirty-two ounces of hard Ash I'd more than happily greet any uninvited visitor with. It resides near my front door. It always resides there. I can find it in the dark if I need to.

Boxes waited near the kitchen to be unpacked. Sure, that was going to happen in the next six months. I can't cook to save my own life and no one who wants to live will touch anything I concocted. My idea of a great meal was take-out Italian and a bottle of cheap Chianti. Mother Tanner would be mortified, and I sometimes think I would say such things to see her face twist in abject horror. Then, we'd laugh.

Before I did anything, I had to check what I'd written about the events and my thoughts on the first meeting with Lockwood. This was essential stuff. I did a once over of my notebook before locking it away with my rod. I'd written all the words and feelings, including my doubt that Lockwood gave me all the facts surrounding his case.

I left off any commentary about how handsome he was. And my, how he got my skin to tingle. I put a stop to those thoughts — I'm a professional.

Yes, I'm a professional, not dead.

I'd need to get myself back to sleep — reading does the trick. I'd save *The Black Mask Magazine* for breakfast time reading, tomorrow. I tossed my copy of *D&S Detective Magazine* onto my bed and started to peel off the remnants of the day.

There were things to do. And if this rain didn't let up, I see getting food for the cat too. I might be able to budget in the cost for some Gaines's hard kibble, assuming Not My Cat didn't go catch his own dinner. Wait, where was he going to do his business?

Oh God, just don't pee on the new furniture …

I got all my lights on, so I didn't trip over something. Frock off. I was out like an unlucky prize fighter — forgetting all about the lights. I'd review those notes in the morning for clarity, as I almost nodded off mid-sentence a couple of times. Never opened my magazine. Never bothered to get under the covers.

I forgot to take my shoes off until morning.

You're being watched

CHAPTER SIX

Beauty Sleep? Forget it. Run in your stocking? Learn to mend it. Good or bad, right or wrong, this is your world now. Take no guff.

-Lou Tanner, P.I., Notes to female Pemberton Graduates, 1935

Morning had that special kind of promise. This morning especially. The fog was burning off, the dampness suggesting a good and hard cleansing had been achieved. The City could be a lovely place when its washed behind its ears.

I rolled over and clutched my pillow like a neglected lover. I couldn't sleep in, but I didn't need to get up quickly. The Lockwood case was intriguing and a good way to stoke the brain-box up to full steam. That, and a cup of hot coffee would be essential.

My place is medium in size. Ah, the view of 10th Avenue, and if I lean into the bay window, I had a full gander at Judah Street. There were two cafes in earshot and an Italian restaurant more than willing to help you pack on the pounds. Tailors. Mom-n-Pop grocers. Mechanical repair shop working on Nightcrawlers and various robotics. It's a good neighborhood. One might think I chose the place for the location and size.

One would be wrong.

I picked it because it's safe.

Three escape routes exist other than the front door. I can see anyone coming up the stairs and down my hallway. Fire escape out my big window. Big dumbwaiter a gal like me can fit in. Back door of the complex a couple of yards away.

So far, my work hadn't required me to mix with the bad crowd. But it was bound to happen, one way or another. My client did say his stepdaughter had some questionable friends and I concurred.

Now that I had a dangerous career, I'd laid off with wearing earrings. They turn out to be good only for the crooks who want to grab you by something. Besides, they were expensive.

And I don't wear rings. Certainly not like the honker that dame was wearing the other night. Wow-wee, somebody liked her. A lot. Maybe too much and she'd sparked a few jealous fires. Was this why Alley-man was chasing her?

I hadn't paid enough attention — I'd been caught up in my self-centered-grumping over Mason. I need to learn to be on alert. Always. No excuses on my part. *Pemberton's* was very clear on the subject — pay attention or get killed.

Today, I had to figure out what the Lockwood business was really all about. Looking after his wayward stepdaughter out of honor? If it turns out he was, I think I just found the perfect man.

Opening the icebox reminded me I needed to put on my domestic housekeeper hat soon and go fetch groceries. No eggs. No bread. Even the coffee tin was down to a teaspoon – not enough to make a cup of raw ambition. Ice, as in "necessary for an icebox," was not as abundant as my mother would require. I'd ask Mrs. McCarthy to arrange for the ice man to come in.

Booze, I had a-plenty.

I'd give up a little coin for a meal this morning. Happily, San Francisco had more cafes per capita than New York. An achievement of significant proportion.

I didn't dress to impress anyone but myself today. Belted navy-blue sweater with a neat white polka-dot bow. Beige rayon skirt with kick-pleats, hemmed just shy of ankle length. Street Oxfords with a functional heel. I laid out a plaid, wool cap. Short, powder blue, leather gloves. And an overcoat, because sunny didn't mean it was warm. This was San Francisco, after all.

I packed my daily-go-to-work-purse with only the essentials, such as case notebook, pencil, and pen. Private Investigator's License and Badge, in a leather case. A small box of ammo for the two-shot Derringer on the leg. Change for cabs and coffee. Cigarette case and freshly refilled lighter. I grabbed out one cigarette and lit it.

The apartment building began to rumble, then shake a little harder. Not an earthquake — quakes were more undefined, unsteady. This was steady. The cable cars and trolleys rattled the place a little while racing up and down Judah, but not like this.

Aero-Passenger Service.

A Zeppelin.

Over my building.

It happens now and then. I sat on the inside ledge of my bay window, smoked, and watched the big vessel float by, its intercontinental-strength engines rattling everything nearby. A dark shadow passed over the window.

Not something you get used to. Service was regular these days, but the airships had only been in service for the past few months. They weren't blasé yet. A couple of neighbors, out with their dog, stopped and stared upward. A guy was trying to use the wall as a wind block while lighting his cigar. Once accomplished, he looked up and let a billow of smoke flow into the air.

A huge Swastika adorned the sides and bottom of the balloon-envelope — my skin crawled, and I tried not to spit.

Nazis. No, no, no! I wasn't thinking about them or any experience I had with them. No. That was the past. I shoved that memory to the back of my head so hard it almost hurt. Gone. It never happened. Never.

I took another drag in disgust and looked out at the trees. The wind was blowing south, hard. I'd need a hat pin, and the Zeppelin would need to approach the Station Tower from the northeast. In other words, the traffic for all aero-service, rerouted due to weather, put the flight path over my neighborhood. Again. Good thing I was on my way out. If I wasn't mistaken, another three Bloated Birds were due in by noon.

Despite there being no damn chance I'd ever set foot on one of those, the idea of luxury living at ten thousand feet intrigued me.

Intrigued, but not anticipating a fancy vacation anytime soon.

Through a brief cloud of smoke, I looked back at a narrow mantle topped with framed photos of me and the parents. I missed them.

There was Uncle Joe's fedora, too. I kept it free of dust. And, that reminded me, I took the hat and propped it on top of my coat rack, as a lucky rabbit's foot for my first case. Sort of like a reminder that Joe was watching — looking after me.

I propped my foot up on the sill and pulled back my skirt enough to reveal a pocket clipped to my garter belt. My little gun fit in my pocket just the way I wanted it to.

I stared out the window. The Zeppelin descended into Downtown and was readying to hook its nose up to the Montgomery Street Rail and Aero Station building, at the 52nd floor. I couldn't see downtown from my place, but I knew the routine. The gangway would be extended soon. People actually walk out on that thing to disembark? I shivered.

Nope! Don't like heights.

Yup! Love to make my own living. And I had best hop to it if I was gonna' solve my first real case.

Every block closer I got to the Montgomery skyscraper, the tighter my stomach twisted.

I hate heights.

And there was no avoiding it.

Well, I could avoid it for a little bit.

Life scurried up and down the big street. Despite the bright sky, things were cold and damp. Fresh, but chilly. The wind wouldn't let up. I stopped to take a measure of the City by the Bay. A few

'Crawlers streaked by. I think I saw a human-driven cab, but I knew that had to be impossible. Those were rarer than Dodo birds these days.

Above us, the City was preparing for Chinese New Year with large, red cellulose lanterns shaped like enormous beach balls hung from every branch, telephone and light pole, and swaying in the breeze. We had paper lanterns, when I was a kid, but I couldn't imagine those surviving in this weather. Bright red cellulose, with gold accents and tassels. At night, they glowed a strange inviting orange, begging everyone to head up Grant to Washington, and to be wary of dancing dragons.

Some creep wolf-called me from his automobile as I sauntered by. Yeah, sure, the kind of fella my Mother wanted me to bring home.

We, the working masses, waited on the corner for that cop to give us the okay sign, and crossed the street, dodging steaming manholes, slick rail tracks, and expensive cars making a turn, disregarding the traffic cop. Some folks crossed Market any-old-place they wanted. Trolleys and 'Crawlers took up most of the center street, with four tracks for the Muni cars and another four for the 'Crawlers. Vehicles and people squeezed in between. A long line of cars waited for their chance to make the turn at Kearny.

Looking down toward the Ferry Plaza, I saw the dome of the Palace Hotel, the Humboldt Bank Tower, and rows of elegant, post '06 stone buildings, all rising above the elevated train tracks that intersected the big street at Fremont and at Montgomery. A pair of aging Fords darted by, missing a line of folks headed across the street to the next west-bound, street level tram.

The City was home to more rails than people. Big locomotives came in from multiple routes, 'Crawlers raced around every small street; trolleys and trams rolled up and down the main avenues, and every hill had a cable car. It was little wonder that anyone tried to drive an auto here. Made no sense to me — I put my car into storage. A pretty '30 Cadillac V16 Roadster in medium blue with cream detail and soft, roll-back roof. A gift, one I couldn't afford on my own. Maybe, just maybe, when I getting settled into a routine, I'll take a day and drive up the coast? A girl can dream, can't she?

People. There were people everywhere. Rushing through the brisk morning.

I felt the interest of a couple of laborers on the back of my, um, back. A little lower than polite to mention. The lot of us scattered in a variety of directions. The construction Joes and maintenance Bobs headed toward the hole at Van Ness and Market that had dreams of becoming a glass and marble edifice to modernity. Several ladies passed me, hurrying to clock in by nine a.m. Well-dressed men, leaving the hotels, headed toward Civic Center to prepare for the liquid lunches they eat.

Ahead of me, I heard the Floaters. Truly, I try not to snicker at that nickname for the motorized hydrogen balloons used to lift cables into place. They were working on the new Emperor Norton — Bay Bridge. On water or in the air, Floater crews worked damn near anywhere. Loud banging echoed, pile drivers likely finishing the last of the piers over near Harrison Street. All the while, twin technologies and crews were performing the same waltz over by the Golden Gate. Two more years, we were promised. Just two more years. Then we could drive from the City to about anywhere across the Bay, without getting our feet wet.

I stopped at my usual newsstand for the Chronicle and the Globe morning papers.

Howie looked up at my approach. His dark skin glistened from hefting stacks of newsprint and arranging his stand. He tugged the brim of his hat. "Good morning, Miss Tanner. Been a while."

"Good morning, Mr. Johnson. Too long. I need my news. Anything worth reading?"

Quickly cutting the strings holding stacks of papers together, he stood up and thought for a moment. "I'd say the most important story is on page four. Germany. Again." Some fellow reached between us to snag the top paper and tossed a coin into the cash jar. Howie Johnson didn't look to see if it was the correct price; in his opinion, he once told me, nothing matters except the honor system. If you don't believe in it whole cloth, it won't work.

He'd owned this stand for as long as I remembered. Grey had sneaked into his short, coarse hair over time, but I felt like it was only yesterday my Dad brought me downtown for an introduction to newspapers.

He was also the most politically savvy man I'd ever met. He didn't just sell the news, he read it voraciously. He analyzed every aspect of government, stock market, and economic growth.

"What now," I asked.

"Trouble. Nobody seems to be paying attention, but I see trouble on the horizon. After that man, Hitler, walked out on Jessie Owens at the Olympics, fuming about a Negro man being a champion over his superior athletes, I've been watching him. We should all be watching him and his cronies. Nothing good comes from his policies. His whole approach to reinvigorating the German economy is based on developing his military. Nothing else to do with a strong military but invade and fight.

"Nobody's saying anything about that?" I was being a little sarcastic.

"Who has time to care about some foreign country when they don't know where their next meal is coming from? Besides, with Germany providing the only viable air travel to the west coast, they look like the good guys, right?"

"Touché."

He nodded solemnly, then smiled for a pair of men paying for another set of papers. Once they were out of earshot, he asked, "Ever hear of Mein Kompf?"

I looked at him, giving him my best, I-clearly-need-to-expand-my-knowledge look.

"Hitler wrote it. I managed to sneak a gander at the first chapter — they have a copy over at the Public Library — well, until I was moved along."

My stomach fluttered, and a cold finger ran across my shoulders. Smartest man for at least a hundred miles and he couldn't be left alone in a public library.

"Nasty stuff?" I asked, sort of knowing the answer already.

"Yeah. And that was only the few chapters I got a look at. Hitler's insane ideas about master races is very nasty stuff. I can't even imagine what else is in that book." He adjusted his cap. "Something bad is coming. I wish more people were paying attention."

So did I.

"They're asking for more space, out at Hunter's Pointe." He exaggerated the "e" at the end of "Pointe." He always made fun of that. Some newspaper made a mistake, added the "e" and it stuck. Someone in the Militia thought it looked classy, so they never complained. I wanted to join him in the laugh, but ice was crawling down my spine. Militia? Forget it. It never happened, I told myself over and over.

Howie looked at me strangely. "You okay, Miss Tanner?"

"Sorry, I was trying to remember if I turned the stove off," I lied, using that fib no one gets away with. All I got in return was a knowing look and respectful inaction.

I wished him a great day and headed down the street. Veteran of the Great War, Businessman, all-around smart cookie; if Howie Johnson said it was so, it was so.

At the coffee joint on Tenth, I settled into my desired routine of morning news and a paper cup of heaven. Espresso, they call it. It's Italian. The owner's Italian. He can call it anything he wants to call it so long as he doesn't stop serving it. Not much to it and the nickel it cost made you wonder if he wasn't ripping you off, until you drank it and briefly considered joining the Walrus Club for a fast swim to Angel Island and back. Yeah, it had that kind of effect. My kind of drink.

News of the day. I sat down inside the door, about a foot away from the radiator.

Spreading out the newspaper, I took in my liquid get-up-and-go, and balanced it with the depressing, revolving door of world disaster.

There it was — as promised — page four.

Adolph Hitler, recently named *Führer* of Germany, held a rally with tens of thousands of saluting followers. I swear the guy could shoot someone in downtown Berlin, and none of his followers would care enough to criticize him. There were people in the U.S. who were tremendous supporters of the Nazi political movement. They saw the government of Germany as efficient, focused, and, I tried not to spit again, pure. Looking at the grainy photograph; people stiff-arm saluting — worshiping — this man. I'd met a couple of Nazis. I loathed the whole idea of a Nazi Party. Howie was onto something.

Some *schmoe* in Cleveland was shooting his mouth off about inventing a Death Ray Machine. Right. But then, I'd seen some pretty unbelievable inventions — okay, one particular invention — three months ago. Still, I didn't buy into it. If some brainiac invented a new weapon, the War Department wouldn't let him keep it, let alone brag about it to the papers.

Sir Malcolm Campbell was planning on breaking the Land Speed Record with his Aero-Automobile. Damn dingus floats on a cushion of hot gas and uses compressed air to propel itself forward. I predict disaster. His rival, Sir Alton Bradley, claimed magnetics did the same and promised to match anything Campbell did. That might be fun to watch.

I set aside the news of the day and pulled out my notebook to review observations and notes from the previous nights. I honestly don't remember writing much of it. Even whacked out with missing sleep, I managed a good narrative of who said what and things worth noticing. A good detective takes notes. *Chapter 1: What it takes to be a P.I.* Not vague, colorless notes, but clear, details, like how people appear, physical gestures, body language, vocal patterns, and what they say by the word. How someone maintains their home or office was as important as the description of a crime scene. Everything counts.

Looking at Elliott Lockwood's list of contacts for Frannie Coventry, I decided to start with family. Nine times out of ten, it's family that's deeply involved. I was thinking that Frannie, perhaps tiring of her mother's demands, ran off to another family member for solace or protection — or both.

I looked at her picture again. There were a thousand things wrong with the photo. For one, Frannie had been in her mid-teen-years when it was taken. I was guessing 1931 by the look of her fashion and hairstyle. She sure knew how to pose for a photograph. She was as confident and comfortable – as a clothing model might be. And she was familiar for some reason. But Lockwood didn't say she had a career as a magazine model. I didn't ask last night; I should now.

Also, for a teenage girl, she dressed much-too-much to the nines. She was tarted up like a movie actress: heavy-handed with the eye shadow, wearing those new false eyelashes, and dark lipstick. This wasn't a portrait of a girl still in school, dreaming of meeting her future husband in college and having five children. This image was a crafted vision of a young, sexual creature, a siren preparing to drag a man to the bottom of the ocean.

Comparing Frannie to me at the same age wasn't fair nor was it accurate. At her age, I was learning what it was like to have money. Dad's overhead rail grips were patented and his stabilizing mechanism, the rescuer of many a sea-sick train passenger, sold like hotcakes. I was in pigtails and coveralls, climbing all over the latest locomotive or Pullman car. The conductors and engineers around New York Central Rail knew me by sight and put up with my incessant questions. If I wasn't being a tomboy, I was playing detective with Uncle Joe.

The bottom line was that I might not have had the average girl's childhood, but I had a childhood. Frannie looked like she skipped out on hers early and wound up being an adult all too soon.

At the strange collision of Market, Larkin, Hayes, and Ninth Street, sat that big, over-decorated theater that I loved. Inside and upstairs, my office awaited.

I heard the phone ringing inside as I worked the key in its lock. Oh yeah, I still needed a secretary that I couldn't afford.

The phone kept ringing, thankfully, and my gut told me it was Lockwood. Who else would be calling me here? I sure hoped he would open up more about this case. I also sure hoped it wasn't Mason.

"Tanner Private Investigations," I answered, hooking my hip on the side of my desk and noticing that Not My Cat had taken over my boss's chair.

"Hello Miss Tanner?" It was Elliott Lockwood.

I love being right.

"Miss Tanner? I've done something …" He couldn't finish the sentence.

"Mr. Lockwood?"

It took him about three tries before he finally spit it out, "Something terrible."

CHAPTER SEVEN

I like strong men, when all that strength comes from their core. Good men are plenty, so long as they can pretend, but a strong man is rare.

-Lou Tanner, P.I., Notes for female Pemberton Graduates, 1935

My stomach wasn't up for this — not this early in the morning. The espresso bubbled away in my gut.

His voice brimmed with shame. "I've done something inappropriate, something I'm ashamed to ... but, but it produced something I think you should know about."

Inappropriate? Did he follow Frannie Coventry? Sleep with her? Kill someone? What? My heart started pounding. "Mr. Lockwood, what is it?"

He didn't answer at first. I heard noises beyond the telephone receiver. He was in a public phone booth. I listened more, while he got his thoughts together. Where was he? A woman's laugh? A car horn? Plates being dropped onto a busboy's tray? A restaurant or café? The phone booth's doors must not close well background clues slipped through as if they were lap-dancing on his thighs.

"I went through Frannie's room and her things." He took an audible breath. "I took something."

Was that all?

Sometimes I forget well-meaning people were mortified by actions I thought of as average. A Shamus goes through people's belongings all the time. Hell, we may even go through their trash. But, to a nice guy like Lockwood, I suppose such actions were downright deceitful, warranting a parking spot in Hell. Had my eyes rolled any harder backward, my thoughts from yesterday would be legible on my inner skull.

Oh well, my sarcasm wouldn't work with him, but boy, I sure wished a few choice words would fall out of my mouth. I was a professional, after all. "I wouldn't worry about that, Mr. Lockwood. You're still acting as a father. And, on a scale including all the other troubles of the world, I wouldn't rate searching your stepdaughter's room as high. In fact, I plan on doing the same thing. Can I arrange my search through you?"

There was another long hesitation.

Come on, Lockwood, don't hold out on me.

"Not today. Let me bring this down to you. I really shouldn't go back to that place."

Stalling? Or, was he being practical. "Your former wife lives in the house you still own. I'm sure you being present is not unreasonable."

After another pause, he said, "yes, but I'd like to not run into her. In the house. I ... she might think I was trying to ... restart ..."

Ah, I understood now. "Then go ahead and come down to my office. Bring whatever it is you found," heaven only knew what it was, "and I can take a look at it."

We agreed to one o'clock, he thanked me, and got off the line lickity-split. This was interesting.

I retrieved Uncle Joe's hat from the desk where I'd dropped it in my rush for the phone. I put the Fedora on the knob atop the hat rack with an almost ritual reverence. From such a prime spot, the sacred Fedora looked at me and me at it. It completed the place. It completed me.

Joe Parnaski wasn't my real uncle; he was one of those guys who was so close to the family, he became part of it. Roly-poly, always smoking a cigar, big smile for the little girl who had all those pesky questions. Joe was the in-house detective for Dad's company. I saw him work. He was a walking encyclopedia of laws, bad guys, tricks, and perfect interrogation technique. Yet, he had a heart as big as Wyoming, and knew when to stick to the letter of the law and when to look the other way. No college degree, just life experience. No one pulled a rug over Joe's eyes — until the time someone plugged him.

I shooed Not My Cat off the chair. He harrumphed over to the window sill and sat in the sunlight, grooming in protest.

Phone calls achieved a few appointments. Family members were more concerned about how Frannie and Irenie were mucking up their social reputations and split between those who wanted to talk about it and those who didn't. No surprise. Yet, the universal thought was Frannie might be worth saving — Irenie was not.

Frannie? Irenie? Did they use a similar diminutive on purpose? They sounded like sisters in a vaudeville act, not mother and daughter socialites.

The more I thought about it, the more I wondered what the terms of the divorce settlement were. What had either gal received from the dislodged hubby? Well, I expected Lockwood in my office this afternoon, and I would ask. I had other questions for him, too.

The first interview was down town. A cousin once removed from the Lockwood family. According to Lockwood's list, Frannie had been close to them, for a while. That suggested a falling out and I wanted him to tell me why. I gathered up my things.

Not My Cat sniffed at the air, screwed up his nose, and headed back to the warmth of my chair. Before plopping his furry butt down on my seat, he gave me a look challenging me to try to move him. Just try.

I left the fuzzy gangster to contemplate his own godhood and headed off to the rest of my day.

I needed to run my own little errand, too. Heeding both *Pemberton's* and Uncle Joe, I actively maintained a few local connections gained from my brief railroad career. No burning bridges if you can help it, right? I had some terrific friends out here.

One of them worked in the Montgomery Station Building. As much as I hate heights, I needed a touch of inspiration and good sense. Marley had those in spades.

As I headed down the street, I caught myself checking to see if anyone was following me. I had to face it; this was my normal operating procedure for life.

Gilbert Halliday was an enterprising man, with inventions galore. His whole office was a chaotic mess with plans, blue prints, napkin sketches, and pencils scattered everywhere.

He stared at my badge, unconvinced, but offered me a seat all the same — after clearing reams of paper off it.

"So, trouble over on Vallejo Street," he asked without me saying a word.

"I'm interested in Frannie, specifically. The family asked me to do this."

He scratched his dark head. "Not sure what I can tell you. We haven't seen Frannie in a year or so."

I crossed my ankles, ladylike, and set my hands in my lap. I was of the mind that pulling out my notebook and scribbling things down as he pronounced them made him itch, like he was being grilled by a journalist — or the police. I needed him slightly off kilter, since he just might make a critical error in that circumstance. All the while, I smiled and jotted things down. "Is there any reason why Frannie and your daughter …"

"Margaret"

"… Margaret stopped spending time together?"

I was direct while looking for a response from him. His muscles tightened up protectively. Good daddy.

"It's important and," I added with emphasis and eyelash batting, "confidential."

He stopped to take all that in and maybe to think about how he was answering me. I knew Halliday wasn't directly related to

Lockwood, so it came as no surprise to me he had little in common with him looks-wise. Halliday wasn't tall, but had strong, masculine features and a thick moustache. His voice was a deep baritone. Dressed in acceptable fashion, I decided he was doing well enough in the world. Now, I just needed him to talk.

His shoulders relaxed when I repeated the word, "confidential."

"I'm surprised, but not really, that Elliott asked for help. I still can't decide what motivated him to marry Irenie in the first place. Have you met her?"

I flicked my eyelashes ever so prettily, replying, "not as of yet."

Well, he had some choice words on that subject. I did not write those down. After a deep breath, he continued, "She got her claws into Elliott Lockwood and held on tight. I won't describe how, you being a lady," something he'd ignored or forgotten a moment ago, "but I think we can both agree she wanted to marry into money."

I appeared innocent and confused — on purpose.

He fell for my deception. "Elliott's done well by himself."

"He struck me as being so shy, so reserved," I exaggerated, hoping to trick a tid-bit of information out of Halliday.

"With you? With a woman? That doesn't surprise me. He's a romantic kind of fellow. Not a womanizer – just a guy who believes every woman is a lady before she proves otherwise."

Not a womanizer? Noted. "And?"

"Well, Irenie proved otherwise. So did Frannie. I caught Margaret and Frannie sneaking off to some club in Chinatown, of all places. Don't get me wrong, I didn't mind it when Frannie was willing to introduce my girl to the folks at the Seal Rock Sports Club. During the day. But one of those nightclubs, with drinking and who knows what at night? I drew the line. Had quite a chat with Irenie, who thought nothing of it, but it upset Elliott."

"Upset?"

"Oh, sure, Elliott has a business to protect. And, since he was splitting with Irenie, we figured keeping Frannie and Margaret apart was okay. Elliott agreed."

"Oh, I see."

"Yeah, you have to be careful with image these days, especially with the industry he's moving up in. Elliott's doing some fine work in import/export, and," he smiled with a tone of conspiracy, "getting involved with some fancy projects, like robotics for the government. He might even have some important friends over at the Pointe. Those soldier-boys need a lot of metal these days."

"The Pointe?" I couldn't bring myself to say, the Militia. I grasped my fingers so tight I thought I heard my knuckles crack.

"I could be wrong. Elliott plays that card close to his vest, if you take my meaning. His company is a supplier of base materials, so he supports all sorts of industries. He doesn't know where most of his product ends up. He runs a clean shop. No funny business. Still, he can't afford a wild girl ruining his reputation."

"Oh, yes, I understand." I relaxed again and gave him one of my best persuasive grins.

His phone rang. He held up a polite finger ordering me to wait, chatted as low as possible, then set the receiver down. "This is for my partner. Can you wait a moment?"

"But, of course."

He nodded with appreciation and went into the other room, demanding where Ralph was.

I hopped up and took a look at the papers on his desk. Some were strange versions of automatons sketched out. Big 'Tons. Bigger than anything I thought existed. Bigger than anything should exist. And guns, if that was what you called them when they were that size. An army of iron? Armed? The shiver down my back showed through my clothes. It couldn't be. It was my imagination, right?

The shuffling at the door told me Halliday was back, and he would find me seated and waiting like a nice, privacy-respecting girl.

"Is there anything else I can do for you? I need to wrestle with a vendor. Ralph may be out of the office. I hope I was able to help."

Holding out my hand I said, "yes, Mr. Halliday. You were very helpful. May I ask one quick question?"

"Shoot."

"How is Margaret doing? She lost what sounds like a friend."

"Doing well, I think. She's out east now, at boarding school."

"Thank you."

"No, thank you, Miss Tanner. If you can, help Elliott out of whatever mess he's in this time."

Well, that statement was the most telling thing he'd said. I forced my gaze to stay off the desk. I didn't want to make Halliday suspicious of my actions. Or maybe, I didn't want to remind myself of what I saw.

I stood and stared up at the Montgomery Street Station. With two major railroad lines, four trolley lines, cabs, and 'Crawlers all meeting up, the place had to look good. Damn good. And it did. Gorgeous architecture with plenty of flourishes and parallel lines, and glass. The trains from around the country came in via the elevated tracks, entering the building around the fourth floor. More local trains came in via tunnels underneath the station. The public transit used street level accommodations. Above all that were offices. None of it struck me as terrifying except the sheer height of the whole structure, made necessary by the Zeppelin Service. To bring those big monsters and passengers into the City, they either had to land or they had to disembark the people while airborne. There was no place big enough. All of downtown was multi-story buildings, so, they built the Station up and up, and up, until the rooftops of its neighbors didn't impede the air service. Fifty-two stories up.

My first thought, when I saw photographs of its construction was it was the last place I wanted to be in during a quake. The last place period.

A small bi-plane buzzed the building, dragging a sign behind it. After a moment, the message was legible, *Support Local Unions*. I figured we, down with the muck of the common street, were not the intended readers. The message was for all the companies and corporations with the pricey square footage in one of the best-known pieces of real estate in the country.

With all the reluctance expected from an acrophobic, I willed myself into the tower and gritted my teeth as the elevator bumped and groaned its way up — and up — *and up.*

At last, I escaped with my life and relative sanity into a comfortable, warm office which occupied the entire floor. To my relief, Marley's office wasn't in love with the view. There were only a couple of windows, and I sure didn't need to go look out either of them.

Marley O'Brien was a Swedish-Irish bombshell, with a sharp wit, life experience, brains, and guts. Naturally, that meant she could only get work as a secretary. Not to snub secretaries, *professional was as professional does,* whether a secretary, president, school teacher, or detective. But with her brains, Marley would make a great teacher or cop. For the moment, though, she worked in one of those pretty offices full of light when the bosses don't close their doors and leave the common staff in darkness. At least Marley had a window at the end of the row of offices providing some natural illumination.

Her floor was above all the other buildings on Montgomery, Market, and Bush Streets, and about five stories below the Aero-docks for the Station. I was happy to sit as far from the window as possible. Only Marley achieved the miracle of getting me up into a skyscraper.

My friend had long legs, long hair, and a long memory, not to mention a brain that was a walking encyclopedia, and she knew where to glean any information she didn't already know. She stood about an inch shorter than me, which was still saying something, as I was not what you'd call a shrimp.

She had a number of things I did not. For one, she was the average man's dream of womanhood. Her smile had the power to stop a runaway cable car mid-hill. Men tripped over each other to open the door for her. If she told me two swells were planning on a duel over her and she had no interest in either, I wouldn't be surprised. Knowing her, she told them as much, and still, I bet they threatened to blow each other's brains out for a chance at a date.

She was light where I was dark, not in personality, but in appearance. She tended toward fashionable hair styles and swinging skirts, fashionable pastels, and adorableness. Me, I was dark haired, tidy, and preferred woolens. Getting us into the same room together created a vision of opposites some men only dreamed of.

Such problems were not those I spent much worry over. I was not at all bad looking. Anyone who can be identified with Myra Loy was high in the looks department. But Marely, she redefined "knockout."

I waited for her by her desk; a lone edifice planted right outside the boss's office. Singular, trapped, empty of anything speaking to her character. Plans, tacked to the board next to her, said someone in her company wanted old pneumatic tubes taken out and new two-way radios put in. The newest in technology.

The door opened, and Marley was on her way out when a masculine voice called out to her. "Thanks. Now, Honey, don't forget we need the report by five, tonight."

Another voice called out, "Thanks, Sugar."

"Of course, Mr. Franklin."

The two faceless voices then returned to low laughter and plain man-talk. Closing the office door, she shut out their chatter.

"So, 'Sugar,' want to hear about my brand-new case?"

Her pale, round nose crinkled. The sweet little freckles bounced. She whispered, taking care of her words, "I hate it when he calls me that. Mr. Franklin just eggs them on, the clients, I mean. Then they start calling me Sugar, Honey, or worse."

Or worse? I'd ask later. "So, you've said more than once. Do any of them actually know your name?"

"Nope," she said dropping into her chair. "Not even the color of my eyes. Entire discussions are held at this level," she said, indicating brassiere level with her hand. She might be exaggerating but I understood how she felt. Dressed as a true professional, and not showing a great deal of skin, Marley wasn't showing anything to encourage anyone.

"They *don't* know you."

"I prefer it that way, Slim. I don't want to know them, and I don't want them to know me."

I pulled out my cigarette case and offered her one.

"Later," she said. "I need to get this report ready by five." With a flourish, she signed and dated a short stack of papers sitting in the middle of her desk, indicating her involvement in preparing, producing, and verifying the accuracy of the document. "Done," she announced after about six seconds.

"It was ready to go long before you talked to him," I said rather matter-of-factly.

"Of course. But, Mr. Franklin needs to be seen being a boss. It's important to him. He says it makes it easier to negotiate with a client if they know he's in control," she added, mocking and quiet. She placed the document in a file envelope, looped the string around the tab to keep it shut, and dropped it into Franklin's in box. Stepping around to the front of her desk, she took the cigarette I offered. "What brings you downtown ..."

A rumble shook the whole building and the only way we were having this conversation was by shouting. Instead, we both folded our arms and waited.

The big airship blotted out what little light made it to Marley's pathetic desk. The roar of its engines and the huge vibrations lasted for another minute before the damn death-trap floated away from the Station.

Marley rolled her eyes and rubbed her temples. "All day long. In and out. They just keep coming and going. I need aspirin powder. Or a drink."

"It's not noon yet."

"It is somewhere." She started to rub the back of her neck, under her strawberry-red mane all coiled up neat and tidy. "So, what did Mason give you this time? Case of the missing Mint?"

"Nah, I checked, it's still over on Fifth Street where it was last seen. Mason can take a long dive off a short pier. Tell you about it later? In the meantime, I have a real client."

"Keep that thought. We need outta' of here."

"We do?"

"Yeah," she said with some trepidation. "We do."

67

CHAPTER EIGHT

Unless you like to look haggard and strained, start preferring the slow track. Living too fast is encouraged by those who don't.

-Lou Tanner, P.I., Notes for female Pemberton Graduates, 1935

"What's going on?" I whispered.

"I'm getting fired."

"You're what?"

"I'll explain. Come on."

Grabbing her umbrella, coat, purse, and hat, she dragged me out of the building, and down to the street. It took a few too many minutes for my liking. By the time we arrived street level, crews with teams of sweeper 'Bots and lifters were cleaning up a mess of glass, fuel, and metal, strewn all over the corner of Montgomery and Bush. Two trucks tried to occupy the same space on the street. Needless to say, it hadn't gone well. Several firemen, all of whom were chosen for their good looks as well as strength, motioned for us to avoid the area.

Little hill-shaped sweepers, with parallel bands of chrome on top near their wind-up keys, and fuzzy brooms swirling underneath, rolled back and forth over the shards — the sound of grinding glass made me shiver and we trotted down the street, toward Market.

Marley turned and blew a kiss to one of the firemen.

Flirt.

She giggled and kept up with me.

A moment later, her hand was in my bag and pulled out my cigarette case. I found the lighter and got her set up. She slowed down only long enough to tilt her head back, drag deeply on the stick, and exhale with a sigh of relief.

"Marley, you alright?"

"You hiring, Slim?"

"Well, now that you mention it…"

Marley stopped mid-stride. "Tell me more."

"Over lunch. I'm starved, and I want to hear what's going on with you. I didn't eat real food this morning, but I did knock down some Italian coffee."

"Geez, Slim, that stuff will kill you," she cracked while puffing on her cigarette.

We walked up to Powell Street, to the Woolworth's Department Store at the Flood Building, stamped out the remains of our cigarettes, and headed downstairs to find a little booth in the diner.

After we ordered, I checked around, to note if anyone might overhear us, and for the record, no one. We were early. At her insistence, I proceeded to bring her up to date on the Lockwood case.

"He did leave a few things open, didn't he," Marley said, running her fingers against the roots of her hair, pushing the Marcel waves back into place. "You took the case, right?"

"Took a retainer too," I added with a tad too much pride.

"Oh good, then you can probably afford me." For a moment, she considered smoking, then decided not to. "If I have to let one more of those 'fine, upstanding businessmen' chase me around a desk, I swear I'm popping him one in the kisser."

"I'm surprised you haven't yet. Or have you? Is that why you think you're being fired?"

"Well …" she looked at her purse, then nails. "I did. Hit someone." She grabbed the abandoned cigarette and lit up out of fury. "An old client needed quotes, papers, you know, the usual Dingus and McGee. I was feeling pretty full of myself. I'd managed it all to perfection." Long drag. "I was reaching for a pen he dropped — God, this is embarrassing, it's the oldest trick, but I thought I was saving the account — I wasn't thinking. Next thing I know, he's behind me, rubbing …" She spit out her smoke.

"Oh Marley." It was terrifying for her. "He didn't do more to you —"

"No, 'cause I turned around and busted him in the nose. I remembered you saying never to hit someone in the jaw. Too big a bone to break with one right cross."

"And?" I asked, thinking of my encounter with Mason, amused by the fact Marley and I engage the same management technique.

"Whaddya think? He didn't take it kindly."

"And?"

"He fired us, the whole company. Yanked his account files out of the drawers and stormed out. My boss was in Sacramento at the time."

"He doesn't know yet?"

"Nope."

"How's he gonna' to take it," I asked, as if I couldn't already guess.

"He'll be pissed at me. He'll say I should have played along for the sake of the company. He'll explain how it's business and if I wanted to be in this industry, I shouldn't be so proud. What else should I expect, being a pretty girl? All in good fun, right? It's not as if the man raped me." She stopped, and glanced about, jaw tightening. "Boys will be boys, he'd say. The client was just playing with me, he didn't mean anything." Her voice warbled a bit. "It was a compliment, right? Who am I to say no to a client?" Common comments, we dealt with them time and time again, always the same. "And then, he'll kick my ass to the door, without references or back pay." She leaned into the booth, her face alternating between pride and fear.

My heart chilled.

Maybe I couldn't do anything to stop bad behavior from men like them, but I would help Marley, here and now. She was a gem. A damn fine friend.

"Whaddaya think about me working for —" she started.

"You're hired," I blurted out, sucking down my coffee too fast. Oh crap! Could I really afford her? Could I afford not to hire her? "Let me lay all the cards out for you, before you place your bet. This might not be the steadiest gig you've ever had." I explained about everything that came to mind about the reality of investigative work.

Marley took it all in and proudly announced she was my new secretary and researcher.

It took us about twenty seconds to hammer out salary, hours, and requirements. She had the guts to ask for a fair wage. I was happy; she trusted me to be on the level with her. Anything else wasn't cricket. We also covered the topic in inconsistent caseloads again. I insisted. I wasn't holding out on her, I owed her that much. Overall, she was okay with it.

She tapped out her cigarette. "I'll call Mr. Franklin and inform him I've quit."

"You telling him about the lost account?"

"Sure. I should. I don't want to leave on bad terms — not too bad. What would my new employer think?"

"You should have popped Franklin in the mug a long time ago. How about your stuff at the office?"

"What stuff? Nothing in that office belongs to me."

I had to laugh. "Well, so we're clear, you can bring personal items to the office. No setting up a boudoir," I winked at her. "Some comfortable things to give the space your own touch."

"A woman's touch?" she asked ridiculously.

"Beat ya' to it." I grinned big as a day. "In all seriousness, you don't ever have to take that from a client of mine. Ever. If they can't treat employees of Tanner Private Investigations with respect, they aren't clients of Tanner Private Investigations."

On conclusion, we shook hands. A strong, mutual promise to one another.

I packed Not My Cat off to his radiator bed when the phone rang. I snagged it before Marley did. Habit. I needed to let Marley do her job. In agreement, she leaned over and gave me a look that said, "No more of such nonsense, missy."

"Lulu, darling! How are you?" Long distance static screeched on the line.

"Nora?" I checked my wristwatch. "Aren't you supposed to be at a bar?" These days, when weren't the Charles's at a bar?

"Oh, Nicky and I took some time off to shop. They don't like us stumbling around so we'll head over to The Gin Joint after."

"Find anything good to buy?"

"No," she said, her voice slipped off into a dismal place. "Winter clothes are so bulky and hideous."

"Well, promise me you'll have a Firecracker at the Joint, in my honor."

"That's what I'm calling about. Congratulations."

Nick made himself known, loudly, in the background. "Tell her to keep a gun in her drawers, oopsie, I mean drawer."

"Tell Nicky I've got both."

Some conversation went on outside my hearing, and I pictured Nora either swatting Nick or telling him to go pour her a Rye.

"Now, Lulu darling, we're coming home next month, and we'd love to see you."

"Absolutely. When —"

Nick interrupted. "Here, give me that. No, you go pour me a drink, you're my wife, aren't you? I married you for more than just your money. Lou, are you there?" By the sound of it, he hadn't waited until after shopping for his adult libation of choice. "Are the boys, and now girls, still meeting at the Marc Hopkins?"

"We sure are. I mean, how else can we steal clients from one another and show off who made it into the news?"

He cleared his throat. "Well, let me tell you, when I first went to one of those gatherings, nobody was a somebody yet. Those weren't merely chances for drinking buddies to hang around together, we were serious about exchanging ideas, information, all that sort of stuff."

I knew that. Nick knew that I knew that. Why did he always explain to me what I already ... Oh never mind, at least he cared enough to say something. "We still meet Thursday nights, Nick. But, warning, Philip Marlowe is in the habit of coming up from LA these days."

Nick grumbled something substantial but incoherent. As it was Nora back on the line, I couldn't tell if he'd grumbled about Marlowe or having to give the phone back to Nora.

I bet she squished up her nose at him, such was her private signal to him. I've seen it before. "It's been a while since we've attended one of the gatherings."

"Marlowe may show up," Nick shouted in the background.

"Oh," Nora replied, her voice trailing off in disappointment. "Well, the bar is big enough to avoid him, I suppose."

"I think Phil's charming, if a little full of himself," I offered. "It's Miles Archer who gives me the willies. He's never been the same since Hammett wrote *the book*, the one where he was murdered."

"Never make a writer angry, they'll put you in a book and kill you off dreadfully," Nora said. "Darling, I called to congratulate you and to tell you we'll be home soon."

"Thank you. And?"

"Well ... be careful. You're smart, Lulu. And Joe Parnaski taught you everything he before ..."

"I know."

"Well, I'm worried about you, that's all. You have a new office and your licenses. You really are in business now."

"So, you did receive my announcement postcard?"

"Just today. I mean ... what I'm trying to say is ..."

Poor dear — always worrying and pretending not to be. "Nora — don't worry. I'm fine. I even have my first case. A simple missing person case. A wild daughter who's misplaced herself at the moment. I promise to watch my back and to keep you apprised of the case."

Nora sighed. "I'd like that. I'm sorry to be such a mother hen."

"Don't be. Now give Nick a kiss for me and we can chat later."

"Tell her, Nora," Nick said.

"Tell me what?"

There was a long pause. "You realize Nicky is still connected even though he's retired? He still gets news on the grapevine. Well, he learned about something he doesn't like."

"Give me the phone," Nick demanded.

"No, Nicky. I'm taking care of this. Where's my Rye? Lulu? Sorry, where was I? Yes. Nicky got wind of a rumor that you are being, oh, how do I put this?"

"Being what," I asked, my heart crept up in my throat.

"Observed. Something about an incident on your father's train a couple of months ago."

I rolled my eyes. "Oh that. The Treasury Department has been doing more than watching. They've been sending me on annoying errands —"

"Treasury? No. We're hearing something from —"

"Give me the phone, woman!"

"Nicky, where's my drink? Heavens. Lulu darling, we're hearing some folks in the military are interested in you."

Trolleys and 'Crawlers rumbled by, clanging bells and making other intense noises.

Every sound, including my own heartbeat, pounded from one side of my skull to the other.

I remembered the note.

You're being watched.

Had Mason gone ahead and sent in the terrible report to the War Department? And were they now surveilling me? If I saw things I shouldn't at the Pointe, was it the Militia?

I shook myself out of it. "Anything dangerous? You know, don't you, I would never do anything to compromise the country?" My mind raced to the collection of papers from Mason. Yes, I read the report he'd held over me. Where was Mason's retraction statement? If I had half a brain, I'd put it where no one would find it.

74

"Of course, you wouldn't, Darling. But Nicky and I think you should keep an eye out. Pay attention to what's behind you as well as in front."

I shook my head, as if she could see me over the telephone wire. Mason. What was wrong with that man? Or, had the Charles's learned of the rumor before I'd finalized things with Mason? That was much more likely. But why the military and not Mason's Treasury Department? Who did the rumor originate from? I asked Nora.

"No one had an answer, but the rumor mill says you noticed or learned something you shouldn't. Not a first for you flatfoots." She called over to Nick, "Right? You're always sticking your nose in where it shouldn't be?"

Sure Nora, as if you didn't do that too. "Not to worry." My anxiety was starting to ebb like the tide. "Everything from my last assignment is all done, nothing out of the ordinary was seen," I lied. "There will be no more assignments from that source. But, I'll keep following Nick's useful advice when it comes to dangerous circumstances. Good habits are good habits, regardless of the case, right?"

"There's the sensible Lulu I know. So Nicky and I don't worry too much, would you give us a call now and then? And we'll get together once we're back in town."

"It's a date. And Nora …"

"Yes?"

"Thank you. Please tell Nick 'thanks' too."

The click disconnected our call leaving me cut lose and drifting in a sea of unknowingness. I missed them. Nick was sometimes more pompous than he meant to be, but it came from years of experience.

The one thing I lacked, I needed to develop more local contacts. Truth was, I hadn't gone to the Thursday gathering of detectives in a very long time, certainly not since Nick and Nora left town for the long term. A good P.I. had contacts. I should be hearing this sort of rumor for myself.

Damn Mason. This was his doing and my blood pressure suffered from it. I told him everything, I gave him everything, albeit the morning after, but I didn't hold back on him. I was on the level with him. I guess he'd never understood the fact you can't squeeze blood from a turnip.

To satisfy myself, I went to the window and scratched Not My Cat on his head while looking down at the street. No one out there. Perhaps the rumor was older than my finale with Mason. Still, I wanted to secure his written statement in case I needed it as my Get-Out-of-Jail-Free card from that board game.

In the front office, Marley was rearranging things and fussing around.

CHAPTER NINE

Promises tend to be emptier than an old bottle of gin,
feel just as great when taken as a whole, and just as
good at giving you a hangover.

-Lou Tanner, P.I., Notes for female Pemberton
Graduates, 1935

One o'clock, and Mr. Lockwood arrived with business-like punctuality. To his surprise, and likely some pleasure, Marley showed him in.

Dressed dapper and swell, Lockwood was the picture of excellent taste. Blue suit, white shirt, grey tie.

From the look of his face, Lockwood still wasn't sleeping well. Deeper dark patches under his eyes. His skin wasn't perfect, which I liked — perfection was overrated. In the daylight, I noticed he had texture to his skin which Nature had graced him with, much to the chagrin of fashion mavens everywhere who demanded flawlessness and perfection. Still, those eyes weren't seeing dreams and his overall body-stance spoke volumes about his exhaustion. Anxiety over missing stepdaughter might cost a man his health, if he liked her, but every move and gesture Lockwood made was telling me a lot more. was it his import business causing him worry too?

Despite all, Marley gave me a look that said, "What a dish."

"So, you decided not to type my invoice yourself?" He sat down. A nice attempt at humor.

Not My Cat hopped off the sill and wandered out to Marley before she closed the door behind him.

I had the sensation he was looking me up and down, now the light was flooding in the window. A rectangle shadow, from my painted name plate, covered my desk.

Confession. I didn't mind him checking me over. Hell, I'd done it to him, and turn-about was fair play. And for every second he got a better look at me, I got a better look at a man who shouldn't be divorced. Where were all the ladies looking for love? Money, looks, manners. Why no new doll clinging to his arm? What was he doing alone?

Keep it professional, Lou. "What did you find in Frannie's room?"

"A cheque. Written to her."

I took a long look at it. Unsigned. Written from an account belonging to Charles Allen Burton Proctor III. People with four names tend to be people from families who pay by the word for their offspring. I recognized the name. Maybe my former railroad princess alter-ego knew him or maybe met him once. I couldn't put my finger on it.

"Blackmail? Is this proof that Frannie was blackmailing this fellow," he asked, with a tinge of guilt in his voice.

"It's unsigned." I held it up and looked at it through the bright light streaming in the window. *Chapter 28: On Forgery* had some very useful techniques for recognizing forgeries. "No pencil marks on the amount or receiver's name."

He came to stand by me and an electric pulse rushed through my body again. "As if copied from another cheque or a letter?"

I nodded. Smart man. "Only means they didn't copy it by tracing in pencil first. That would be an amateur move. The writing is fluid, so at first glance, I'd say this was written by someone comfortable with putting their writing on paper. Do you have anything by Proctor we can compare it to?"

I looked out at the street as a hack and two 'Crawlers raced by.

I saw the guy leaning against the light pole. Tall stature. Overcoat. Big-brimmed hat. The indigent from the other night? Was he following Lockwood? I only saw him when Lockwood was here, otherwise he might be following me. Nah.

Maybe I should worry.

You're being watched

Lockwood shook his head. "Cab Proctor and I don't move in the same circles." A strand of hair fell in his face. The circles under his eyes were bothering me. Maybe I was just being a Mother Hen. Then, he looked at me — dead in the eyes. We stood trapped in place for a moment. Voltage was arcing between us. He smelled good.

"How about something of Frannie's? We can likely establish whether or not she forged this."

"Nothing with me, Miss Tanner, but I think I can find something."

I hurried away from my window and any dangerous attraction I had to my client. At my desk I lined up the cheque and pulled a camera out of my drawer. Same drawer my bourbon bottle resided in. He saw it and raised an eyebrow. I did not choose to reply.

I took several camera shots of it, close and further away. Once done, I handed him the cheque. He didn't take it from me.

"Don't you want to hold onto it?"

I shook my head. "I have copies now, once my roll of film is processed. You should put it back." I removed the roll of film, asked him to wait a moment, and stepped out to Marley.

"Think you can check on someone I think is tailing Lockwood? And not get caught doing it?" I whispered.

"Of course. I can drop that," pointing to the roll of film, "at the drugstore. Where's the tail?"

"Light pole, down from the big window. Thin guy. Cheap overcoat. Cheaper hat. Can't make out his face. Smoking right now, I think. Kinda' tall."

Marley winked, grabbed her coat, and headed out. Not My Cat took up her seat, enjoying the warmth she'd left behind.

"You be careful," I whispered — out loud. She gave me a sharp nod before closing the door.

I walked back into my office, to find Lockwood was still holding the cheque.

For a moment, I was sure he was ready to panic. "Must I return it?"

I kept seeing him from different angles and in different lights. He was the kind of man who melted into his environment by choice. It was a good habit for a businessman. Yet, in the light streaming through my window, he looked lost. Not incompetent or weak, simply lost by all the unfamiliar, uncertain landscapes he was roaming.

I found it attractive in an odd way. "It's unsigned and uncashed. Put it back exactly where you found it. If it turns up at the bank," I held the cheque out to him again, "then you have proof she's still around. You'll also have proof she's been to your house."

With reluctance, as if touching a canister of mustard gas, he took it back.

"Mr. Lockwood, you *are* able to get back in again?"

He blushed a little. "Yes. I think I can. Irenie has a regular schedule. I have an idea when I can go there — safely."

"Thank you, Mr. Lockwood. It's important. Of course, I wouldn't mind a chance to examine her room on my own. From a PI's point of view. At which point, I can return the cheque for you. You wouldn't need to be involved unless I need to prove I have permission to be on the property. In case I'm seen."

"That would be nice. But it might cause too many problems. I need to take you. You, and this cheque." Ah, so he had a bit of the backbone he had been holding in reserve.

"When Irenie is not at home."

He chuckled. "Wouldn't it be ironic? If Irenie came home and found us ..." He broke it off. "She wouldn't believe you were there on a professional level. As an investigator, that is."

He smiled. Damn. I realized it was the first time he'd relaxed with me around. I had so many questions, but not now. Beyond anything else, he needed confidence in me, certainly enough to sneak us both into his house. Too many questions now would ruin everything.

"Irenie goes to dinner at a club every night now, unless she's hosting what she calls a 'party.' According to the housekeeper ..."

He had a housekeeper? Interesting. Said housekeeper hadn't abandoned the job when Lockwood abandoned ship. Either Irenie wasn't so bad, or the housekeeper had high hopes that Lockwood would be back. Or, Lockwood was paying her to stay put.

" ... Irenie doesn't have any of her Salons planned this week. Thank God."

Or maybe the housekeeper had something on Irenie? "I gather her Salons are," I thought of the words best to use, and chose, "intriguing?"

"That's one word to call them. I guess divorcees live by a different set of standards these days."

"We are in the Modern Age, I'm told."

He huffed a half-stifled laugh. "Meet me at, say, eight o'clock, this evening? We can take care of these two birds with one stone."

"Leave me the address. I'll be there. Eight o'clock sharp. Anything you'd like to tell me before then? Anything you've thought of?" *Come on, Lockwood, there's more to your story.*

I thought for a moment he might say something. It looked to me like he wanted to. Instead, he prodded at his pocket, as though he couldn't find the cheque inside. "No, I don't think so. Until eight. Thank you." He took up a pen from his inside pocket and wrote down an address on the slip of paper I offered.

To say the least, I was both disappointed and unsurprised by his response. I had to earn his trust. That, or I needed to discover what he was hiding.

Both.

I thought about asking him if he wanted a drink, a little because I wanted one and a little because I worried Marley might need more time. A little booze can loosen a man up, start him to talking about things. Maybe later. I didn't want to spook him. There was no chapter in the *Pemberton* manual covering this in detail. Maybe because encouraging the use of alcohol only a couple of years after they revoked Prohibition was not a wise move for a company maintaining its national accreditation. Besides, timing and reading the client were things one couldn't be taught in a book. It required instinct, something Uncle Joe said I had in spades.

My front door opened, and I recognized Marley by the shapes and colors coming through the frosted window.

After an awkward moment, I couldn't quite read, he politely offered his congratulations on the new office and his wish for me to have a pleasant afternoon. His eyes said one thing and his mouth another. This was becoming par for the course. I didn't yet sense he was outright lying to me, but I did gage how much he was compromising my investigation through omission of facts.

Lockwood stopped at Marley's desk and asked her for her name. It was a professional move from someone who thought he might need that information at some point. Wise. He even went so far as to pet the cat. How do you dislike a man who was nice to animals? I took the moment to write everything down in my notebook. I needed to record everything while it was fresh. Word for word. Narrative style, like a novel. I penciled down every detail I recalled, then I scribbled things in the margins about tone, actions, body language.

After his departure, Marley sidled in with a scrap of paper in her hands. "Here's Mr. Wonderful's address." I held up the slip of paper he'd given me.

She was right. Something was wonderful, yet not quite trust-worthy about him. I dismissed it as attractiveness combined with mystery.

"How about our friend from downstairs?"

"Fled the moment I walked near. He figured out who I was. That means this guy isn't necessarily following Mr. Lockwood — he might be following you."

You're being watched

"Damn." I leaned back, hoping my guts wouldn't try to escape. A couple of deep breaths, and a mental assurance I had Mason's statement safely tucked away, I settled back.

"Is he part of this?" Marley held up a rumpled piece of paper. *The note.*

"Yes. Where did you find that?"

She looked a bit surprised I would even need to ask. "Trash can, where I presume you tossed it, Slim."

In fairness, I told her about how I got the note and the instances I thought might be the same guy. Of course, she wanted to understand why anyone took such a creepy interest in me.

I told her about Mason. She promised to knee the agent in the groin if he showed up at the office. Professional to the nines, of course, since we were a legitimate outfit.

I left off on the details about the Pointe job, and I told her I was. Some things she was better off not knowing. "Okay, Slim. Your call. But, I can handle the information?"

"I'm not worried about you, I'm worried about them dragging you into the middle of all the stupidity. I'll keep it to myself, for now. That way you've got plausible deniability."

"And the creeper following you?"

"Let him. For now. You got his measure. What did you pick up about him?"

"That's one tall drink of water out there. Couldn't be less than five-feet-eleven. Never saw his face. Good quality trousers and shoes, though you're right, cheap overcoat and hat. It's a disguise."

"It sounds a bit amateur. And he ran away?"

She nodded sharply. "Definitely amateur." Marley picked up a cigarette, lit it, and handed it to me. "So, Slim, anything else dangerous about this case, other than Mr. Wonderful's dark baby-blues?"

"Maybe."

She lit her own cigarette. "Are you worried? You look a little worried."

"I don't like this office being observed, especially if that mug is following me and not Lockwood."

Her face contorted a bit. "If you have a promissory note from Agent Mason, then why would the government send anyone to follow you?"

"He may not have told anyone. Let's just say I obtained it under duress."

"Break a man's nose, he's bound to be a little upset."

"More embarrassed than injured."

"To a man, it can be the same thing." Marley's eyes followed her smoke curl up toward the ceiling. "Is it related to this case in a different way? Is someone tailing you, because of Lockwood?"

I shook my head, realizing I was jumping to a conclusion I couldn't support yet. "I haven't started poking my nose around any of his stepdaughter's questionable friends. I did talk to a Lockwood connection." I gave her a rundown of my meeting with Gilbert Halliday. "I do have one big target. It's a doozy. One of Frannie Coventry's friends is a real winner." I held out the sheet Lockwood gave me last night.

She almost dropped her cigarette. "Willkie Valentini? The Willkie Valentini."

"Yup. *That* Willkie Valentini."

Marley backed up a step. "Slim, he kills people."

"No, not really. He has other people kill people for him. According to what I've read in the papers, he never does it himself. That's why the cops can't catch him. And more than one cop has been riding him pretty hard, hoping he'd slip up."

I estimated about a mile developed between her thoughts. "Slim, I think his involvement makes this case very dangerous. Are you sure you want to be involved further?"

Fair question. "Right now, all I'm doing is working with my client. I haven't started on the more illustrious friends of Miss Frannie. I may not have to."

"And if you do?"

I set down my cigarette and opened the drawer opposite my bourbon drawer. The automatic I set down on my desktop impressed her. "Savage 1907. .32 Caliber, ten-shot, made in the good 'ole USA."

I then pulled my derringer out of my stocking pocket and pushed it over to her. She liked it, though I couldn't tell if the gun or the handy holster caught her attention. "Ever strip search one of these?" I knew the answer, but I suspected her response would be more than satisfying and I wanted to see her do it.

Marley jammed the cigarette between her teeth, picked up the little heater, and pulled it apart like a pro. Once she'd inspected all the parts, she popped it back together and held it with pure confidence. Proper muzzle control, safety locked in place. She grasped what she was doing. I took a box of ammo out of my purse, making it much lighter. "You got something against Lightning guns?"

I tried not to laugh. "The big ones are messy as hell. The little ones you and I can plant our hands on tend not to work when you need them to. Bad batteries. One big blast that had best count or else."

"They look pretty darned dangerous, working or not. They have that advantage."

"So do these. And they work ninety-nine percent of the time. I don't know," I admitted, "call me old fashioned."

"Ha! You? Old fashioned? Who's the first female Detective in the City? Who's bucking every social norm?"

"Okay, you win. But I'm not getting a Lightning Gun. If you want one, have at. I won't stop you."

This partnership would work out fine. "In the meantime, keep it handy, Marley. They haven't gotten into the habit of shooting the secretaries yet, but if I can be a lady dick, they can change their rules too."

"Do I need a license for this rod, and for snooping around?"

"Yes, and maybe. We'll get you your own gun — licensed properly. As for a PI's license …"

She looked at me, wondering what I planned say. Hell, I was wondering what I'd say.

"As for that, you'll need to graduate from an accredited school, take a couple of tests, and register with the City and County." I tilted my head, as if seeing her from another angle changed anything. "Then comes the leg work. Lots of leg work. I got lucky, my experience included years tagging along with Uncle Joe. Are you sure you really want to this?"

She made an attempt at appearing very thoughtful. "*Pemberton's*, of course." She pointed the derringer at my diploma.

Of course. Go sign yourself up. If you don't graduate, you'll learn a lot about this business. If you graduate, the office can reimburse you. Fair?"

"Fair e'nuff." Smoke slipped out between her lips. "O'Brien and Tanner, Private Investigators. I like the sound of it."

I didn't, but only because it should be Tanner and O'Brien. And, because, *Pemberton's* doesn't hold back in telling you what to expect from the life as a Shamus. Marley was smart — she might decide it was better to be the secretary than the Shamus. I'd leave it to her. One way or another, today I had the best help ever asked for. Last night, I didn't.

Looking at the Savage .32, I felt my stomach tighten. I was treating my job and this case as if it was a safe hobby, I'd invite all my friends to come and try. It wasn't. It was time I settled into reality.

It was also time to visit the police. And I couldn't decide which was worse — Valentini or the cops? Neither one of them followed the rules or had any use for a lady dick.

CHAPTER TEN

Make friends with the cops. It never hurts to have a
friend with a handcuff key.

-Lou Tanner, P.I., Notes for female Pemberton
Graduates, 1935

A regular hack. Yeah, I lucked out and found one of the City's
ten real cabbies. Dropped me off at Drumm and Washington Streets.

The San Francisco Police Department, Homicide and Vice
Division, looked like every police set up you ever saw in the picture
shows. I felt a little twinge of guilt: old desks, beaten up chairs, files
stacked to the ceiling, mail delivery 'Bots sliding awkwardly up and
down rusting cables, and a fleet of cars from 1922, I'd walked past on
the way in. Chairs looked to be older than me, and the desks were
positively ancient. My new office was better by far. Newer, cleaner,
more graciously appointed, compared to this joint.

Marley finagled the name of a Vice cop who might give me
some details. She warned me he had a thorn under his saddle about
Willkie Valentini. She didn't warn me enough. Newspaper men got
their statements from Detective Sergeant Milton Somerset every time
Valentini was into something nasty — by implication or otherwise.
And every time, Valentini wiggled out of it.

It was no surprise to me when Somerset stopped watching me
from an impolite distance, put down his cup of coffee, and acquiesced
to speak to me, he looked like he lived his life as a three-act play about

frustration and disappointment. He was medium height and broad in the chest. He wore a light brown, narrow-brimmed Tyrolean, complete with wide hat band, narrow brim, and ity-bity feather, which made his head look a little too small in comparison with the rest of him. Nobody at home making sure he dressed right. His shirt had seen better days but was clean and neat — professional laundry style. His muscles pressed out from underneath, and, as he casually disrobed his coat in front of me, he kept a brown cigarette clamped in his down-turned mouth. Cheap smokes. Clean shaven — just to be sure everyone noted the frown lines around his mouth and the small dimple in his chin. On the street, I would mistake him for a former boxer-turned-manager.

Rolling up his sleeves, he revealed a set of thick-veined forearms, took his seat, and pulled the cigarette out of his mouth. No handshake?

He looked me over hard, like he'd seen me somewhere before. He'd been looking at me since I moment I walked in and asked for him. Then he held my badge with disrespect and even held it up to the light, as if it were a fake. I was expecting him to try to bend it with his teeth, as if it were a forged coin made from cheap metal.

Tossing it over to me, he leaned back in his chair and folded his hands across a taught-muscled abdomen. "You wanna' know about a friend of Willkie Valentini? You've come to the right place, Toots. What do you want to know? Did he lose a pet dog and you're looking for it? Can't he find his house keys?" Such a nasty sting to his words. Bitter. Disappointed. Angry.

"Nah, I'm here to waste your time." That didn't come out the humorous way I wanted it to, but sure came out the way I was feeling. Sarcasm was my best friend, most of the time. This time, perhaps not so much.

He glared at me. No sense of humor. Can't take that route with him.

"I'm quite serious, Detective, I'm here to find out if the SFPD's expert on a notorious bad guy ever heard of a gal named Francis Coventry and can tell me about her."

He attempted to hide a laugh by staring at the ceiling for a moment. "Frannie, huh? What's she done now? Fleeced another lover? Is her mommy pissed off at her again?"

"From what I hear, there's an unlimited number of reasons Irenie Coventry might be mad."

"And you want information, for free?"

"Better to hear it from you than spending hours in the library, looking at microfiche copies of the papers. Besides, you now more than the paper men." A truthful compliment, I hoped he'd accept. Hook the fish with bait not stone, as my Gran would say.

He bit. "Sure, I do. What's in it for me? Why should I tell you anything?"

"I like to have friends in high places. I like smart friends in smart places even better. I'm not after Mr. Valentini. I just want to learn a bit about Frannie and how she links up to Valentini."

I opened up my special, *make friends* cigarette case and offered him one. Each one of those cigarettes was worth a whole pack of the regular stuff. Quality. I don't mind investing in conversation starters.

Intrigued, he leaned forward to look. After giving me the once over again, which sent blood rushing to my cheeks, he took two cigarettes.

I didn't think one of those cigarettes would be lit and offered back to me, so I closed the case and waited while he stoked up one and pocketed the second. Other than showing up with coffee and doughnuts, I figured good tobacco was another way to warm up a cop.

"Also, Detective, I'm on the level. Willkie Valentini is yours. All yours. I'm only looking for some background on Frannie. Anything bad points to Valentini, I'll give you the goods. No holding back. That's a long-term promise."

He thought about it, while enjoying his smoke. I figured he'd already decided to share but liked to appear thoughtful, and maybe just a little bit like he controlled the deck. For the moment, he did. I respected that.

"Not enough."

This guy takes bribes in the middle of PD HQ?

He breathed out a puff of smoke. "Who you're working for and how the hell some doll got past County officials to win one of those," he pointed to my badge. "I think you either have something on a county official or flirted your way in. That's what I think."

What was I thinking? I know. I was thinking: *Look, Sparky, you don't know me from Eve. I worked hard to earn my piece of bronze you were pitching around like a horseshoe. This was my career. Career, you goon! Why I became a P.I. was none your damn business. For the record, I was fed up having to do better and more just so that some low-brow, flatfoot like you can sit on your ass, smoking my cigarettes and staring down your nose at me. If I didn't look so lousy in black and white stripes, I'd sock you in the yap and try to slap some common curtesy into you.*

What I said, however, while every angry thought raced around in my head, was, "Meet you half way, Detective. I give you my story and everything, except the name of my client. You know, and I know, that information is confidential. Everything else up front and cricket."

"Yeah, well you know, and I know that if I find out your pretty little badge is a pretty little fake, I'll throw your pretty little ass into the clink."

Okay, big boy, I can play this game too. "You know, and I know, my license is not fake, and neither is my promise to give you anything I learn about Valentini. He's bad news and you're after him. I'm not planning on getting in your way and I can even help." I stared him straight in the peepers and I still wasn't sure if he would blow up or calm down. Instead, he laughed.

"Okay, Dollface. I'll bite — for now." He dragged twice on the cigarette and exhaled in my direction. What a Gent. "What have you got so far, Toots?"

A searing hatred for being dismissed and diminished by being called Dollface and Toots. "Frannie's a wild child. A parent's worst nightmare. Hangs out with the wrong crowd. Not the apple of her doting mother's eye?"

"You're right. A doting mother? That ain't Irenie. Have you met Irenie?"

"Not yet. I came here to sharpen my claws on your desk first. That way anyone else I need to contact will think I'm a pussycat. Tell me about Irenie. What should I expect?"

"She's a real piece of work. Managed to snag some sap who gave her two favorite things in the world – money and status."

The "sap" was my client, but I kept my expression neutral.

He kept going. "She'd sell her own daughter. May have, though we haven't caught her doing it yet. I get the idea Frannie has some sense, but she's made some pretty bad choices, Valentini being one of them." For half a second, an expression of sadness and resignation controlled his features, then he tightened up. "Truth is, Irenie is more jealous of her own daughter than anyone else, and that says something. Still," he inhaled, "she protects that girl."

"Maybe she has a little bit of mothering in her?" The end of my sentence raised — I anticipated what he might say.

"In Irenie? Hell no. She sees Frannie as income, nothing more."

"Anything else?"

"If she invites you to one of her salons, don't go."

"Oh?"

A darling, roly-poly man wandered up. He wasn't nearly as tall as Somerset, but twice as round, and he had a neat moustache, clean suit, and a warm handshake. "This is the lady dick everyone's talkin' about? You didn't say she was nice looking lady dick. Gee, you're sweet," he gave Somerset the stink-eye, I suppose for not making a better introduction. "Detective Bernard Rollins, but you can call me Bennie."

I took his hand, like one of the boys, and gave him a handshake worth remembering. "Hello Bennie. You can call me Lou."

"Ain't that swell? She even sounds like a real Shamus."

"Probably 'cause I am a real Shamus. Ain't *that* swell?"

Somerset blew his smoke over at Rollins. "What do you want, Bennie?"

"Heard this lady might have some info on Willkie Valentini. Whaddya got, Honey?"

91

"A missing person case," Somerset snarled at him before I could reply.

What was between those two men was not a friendship, but then sometimes you don't get lucky in your partners and colleagues. I didn't doubt Somerset would go to the moon for Rollins, and vice versa, if for no other reason than they shared dangers and goals. And the blue uniform.

Didn't mean they were friends. In fact, my woman's intuition said they didn't like each other much.

"I'm looking for Frannie Coventry," I said before Somerset, taking control the conversation away from him. "Rumor has it she's friends with Valentini."

"Nobody's friends with Valentini," Rollins said. "He just puts up with folks until he decides he doesn't need them anymore."

"Frannie?"

"She fit the bill for a moll. He put up with her, I gather. Can't picture him falling for a broad. Can't picture him caring enough about anyone else. He's ugly that way."

"Violent? That's what the papers say."

"The worst kind. Don't matter if you're a cop, a priest, or a kid. If you're in Valentini's way, you're as good as removed."

Nice guy Frannie was associating with, but then I understood it as fact before I came in here. Valentini liked to make the papers. "Based on what you two have gathered over the last couple of years — sounds like Valentini got tired of Frannie."

They looked at each other. Rollins shrugged. "If he has, she's as good as gone. He doesn't keep his molls around for more than six months."

"Sounds about right for the timing. I understand she hooked up with Valentini about six months ago," I shared. "What else can you tell me?"

"Shut your yap, Bennie. Don't be such a sap for a girl with a badge. We don't have time for a lost and found." Somerset put out his cigarette.

Bennie rolled his eyes and then smiled for me. "Look, I don't know if you're on the level or not. But if you are, I hope you find her. Her mother won't be of any help to you."

Somerset waved his partner away. "Don't waste your time. Keep your ears open, for where Valentini's dumped the body, and keep your mouth shut, so you don't go catching his attention. Leave the rest to us. This is too big for you, sister. It was all too big for Frannie — she shouldn't have gotten involved with Valentini. And neither should you." He stood up, still not offering his hand. "Come on, Bennie. We have real work to do."

Rollins looked embarrassed. "I'm sorry about him. He's got one song to play in this band."

"It's called Getting Even with Willkie Valentini. And he plays it over and over and over."

"That's it. Listen, Honey, he does have a point. He's been after Valentini for eight years now and he's got nuthin' to show for it. Slicker than a wet fish. I'm not sure who you should avoid or who you should visit, but whatever you do, don't land in between Valentini and Milt Somerset. That's where people die."

"Even if his partner got in the way?"

"Oh, he'd shoot me first, then take on Valentini, if I got in his way." Rollins laughed. I didn't think it was so funny.

"Thank you," I said, in earnest. "Bennie, here's my card, in case you have anything for me. A pleasure meeting you."

"Likewise, Lou. You be careful."

I headed out of the department, stopping to look back. Rollins was chatting with another officer, I guessed he was explaining who the dame was. Somerset was glaring at me, studying me, over the other cigarette he'd taken. I got the message; he controlled the flow of information out of the Vice Squad. I got it, loud and clear.

Outside I sat down on a bench and took out my notebook. I was too new to the job to trust remembering everything. Word for word, I wrote it down, while it was still fresh in my bean.

So, I thought as I smoked one for the road, chances were good I'd face the infamous Willkie Valentini sooner rather than later.

But first — Irenie Coventry. The Dragon herself.

CHAPTER ELEVEN

Be prepared for there to be two sets of laws: those for us and those for the rich. And, they are not even close by comparison.

-Lou Tanner, P.I., Notes for female Pemberton Graduates, 1935

Eight o'clock, fully-loaded Savage .32 in purse, I passed any number of harried and tired servants heading home for the evening. Some people put their staff up on site and others, with smaller homes, not enough room. It was like watching the bruised and damaged from the poorer parts of the world. Come to America, survive underemployed and underpaid. Better than getting killed by that Hitler creep, or Bolsheviks, or any of the jackasses who want to rule the world.

I stopped at the intersection of Jones and Vallejo. Russian Hill. Nice homes up at the top. Further down the slope, past Jones, were nice but affordable houses and apartments. 1021 Vallejo was at the top of Vallejo Street, next to a hillside park with a stone balustrade and enough grass to accommodate expensive breeds. Dogs, I mean. Mr. Lockwood was doing alright for himself.

Two flat disks with spinning brushes whizzed past me, snagging any number of cigar butts and other detritus of the living and sucking them into big canvas bags they dragged behind them. Cleaner 'Bots. My Dad once told me they were called Bummers because of the collection bags. Not at all what they were called in reality, but to a seven-year-old, such details were fascinating. Top of the line street cleaners, expensive, and they're never used outside of this neighborhood or any other high-class quarter. Their handler, watcher, and wind-up key man strolled past me, barely taking notice. My tax dollars at work.

They split and went down the perpendicular lanes of the street, built at an angle to keep the street grade navigable while providing access to Jones. I waited, a little amused, when they passed me and then continued climbing to the top. Big townhouses clustered together on both sides of the cul-de-sac. Vallejo Street cut off at the top of the hill, then continued below the steep cliff to Mason Street. Mason? A flash of irony.

From the balustrade, I looked out over the City. Fog was laying off the coast and the area had a spotty set of high clouds above it. Lights glowed orange, yellow, and blue. Flashing neon on lower Broadway and Columbus called attention to all the clip joints and sex shops.

Lockwood was late.

A punctual man and tonight he decided to be late?

At the bottom of the street, before the split road, a large Buick turned off its lights. No one got out. I didn't like that. I suppose it was a chauffeur napping until he was to drive someone home, but ...

My gut said, "Watch the car."

The Lockwood House fit the upscale hillside it perched on. Some houses wore a nightgown of darkened wood shingles, bay windows, and interesting decorative gables serving little to no purpose but to show off how much material created them. A couple of the buildings were townhouses in dinner gowns; square and boring, were it not for the exceptional accessories of landscaping, hinting that the most important form of life in residence was plant not human.

Then came his house. Soft turquoise green with cream accent. An evening gown of flowing curves, simplicity in design, and the ability to effortlessly hug the hill without tumbling one hundred feet below to Mason Street. The perfect ultra-modern design. One of the few things I learned in finishing school that was of any use to me now, was a laundry list of residential design styles, what was chic and what wasn't, and who to blame. Expensive. Impractical. A show piece. I guessed it was about five years old at most, built right at the start of the Depression. Lockwood took the same economic punches we all had, yet he coughed up the coin to build the thing with his import/export company. He was one hell of a businessman, it would seem. Sculptured hedges and trees matched the modern esthetic. A bracelet of cement surrounded the whole garden, stating without exception that trespassers were unwelcome.

I thought I heard a tune with Billie Holiday's silky voice sliding into the depth of the music. The smell of cooking meat and still-damp mud sent a photograph racing through my brain. Not one of unbridled wealth but of an upstate New York family picnicking at the park. A sharp pang gripped my stomach and I pushed the mental picture to the back of my head. Not now.

The view was breathtaking, and I couldn't help imagining it in daylight. For now, the City, facing east to Yerba Buena and Treasure Island Naval Air Station, was a blaze of blinking lights, vehicle headlamps, and streetlights. A couple of searchlights burst out into the sky, south of the view. The Pointe.

Out in the Bay, a lighthouse sent its beam of light rotating around its tower. Alcatraz Island Prison.

Such a waste of land.

Around 8:20 pm, footsteps arrived behind me, casual but quick. I wasn't surprised they belonged to Mr. Lockwood.

"Good evening," I said hopefully.

"I sure hope so. Sorry I'm late." He looked a little disheveled, and it looked good on him. He explained, before I asked, he parked his car elsewhere and walked up the hill to me. He didn't want his car seen. By Irenie, I suspected. Ah heck, I *knew*.

"Shall we go in," I asked. He hesitated. "You do have a key, don't you? I charge extra for breaking and entering."

"Yes, of course." That smile he'd held back before, arrived just in time. "I have bad memories every time I come here. And, I'd prefer not to run into Irenie."

"Well, Mr. Lockwood ..."

"Elliott. If we're facing the dragon together, we might as well be on a first name basis."

"Okay, Elliott. It's Lou, by the way. Listen if we run into Irenie, I can handle it. I can say I'm writer for a magazine. I'm confident I'm prepared for her, just in case."

His expression said he believed otherwise, but I was ready. Up the wandering stone path, we wound our way to the gracious front door, made from the corpse of a gigantic oak tree. A sweet-faced woman met us. The housekeeper? Of course. She looked at Lockwood as if he was the best thing she'd seen in years. Like family coming to Thanksgiving dinner.

Lockwood introduced us and the look of satisfied conspiracy on the woman's face was a good sign.

I should have been, but I wasn't prepared for the Lockwood house's interior. Clearly someone spent a fortune paying for affection from a gold-digging wife. As if he heard my thoughts, Lockwood removed his hat and offered me a mild, embarrassed grin.

It was money spent on luxury, selfishness, and failure to recognize the crumbling world around it.

The walls were a base of smooth, eggshell white, with soft gold filigree stenciled in diamond shaped patterns from floor to ceiling. Modern crown molding and chair rails in sets of simple threes, painted silver, accentuating the shape of the room. A single mirror took stage on the left, hung above a narrow table of light marble and light wood. A "V" shaped vase held fresh flowers and blocked access to the mirror. Clearly no one was expected to do something crass, such as check the tilt of their hat. It was an old trick to use a mirror in narrow areas to broaden the room's appearance. It wasn't needed but who as I to critique?

Centered in the middle of a white rug was another table, with palm fronds carved into its legs. More flowers. It was an expensive place to dump your hat and gloves.

Beyond the wide entry was a living room with a view to kill for. Sweeping down from upstairs with a gentle curve was a staircase sporting a fancy iron banister painted in white to match the walls.

Everything was new. Sleek, expensive, modern. All for show.

Pointing and almost rushing me, Lockwood led me up to Frannie's room.

If I didn't know better, I'd assume the occupant was a twelve-year old girl hoping to reach puberty with some grace, straight teeth, and clear skin. Everything was white, fluffy, and accented with grey and pink. Toys waited in a corner, not discarded but not a primary focus either. Her vanity table was tidy, with lipsticks, nail enamel, and powder. If I'd found photos clipped from the magazines of Gary Cooper or William Powell, hell, Andy Rooney, I wouldn't be surprised.

Pointing to where he planned to return the cheque, Lockwood looked around, uncomfortable and ready to flee. Finally, he slipped the check between two magazines, making sure an edge poked out. Balling-up his fists and releasing them, a relaxation technique I use too, Lockwood walked back to the door to peek out.

"Would you like to wait in the hall? I won't steal anything. Scout's honor."

Nodding, he abandoned the room with a bit too much speed.

In her drawers were some decidedly un-childlike pieces of underwear. Silk and lace and plenty of see-through-in-all-the-right-places gowns. Impractical garter belts. In the bottom drawer of a rather large chest waited too much leather. A pair of kid gloves, I wouldn't question, but this stuff was the sort of leathery accoutrements that would make any man fearful — unless he was hoping to be a little terrified. Some men liked that sort of thing, or so I've heard.

The locked drawers in her vanity piece were a challenge — for a moment. *Chapter 29: Lock Picking.* I was grateful for the lessons in the chapter. I got the drawers open fast. Some letters and picture postcards were inside. Half empty perfume bottles. A small but thick photo album, hidden under sections of newspaper.

I took out the album and started to look through.

99

I caught myself holding my breath with each turn of the page. The subject of the photos was Frannie. None were pornographic in that you couldn't see any naughty bits. But I couldn't think of a different word for them.

Frannie, underage without a doubt, had been posed in sexual, provocative ways. If nudity was at issue, she'd covered her exposures with fabric. I was sitting on the very bed where some of the shots had been taken, props, girlish toys, and all. I felt a little unclean. This whole space had one purpose: turn on adult men with inappropriate, and illegal, interests in sexual innocence. Not to mention sexual innocents.

Sure, I was learning all about this stuff, about the trade in pornographic photos, but something about the child glaring into the camera lens made me very uncomfortable. I couldn't tell if she was posing against her will or enjoying the hell out of herself.

Later in the album, Frannie's role in the indecent story changed. Now she was the aggressor: leather, chains, implements of torture, boots, and body parts barely hidden. Black lace. Sometimes the victim in control. Sometimes Frannie the Sadist. Out of habit, I kept my face expressionless, but inside, I felt shocked. Sure, I was aware of these things, but I hadn't seen them as graphically presented before. I had to keep it all inside — a detective needed to be beyond shock.

Despite the nature of what I was seeing, Frannie's photographic evolution, moving from helpless little girl to assertive dominator, struck me the hardest. Who was the photographer and who were they taken for? Who guided her on this journey of hers?

Was Elliott aware? Had he looked in here and seen what his stepdaughter was wearing when polite society wasn't looking? I checked her armoire. No demure dresses and school-girl socks inside. Only slinky negligees and evening gowns.

Somerset and Rollins were right. This gal was in over her head.

I sat down on the bed and gave it a bounce. The sounds of paper. I searched under and through her mattresses and snagged the brass ring. Letters. Lots of letters. The handwriting was atrocious. I wanted to read them, but the door downstairs slammed.

A woman began shouting.

Irenie.
Oh brother.
We'd been caught.

CHAPTER TWELVE

You're going to meet a Dragon Lady now and then.
Beware the fire breathing. Always bring your badge
to protect you from the flames.

-Lou Tanner, P.I., Notes for female Pemberton
Graduates, 1935

Irenie.

She'd come home early.

Stuffing the letters into my purse, and the album into my bag, I hustled downstairs. I couldn't leave my client to face Irenie alone. From the top of the stairs, I announced, "Thank you, Mr. Lockwood, you are a life saver. That's a lovely water closet, by the way, and …"

Irenie Coventry turned on me like a cobra who'd grown aggravated at its handler.

I felt instantly out of my league, just staring back at those raptor-like eyes.

Her hair was bombshell blonde-white, ala Jean Harlow, with perfect Marcel Waves formed from scalp to chin. Her eyes were bright blue, large, round, and exquisitely made up. Long lashes and a pouty mouth. Not a wrinkle on her. Porcelain skin. Flawless. Her dress was a pale jade silk, a bias-cut gown clinging to her gorgeous figure and revealing her back from neck to tailbone. In her arms was a matching coat decorated with green marabou feathers.

Her arms were slender but muscled. Diamonds dripped from her neck, ears, and wrists. At the end of each, pale finger was a painted claw I was fairly certain she wanted to use to gouge my eyes out.

Irenie Coventry looked like a model from any number of European fashion magazines. No wonder Elliott Lockwood fell for her. She was perfection.

Until she opened her mouth.

"What is that," she squealed, pointing at me.

Before Lockwood spoke, I recalled I promised to handle Irenie, and so I did. "I'm with San Francisco Magazine. The City Architecture and Design Section." I started down the stairs toward her, bouncing a bit on my toes as if I was just too-too dramatic for the situation. An over-the-top social flitting bird. "As you are aware, our quarterly publication ..."

"What?" She spit the words out at Elliott. "You brought your mistress into my house?"

"No." Lockwood tightened up. "And technically, I still own this place. No, she is not a mistress, I brought a —," he scrambled for a viable lie, "A magazine writer here because ..."

Nice move, Elliott.

I was ready. "San Francisco Magazine periodically does a piece on unique and elegant homes in the City. This little chateau of yours is outstanding, and we've had several requests to take interior photographs and interview the occupant. Mr. Lockwood was allowing me a tour," I waved at the upstairs, "and a little break."

Irenie recognized the name of the magazine, as her finely plucked eyebrows shot up, and now it seemed, we were the best of friends, as ever could be. "Oh. Oh, I'm so sorry. It's been a difficult evening. I hope you'll excuse me. Mr. Lockwood really ought to communicate his plans better in the future." She shot him a look that shriveled lessor men.

I tisked appreciatively. "How dreadful. You look like this evening was a bit of a trial," I said, tapping my old Mid-Atlantic voice and upstate New York manners. My glance moved down to her hemline.

Mud coated her feathers and she had a sheen of perspiration on her arms and face. Irenie pulled her fancy coat out of my easy viewing and sauntered over to the housekeeper, on whom she dumped the thing, along with her purse.

The door opened again and in walked a couple. You could tell they were a couple by the way they managed to not touch one another while completing each other's sentences. The woman of the pair was short, dark haired, and perhaps a little past her prime. The man wanted to be somewhere else. A bit too obvious — body language can tell all.

Irenie drew up her energy and ignored both Lockwood and me as she swept over to the couple. "Gem, darling, how are you this evening." She rolled the "darling" out with great emphasis.

"Terrible," the woman replied. "I just heard from Donald Temple, you remember Donald, and he said the fund-raising dinner for Councilman Martens is cancelled. They can't find a chef. A chef! This is terrible. It's the worst possible thing to happen."

I had a list of about twenty things far worse, off the top of my head. Instead, I stood in place with a purposeful, bored look on my face.

"Oh, how ridiculous." Irenie coddled the woman. The two turned their backs on us and nattered away about the appalling lack of good chefs and why the depressed economy didn't help make more of them available — at a cheaper price.

I never worked out why the rich were so stingy.

The man walked over to Lockwood and offered his hand. "If I have to listen to them go on about another chef, I might just …" He stopped when I caught his eye. I was standing next to Lockwood the whole time, but only now did he notice.

Lockwood jumped in. "Miss Tanner, may I introduce Harold Harrison? Harold, this is a writer for San Francisco Magazine, Miss Tanner."

Harrison took a gander at me, checking if I was some sort of temporary toy Lockwood was availing himself of or if maybe I wanted to be his toy for a while. Ten feet from his wife. The rich. Can't explain their reality.

"How do you do," I said with a sweetness I didn't realize I still kept in my bag of tricks.

"The lady is Jemima Harrison," Lockwood added with a shift of his chin.

"Yeah, that's my wife," Harrison said. "Ain't I a lucky man? Damn women." With that, he shoved his hands in his trouser pockets and sauntered over to listen in on a conversation that was likely costing him a bundle.

Irenie turned back to us, with a look asking, oh are you still here. "Well, Elliott?" she asked. "Are you staying? I'm sure Miss Tanner doesn't need you, as you are hardly familiar this delightful home now that I have improved on it. I would be happy to provide Miss Tanner with all the information she needs for her article."

"Uh — we may be done." He faced me. "Have you seen everything you need, Miss Tanner?"

I smiled in a cultured way my mother approved of. "Yes, Mr. Lockwood. I believe my editor has green-lighted the article."

"I hope, 'Mr. Lockwood' will be so kind as to inform me when this interview is to be conducted. I like to have gatherings of my own and I wouldn't want to have them collide."

Lockwood took a heavy breath and held it in squeezed lungs — like a man dying to do some serious damage but trained well enough not to.

My smile was tight enough to bounce coins off of. "Of course, Ma'am. I'll be sure to contact your social secretary to make proper arrangements." I kept smiling.

Irenie's face fell. She glanced over at the Harrisons. "Oh, don't bother. I'm between, I mean, she's on holiday. For the moment, I control my own calendar."

"I understand."

Jemima Harrison toddled over and seemed to be a bit confused, which made sense since she wasn't part of the original conversation. "You are …"

"From San Francisco Magazine." Out went my dainty, limp hand.

"Oh!" She squeaked with delight, nearly reaching the sound only dogs can hear. "Perhaps you would consider our modest home. Nob Hill? Other side of the church?" The woman was a flurry of gestures, like a chicken attempting a long-distance flight. Irenie ignored it.

I couldn't tell if she was serious or testing me.

"My husband is a Vice President with one of San Francisco's most prominent banks. I'm sure many of your subscribers would be excited to read about how business leaders of San Francisco live. Might I have your card," Gem asked.

I heard a sharp intake of breath from Lockwood. It was a trap and I sensed it. "Card? My cards are in my auto." Big lie. A little risky too. "We didn't expect to meet anyone. But I'm sure if you give Mr. Lockwood a call tomorrow he can provide you with my contact information. And I'll leave a set of cards with him. Would that be acceptable?"

Oopsie, I might have blundered. I didn't think of that when I made up my disguise, and it cost me. No one to blame but me.

But, before Gem grilled me more, Harold made a go at me. "What do you drive? Gem wants me to buy her a car. I haven't got the notion of what a woman wants to drive these days and Irenie doesn't drive." Oh, I had an inkling a little insult was tucked in his comment.

"Auburn Cord L-29. Prettiest thing Duesenberg ever put out."

"They don't build those anymore."

"For me, they did. They should build them again," I answered in my brightest voice. "V8 engine, 125 horsepower, front wheel drive. What else would a girl want?"

It was the perfect answer, and I felt a twinge of pride that I managed to impress Lockwood with my broad range of knowledge. Another spot the *Pemberton's* manual didn't quite cover. It was good, old finishing school to beat that education into me. If only people knew what a bizarre and ridiculous childhood I had.

Lockwood took me by the elbow. "Gem, Harold. Irenie. Good night."

Irenie made a move to take him by the arm. "Elliott, I need to talk to you." She glared then smiled at me. "Alone, if you please."

I couldn't help him out of this one. He either had to refuse or deal with her. I waited near the door.

It was an animated talk, they had. The Harrisons acknowledged their allotted place in Irenie's magnificent world. They stayed over by the large mirror.

Irenie was keeping her voice down, but it did little to hide her demanding nature. She gesticulated wildly. He stood his ground, folding his arms and bracing his stance. Good man. She pleaded. He stayed still. I thought she might cry. Yeah, he didn't hold out too long after that. He gave her some cash and hurried to my side.

She stared after us. "I warned you she would lose interest in your company."

He ignored her and hurried me along.

"Lovely meeting you," she said with no sincerity.

Wait, this was an opportunity to go fishing. "Oh, might I ask for your opinion?"

Both Irenie and Elliott stood stunned for a moment, but for different reasons. Even the Harrisons looked up.

"I've been given the name of Cab Proctor as a potential interviewee, and I —"

Irenie was up on her haunches in a flash. "That worthless souse? Why would you even want to interview him?"

"I was given his name as a member of society."

"He's a dirty, no-good miscreant. Gem, tell her."

Mrs. Harrison joined Irenie up on the high seat — metaphorically speaking. "My dear Miss Tanner, whatever you do, do not associate yourself with Cab Proctor. Men like him …" she gave Harold a dark, brief glare, "… are not to be trusted. You wouldn't want your magazine's reputation and business sullied."

Shrugging, Lockwood gave me the I-don't-know look.

Irenie did one better than Gem, which I suspected happened often. "He was after my daughter, Francis. Don't you remember, Elliott? Of course, you don't. You don't care anymore, do you?" She looked me in the eye and lied like a seasoned, professional shyster. "All he wanted was Frannie, because she has money. Access to money. Anyway, he was quite relentless. Wanted to be seen with her, to take her picture, you understand how these young brats act." I wasn't quite sure who she was referring to. "Well, I put a stop to it. Frannie is destined for bigger and better things, even if her stepfather won't help."

"Frannie? 'Bigger and better?' Like what?" Harold started smiling. A smile you'd expect on a lion after catching and eating its prey. Gem glared at him, and he stopped smiling — put in his place — and declined to speak further.

I had to wonder if that was firsthand knowledge Harold tapped for his opinion. Was he one of Frannie's trysts? From the look on Gem's face, a mix of rage and hurt, I didn't think my imagination was over-working by suspecting Harold. "I hope he didn't compromise her reputation."

"No chance of that," Harold shot out, a little surprised at his outburst, before turning his back on Gem.

Well, that verified my hypothesis.

Gem turned the whole of her small body toward her husband, marched over to him, and started chastising him in a furious whisper.

Irenie rolled her eyes and whispered to me, "Nouveau Riche. You'll have to forgive them. They do have an acceptably nice home, on the lower side of Nob Hill, but it hasn't this view." She swept her hand out toward the front windows while simultaneously sweeping her friends under a proverbial on-rushing train. "Perhaps, you would like to bring your photographer over during one of my gatherings?" She hugged my arm as if we'd been school chums for decades. "Cab Proctor is also new money and," her laugh was a light, artificial tinkle, "so unsure of good manners. I'm sure you'll enjoy one of my dinner gatherings. All the best people and only the highest matters in discussion."

Says the Kettle to the Pot.

"Some of the most eligible men attend my gatherings."

Lockwood coughed. "Not one of the salons?" The level of resentment in his voice surprised me.

"My salons are private. My dinner gatherings are much more to Miss Tanner's wants and needs," she spit back at him.

"Will your daughter be at your gathering? I would very much enjoy meeting her."

"Oh no," she blurted out, before covering by using her practiced laugh. Irenie appeared mildly annoyed, either by Lockwood's faux pas of bringing up the topic of her notorious salons or by the suggestion that she include her daughter in her fancy dinner parties. "Frannie is not fond of intellectual discussions."

Ouch. I glanced in Lockwood's direction. He looked far more than mildly annoyed. "She's busy, learning the family business. My family, that is."

I pulled a little on my arm, forcing Irenie to look at me. "Perhaps I can reach her —"

"No need," she said with a slight panic.

"Does she still live here?"

Irenie let go of my arm. "Sometimes. These children today. Always out and about. When I talk to her next, I'll tell her that you might want to chat with her. But, in the meantime, I'll make sure you have my schedule for gatherings."

Dear God, how had Lockwood been so blind? Had she been like this when they'd met? Her daughter was missing and yet all she wanted was the fame of a magazine article. No doubt this woman had everything that exuded beauty — except compassion.

That close, I had a detective's epiphany. I'd been slow on the uptake regarding the pictures of Frannie. The ones I was stealing from her room told a more interesting story now that I took a long gander at Irenie too. Frannie's haircut and style change, from a year ago? Frannie remade herself as Irenie. Or Irenie remade her daughter into a dark-haired image of herself. I left my stomach knotted and twisted.

"I'm glad I asked about Mr. Proctor. Thank you so much — a disaster averted. Perhaps I need to send Mr. Lockwood a list of those we expect to speak with."

Irenie harrumphed. Gem looked hopeful, having overheard my comment, as if she expected to be on that invitation list. Gem practically ran to my side, as if I was giving away free candies and stockings. And Harold looked like he wanted to escape through the mirror like Alice through the Looking Glass.

Putting her hands on her hips, Irenie snapped, "I hope Mr. Lockwood is more careful with scheduling, since I expect to be hosting several salons and dinner parties in the upcoming months. A pleasure meeting you Miss Tanner. I fully expect to see you again soon at an upcoming gathering?" That was, what, the twentieth time she mentioned the damn gatherings? I tried to look impressed. With that, she sashayed off to the parlor, the Harrisons hot on her trail.

She was a magnet to desperate people who wanted to be like her.

Once outside, all Elliott and I did was sigh, take a deep breath, and then laugh.

"You're good," he complimented.

"My Mother was good and I paid close attention. Can I ask how much that little argument cost you?"

"Less than last time." He pulled off his hat for a moment and ran his fingers through his hair. He looked rather good as a rumpled fellow. Why was he so good looking?

"And, gatherings versus salons?"

He nodded reluctantly. "Her so-called gatherings do draw in some prominent people, and a few politicians. They're not bad. She usually brings in some popular Chef. It's the monthly salons …"

"Not quite the same respectable crowd?"

"Let's just say they aren't advertised or promoted by anyone's social secretaries."

The big Buick from the corner drove past us, having turned around in the cul-de-sac, lights off. Further down the road, he still hadn't gotten his headlights working.

That was interesting.

Correction — *that* was strange.

CHAPTER THIRTEEN

Your casebook is your friend, your lover, your
annoying next-door neighbor who constantly reminds
you of chores.

-Lou Tanner, P.I., Notes for female Pemberton
Graduates, 1935

You're being watched.

The Buick made a beeline for Jones Street at the bottom of the
hill. With lights off? He might have killed someone.

"So," I began, still watching the Buick until it was out of sight.
"I gather the comment about eligible men was a swipe at you?"

Lockwood stopped walking.

"Elliott, I'm a detective. I'll need to find out sooner or later.
Her salons have a reputation."

He shrugged and pushed his hands deeper into his trouser
pockets, making him look like a child who'd been sent outside while the
parents argued. "Perhaps. I probably shouldn't consider them. Irenie
had been the toast of the town, but these days, her so-called salons draw
smaller crowds. As I understand it, the boys come out of curiosity, but
the men are on the lookout for younger women." Lockwood turned
and stared up the street for a moment. "I don't have a say in what she
does anymore, though what she does has consequences she doesn't care
about."

"Fits with what I watched. And the police?"

"What do you mean?"

"Have they raided any of these salons?"

His face squished up a bit. "No," he said.

"She's got someone," I wanted to say, 'by the short hairs,' but decided against it. "She's got someone either on the police force or at City Hall making sure her salons go on without any interference."

"I guess I left just in time."

Around the corner and down the hill from the Lockwood home was a popular watering hole, at the corner of Green and Powell streets. It wasn't one of those fancy joints with a bandstand, sequined singers, and white table cloths. It was a beaten-up gin mill with a long bar and bar keepers dressed in button collar shirts with loose ties. Patrons didn't bother to take off their hats. They swarmed around the stools and chairs, cheering a clarinet player and his band of two, with drums and big bass. Tonight's player was a good reed-man and he energized the place.

From the look on Lockwood's face, he'd never been in the joint. Four blocks from his house and you'd think it was six-hundred miles for him.

He settled his hat deeper onto his forehead, and unbuttoned his jacket, trying to fit in. Got to appreciate the effort. It didn't work, but I appreciated it all the same.

I pointed to the telephone booth and he had the decency to order us a pair of drinks. I had no idea what he'd ordered but for some reason, I was willing to trust his judgement. For the most part. He wore good clothes, had good manners, and the house had been the epitome of excellent, upper-middle class design. He had lousy luck in women, but I had to admit Irenie was the sort who drew any and all men in. Yeah, I trusted him to order something alcoholic and useful. It was a hell of a day.

I dropped a nickel in the phone and asked for Klondike 7537. Marley said she'd stick around the office to about 10 p.m.

"Oh my God, Slim, I was hoping you'd call."

She sounded a little panicky. Marley did not panic by nature.

"What's happening? Are you safe? Are you okay?"

"Me? I'm fine. The police have been calling all night. Seven times. Some fellow named Rollins needs a call from you. Right now. He sounded serious and said it was urgent. I didn't think he needed to have every detail on you, so I didn't say."

"Good egg. I appreciate it."

She took a deep breath. "Discretion is my middle name. Here's his number — so you don't have to dig his card out of your purse."

I listened and memorized the number, repeating it back to her. I told her she should go home, and I'd catch her up in the morning. I don't think she liked the idea of having to wait for more details, but, she wished me luck.

Another nickel and a five-minute run around later, I managed to reach Rollins.

He was forcing his whisper through the phone line. "Hiya Lou. You still on that case, looking for Frannie Coventry?"

"Yeah."

"Do you have any idea where either Elliott Lockwood or Irenie Coventry are?"

I sure didn't like where this was going. "Both. Mr. Lockwood was with me from 8:20 to about 9:45 tonight. I met with Irenie from close to the same time to 9:00. What's going on Bennie?"

He didn't say anything for a moment. I pictured him shifting, hiding that he was on the phone. His voice was even softer than before. "We found someone. A gal. It ain't good."

My stomach knotted. "Frannie? She's dead, isn't she?" I looked out of the booth doors at Elliott Lockwood. He looked a little out of his depth in a brew house filled with Joe and Jane Average. But he was trying. He was genuine but not hip to this scene. And, I would have to give him bad news in a matter of a minute.

"Yeah. It's Frannie." He paused. "Dead."

"Ah hell, Bennie, you sure? One hundred percent sure it's Frannie?"

"Yeah," he sounded a little crushed. Maybe being jaded didn't always protect a cop. "We found her in the lot ..." Behind him, voices were shouting, and I swear I heard Somerset barking orders about guns and ammo. "... in the lot behind Willkie Valentini's place. Grant and Green streets."

"Good God."

"We got a tip about a body behind Valentini's place. Just when my partner walked in, too, we got that report. You can guess what happened after that. Pretty much everything exploded after that. He's convinced Valentini killed her his-self. We're heading over, now, to arrest him."

"Bennie, that's going to be a blood bath."

"Yeah, yeah. But Somerset's the lead on this case and a guy has to stand by his partner."

I snorted, "More like you need to hold him back."

A flurry of noise and shouting erupted behind Rollins. "I got to go."

"Bennie?"

He'd hung up.

Oh God, how was I telling Lockwood? There was a chapter in the *Pemberton* manual for this moment, but it didn't occur to me that someone with first-hand knowledge wrote it.

Must I tell him now? Nothing was one hundred percent, I don't care what Bennie said. Before I told Lockwood, I needed to see for myself. I had to be one hundred percent. Maybe, save him from the pain of grief if it turns out the police were wrong. That Somerset jerk-off was wrong about who and how — I sensed it — unless I was too hopeful it wasn't Frannie. Even if my gut was wrong, Somerset might be, since he was too dead-focused on Valentini not the dead girl. Hell, was Lockwood likely to grieve? He'd said he didn't entirely like Frannie. He only felt responsibility for her.

Uncle Joe said he hated domestic cases. Now I understood why.

I set the receiver back in its cradle.

Notebook. I scribbled as fast as possible, every word, every mention. Bennie worried. Somerset arriving just in time to overhear the report and go nuts. Frannie dead. I checked my watch for the exact time of the call.

Any character James Cagney played would simply tell Lockwood. Straight up. No boo-hooing, no pity, no judgement. Man to man. But Cagney wasn't here, and I was. My call. And I wasn't putting Lockwood, my client, Lockwood, through the hell of learning his stepchild was dead until I can say so from my truth. Not until I lock eyes on her.

Pushing the glass doors open, I planted a smile on my face and joined him. He was watching the player waile on his reed. He'd ordered Scotch — neat. While he was watching the musicians, I downed my Dutch courage in a quick swallow and tried to keep as neutral as possible.

Elliott Lockwood looked at me with big blue eyes from under the brim of his Homburg. Damn, those eyes. His eyes were deep pools of ocean water. They were full of shadowy places to hide masculine emotion. They appeared hauntingly still, unemotional, yet screaming with every injustice they witnessed. Some injustices he may well mete out as the president of a business. Underpaying employees, halving women's salaries, perhaps even blocking trade unions from forming, all the while serving the needs of profit and wants of the shareholders. What had those eyes witnessed? Why did I want him to be the bad guy? What was I afraid of? Intimacy with a handsome man? Or a man I was only now learning about by investigating a big mistake he'd made?

He'd said it himself; he was expecting something exciting to happen with his marriage to Irenie. She was a bombshell alright. Was his day-to-day life so dull he took refuge in the promise of the exotic? He wouldn't be the first man to be taken in by beauty. I hoped I was wrong. I wanted him to be the good man he appeared to be.

He handed me his cigarette case and waited while I withdrew one. Dunhills. Imported. Nice. Before I asked, he held a lighter up for me. Did he blink? Or were those eyes still locked onto mine. We were about six inches apart, if that much, with smooth tones sliding down the length of a clarinet and rolling between the heart-beat rhythms from the bass.

Voices blended into a distant murmur.

I had to look away for a moment.

Staring back into his eyes, I wanted to stay put. To drown in that sea of blue.

But he was my client. And there were things that had to be done before I walloped him with the worst news.

"Listen, Mr. Lockwood."

"Elliott."

"I've got a lead I have to follow."

"Great. Let's go."

"No." I hurt him with that answer, damn it. "I need to do this. Only me. Can I reach you at your hotel later? I want to call you. Bring you up to date."

"What kind of lead is it, at this hour, that you can't take me?"

I gave him the PI-damn-serious look rather than a response.

He knocked the ash off his cigarette and left it in the ash tray. "I'll be there. Do you want to drop by?"

"I prefer calling."

"It's bad, isn't it?"

"It's late and it's best I call."

"It's Frannie, isn't it?"

With all the honesty in the world, I replied, "I need to find out."

"Then let me go with you."

I shook my head. "This sort of thing isn't for the client but the Private Investigator. It's my job."

"You shouldn't do this alone."

"Why, because I'm a woman? A doll, a dame, a skirt? No Elliott. This is my job and I do it damn well. You hired me for reasons, none of which are that you think I'm a helpless damsel. Let me do my job." He was still trying to protest. I put my cigarette down in the ashtray and got close — too close. "The one you hired me to do."

He was thoughtful for a long time. Far too long. "I didn't mean to be disrespectful."

"You weren't."

"Lou?" He closed the distance between our lips to about three inches.

Oh God, if he kissed me, I will have blown it with my very first client. I couldn't.

I wanted to.

But, I couldn't.

And I didn't.

"I will call you. One way or another, I'll call you. You will hear from me tonight." I wanted to run out of the place. That terror used to experience as a kid, when I'd jumped into a pool and water rushed up my nose, giving me a sensation of drowning. Yeah, I had that same terror. I had it. I had it big time.

I knew what I was about to find.

Dead was never pretty.

CHAPTER FOURTEEN

That guy had a face like it was married to a pair of
brass knuckles.

-Lou Tanner, P.I., Notes for female Pemberton
Graduates, 1935

Willkie Valentini had more than one gin-joint, but his home base was at the 500 Grants Club, at Grant and Green. The play on the name, being on the five-hundred block of Green at Grant, and the fact that five-hundred Fifty Dollar bills with U.S. Grant's face on them was a cool twenty-five thousand. According to *D&S Detective Magazine*, it was a reference to what Valentini made the first year it was open. It wouldn't surprise me if the gangster gave them a full interview for the publicity.

The exterior evoked a sense of old California, with a Victorian façade and painted-lady colors. It ate up the better portion of the northwest corner of the block. Only one half tamed and developed. But the lower half was still wild. I'd heard about an argument with the City fathers who had other ideas about what should be done with the vacant half. Nowadays, no one at City Hall had the tax revenues to contest ownership or to develop the empty property. Valentini likely enjoyed leaving it scrappy — just to spit at the politicians.

Tonight, search lights focused on the club's entrance and the place surrounded with cops. A line of shields was in a row between the gangster's hold out and the police. A blimp had been maneuvered into place and it blared a recorded message and blasted a bright light down onto the entrance to the 500 Grants.

Police work like that; isn't my cup of tea. They make 'Bots to clean up the streets and to help with industry. But they never created a 'Bot that took on the dangers of police work — not according to every cop I ever met. And if any of those boys were bragging and were now down there. Well, they might be designing a new Cop 'Bot at this very moment.

The recorded message blared again, only partially comprehensible.

I stood on the sidewalk like a sap. Nothing to do. I kept back, sure of the rod in my purse and comforting myself in the knowledge I had it.

Guns drawn. Bull horn out. At any minute, the crowd of civilians I around me expected Chicago Typewriters, aka Tommy Guns, to cut loose and the whole place to go up in dust. Somerset signaled for the blimp recording to stop.

Before he started his demands via bullhorn, the front door opened, and out sauntered the man himself. Willkie Valentini.

A little thick but still fit. He wore a tuxedo. Over one arm, he'd draped his coat. A hat covered his dark hair.

He was sauntering, and another fellow, not so well dressed, was keeping behind him. Lawyer?

"Put your hands up," Somerset shouted into the bullhorn. Ridiculous. Jones was ten feet away. This was all for show.

"Officer Somerton. What's the problem, officer?"

Nothing quite makes a nasty point nastier than getting someone's name and title wrong, especially when you know damn well who they are after all the years they put into chasing you.

Somerset lowered the bullhorn and stomped up to the alleged gangster. I couldn't quite make out the rest of their conversations, but the body language said enough.

Valentini wasn't worried. He wasn't bothered. He was even dressed and ready to go downtown.

The other man — definitely a lawyer. Somerset, yeah, he was plain obsessed. In all that light, the tension in his movements and the red burning up his cheeks was visible. While Valentini stood solid and still, Somerset was wild and animated.

Across the street, Rollins wanted my attention. He signaled me, pointed to his badge then back to me, and then waved for me to come over. All this semaphore was confusing to a couple of the shield-bearing cops.

Whipping out my P.I. Badge, I shoved my way past the crowd, and dodged a car coming down Green too fast.

I trotted across, waving my badge like a white flag, hoping none of the regular cops would be aggressive in trying to stop me. After some side-eye glances, Rollins ushered me into the take-down's inner sanctum.

"You're not up with him, Bennie?"

"I like not getting shot, Sweetheart. This is a situation waiting to go bad."

I turned my back on the whole Valentini-Somerset standoff and leaned closer to Rollins. "Where is she?"

He indicated with his chin, down into the undeveloped half of the lot. The slope was deep from the sidewalk to the lot. Weeds sprang up everywhere that hadn't been trampled down by kids playing or indigents camping. Plenty of garbage, food and newspapers. It was a complete reversal of the 500 Grants Club, with its swept and maintained façade.

Lying on the dirt, face up, and partially covered by a tarpaulin of some sort, was what Rollins said was Frannie Coventry. With all the lights focused on Valentini, the body wasn't as obvious. Neither was the Medical Examiner and two uniforms crouching next to her.

Rollins grabbed me by the arm, making sure he had my attention. "Listen, Lou, go down there and, I dunno, find as much as you can."

"You're letting me near the body?"

"No." He bit his bottom lip. "I'm telling you to go detect. That's what you are, sweetheart, a detective. If I could afford to hire you, I would. I can't, so I'm hoping you'll do me a favor."

Weren't you the cop here?

Never argue when you're handed special favors or treatment, Uncle Joe always advised. Maybe we were both hoping it wasn't Frannie. That this wasn't about to shatter a family. But, there was a dead woman, and I'd bet my automobile that someone's world was about to be destroyed, even if it wasn't Frannie's.

"Officer. Ain't you tired of pestering me? You got nothin'. I'm only a —"

"A racketeer," Somerset filled in. "I'm here to arrest you for murder?"

Valentini's voice drowned in sarcasm. "Who am I supposed to have killed this time? Huh? Who are you blaming me for?"

Somerset leaned in, said something, and pointed to the vacant lot.

"He hasn't been told, has he," I asked, pushing back against the panic rushing up my chest.

"Ah, Christ. Just get down there," Rollins said, as he shook his head and gave me a shove.

Valentini dropped his overcoat, pushed past the lawyer, past Somerset, and ran to the lot. Every cop kept his heater on the gangster despite no threat from the gangster. Valentini didn't care. He made a bee-line to where Somerset said Frannie's body had been found.

I arrived first and I didn't like what I found.

No one likes seeing a dead body, but this was different. My every thought telescoped into the crime scene. My fingers were cold, when I noticed them at all. The painful thumping in my head was my pulse.

I met her. Damn it. I knew her.

In the lot, they'd started to light up the place and to collect evidence. I held up my hand to shield my eyes from the strobes and the light beaming down from the blimp.

I got closer. The damage was unstomachable. The woman had been strangled, easily deduced by the abraded bruise around her neck. A hat was lying about five feet away. A grey fedora. I was seeing a bad case of déjà vu,

I got closer. A scarf was by her side. I'd put money on it being the murder weapon. A patterned scarf with roses and leaves. I recognized that scarf.

I got closer still.

It was the dame who stole my hack.

Resisting the urge to toss my Woolworth's lunch, I kept moving around, looking, seeing, and doing what Uncle Joe did with greater ease in these circumstances. Rollins was watching me. It was his job to watch me.

It was the dame I'd cursed for leaving me alone, in the rain, with a man who had been following her. Had he killed her? I looked at her neck, ignoring the odd stare from the Examiner.

Valentini hammered his way through the barricade of policemen and blundered into the crime scene.

I doubt any of us expected what came next. As I kept looking for anything that might be of value, ignoring Somerset who was annoyed, the lawyer who was astonished, and any number of uniforms who had lost track of what was happening, the tough guy extraordinaire knelt in the mud and cried out in agony, cradling the body of a woman in his arms. Rollins gave me such a look of shock.

Valentini pulled a rod out of his jacket and pointed it at the Examiner, then the rest of us. "Don't you goons touch her! Don't touch her!"

God almighty, his face had tears all the way down to his jaw.

The uniforms responded by drawing whatever heat that wasn't already drawn. Rollins was right, this was about to be a bloodbath, with Rollins, an Examiner, and me as collateral.

Call me stupid, but don't call me stupidly useless. I held out my hands to stop all the rod waving. Looking to Rollins, I said, "Let me talk to him. I can calm this down." I have no idea where that came from. I'm no negotiator, but I did have an interest in staying alive.

Rollins glared, softened, and once he got a long look at the nervous heat about to shoot, waved me forward. Guess he didn't feel like being accidentally blown apart any more than I did.

With my hands up by my shoulders, and the okay from Rollins, I took the last few steps toward Valentini. "I'm not a cop. I'm not the police."

"I don't care!" Valentini turned his heater on me.

The look of a muzzle pointed at your face was enough to start a news-reel rendition of your life — mostly your own mistakes. "Well, I do. And I need to learn who this woman is. Who she really is!"

"Frannie! It's Frannie. Goddamn it, don't you goons know what you're doing?" He didn't shout that at me as much as the confused police line, some of whom had the brains to lower their weapons.

"Look, Mr. Valentini." I glanced back to Rollins who was holding his breath. Somerset was above with the other cops, and he was giving me a look of death. To hell with him. "Mr. Valentini? Willkie. I'm not a cop, I'm a private investigator, and I believe I met this …" I chose my words carefully, "This lady two nights ago. Over by Bayview. I remember the scarf, the hat and — she was wearing a beautiful ring." My brain finally returned from vacation, because I finally had a clear idea of where I was going. "The kind of ring a man gives to his greatest love." I swear, the whole City held its breath. "You gave her that, didn't you?"

Valentini didn't speak at first. A moment later, not looking at me directly, he nodded. His voice was lower, broken. "I gave it to her. I did."

Slowly, he raised her hand to show me. Damn. It was the woman who took my hack. No doubt about that. The ring was lovely. She was lovely, even in death. And she matched the photograph Lockwood gave me. It was Frannie. Deep inside, I felt heartbroken. I hoped …

So, I turn into a sap when a dame gets killed. I get seriously protective. A Mamma Bear, if you like. Too many of us are killed by lovers or men who don't take "no" for an answer. Most of us are blamed for becoming victims. Every one of us wonders if the next man we pass will be the one who kills us.

"It's beautiful," I said, in a soft, soothing, please-don't-shoot-me voice. "Your gift is exquisite."

"I asked her to marry me. Where was she when you met her?" he whispered.

"Bayview"

"She had no reason to be in Bayview."

He wasn't wrong. Were it not for my little errand for Agent Mason, I had no reason to be in Bayview either. "Mr. Valentini, I will tell the police about the details of when she and I almost shared a cab. That helps them find the real ..."

Willkie drew up and shouted at the police, "These goons? They can't find piss in their own toilets."

"But I can." It was the only thing I thought of to say. No, I wasn't that old. No, I wasn't a veteran cop. I was P.I., and in that moment, I was enough.

"What? How?"

"As I said," I carefully, calmly stated, "I am a private investigator. And as odd as that may be, as a woman PI, I take my job very seriously. I'm good at what I do," though not for all that long, and I stumbled on my words while telling my brain to shut up, "and I gave the police everything about what happened when I met Frannie. I didn't realize who she was at the time. But I do now. And I want to find out more."

His eyes glazed over, like a man lost in the remnants of a dream. "We're gettin' married. She loves me," he babbled.

Oh my God. Married?

"May I ask you, Mr. Valentini," I kept talking very softly, "to put down your gun?"

"Let them shoot me."

"I'd like it if they didn't. They might hit me and your colleague, and then what use are we in finding out what happened? Please? I'm on the level."

Any sort of confidence between me and Valentini was too much for Somerset to bear. "Come on, Valentini. I'm arresting you for the murder of Francis Coventry."

To his credit, the shyster put his hand on Valentini's heater and effectively disarmed the whole situation. "I'll go with you, Willkie. They got nothing on you. Nothing."

Valentini didn't give him more than the minimum attention — he was too busy silently pleading with me — an unforgettable look.

I admit, I was in shock too. None of this made sense. Francis Coventry was the woman who took my cab, but why was Frannie over near Bayview that evening? Who was the man following her?

Was Valentini putting on a performance for Somerset? Was he faking? It sure wasn't the performance I'd expect from a powerful underworld kingpin, reacting to Frannie's death the way he did. If other gangster's reactions were the norm, tears were not their first response to arrest.

I got out of the way when they led Valentini off in cuffs, and I assumed it wasn't the first time. But the big-time crook, Mr. Bad Guy, gangster, he'd crumbled into a pool of tears at seeing Frannie's body. No faking at all. Now of course, he'd wiped his face and set it in a fearsome expression. The gangster was back. The bridegroom gone into the dark.

The Examiner rolled Frannie onto her side. Nothing but mud. I saw the ring again. It was beautiful — unique and special. Valentini said he'd given it to her. Marriage? Did Bad Boys marry and live happily ever after?

I started thinking about how long Frannie had been in the lot. I remember the last time I saw her alive was four p.m. two nights before. The instructions she'd given the cabbie were in this general vicinity. Giving the cab a half hour to drive over here, that meant she was dead for close to 48 hours. I needed to narrow that down.

The side of the 500 Grants that faced the lot had only two windows. A creepy Bruno occupied one of them and glared down at us, then shut the curtains. I got a clean look at him.

Think. Yeah, I'd seen his face before. Line up photos *D&S Detective Magazine* had in their news section. Skates Berk. A guy with a memorable face, memorable moniker, and memorable temper. If I read the article right, he was Valentini's right-hand man.

Maybe that mug of his only had one expression, but he didn't strike me as all that choked-up about the body in the lot. I only caught him for a second. Maybe that was enough.

Rollins crouched down next to Frannie.

I showed the photograph to Rollins and told them what Valentini said. I promised I would.

"Geez, Lou, talk about being in the right place at the wrong time," Rollins sputtered out around a cigarette.

"What happens now," I asked.

The Examiner signaled for a stretcher to come down and started shaking out a sheet to cover Frannie.

Rollins shook his head. "Milt may have gotten his man at last. Still, if what you say is true, then he wouldn't want to kill her. Maybe he did it in the moment, like a crime of passion."

The Examiner stood up. "I don't think so. I should have more details later on, but this doesn't look like a robbery gone wrong. This was deliberate and yet messy. But —"

"Yeah, yeah," Rollins held up a hand, "you gotta' do your job first."

"When did it happen," I queried, wondering if he'd answer me. He didn't know me from Eve.

"About five to nine p.m. I'm told we got some kids who played here until five."

"Today? Well, the space isn't that big, so after five seems like a good assumption."

He nodded.

"Have you checked with the local indigents?"

"You think some bum saw something," Rollins said incredulously.

I pointed around the lot. "Cheap wine bottles and beer bottles. Trash. Some bedding over there. An open lot is a magnet for folks who don't have a place to sleep."

"You think some bum killed her and left that rock on her hand?" Rollins was being obtuse, either that or too shaken up himself. Just 'cause you were a cop doesn't mean you see everything in your career. The corpse of a beauty like Frannie would shake anyone up, I was shook too.

"No, I think one of our indigents might have seen the murder or can help narrow down the timing. As you said, whoever did it, left valuables on her. If it was someone committing robbery, they would have taken that rock. And the silk scarf. And the hat. Plenty of time to snatch up her purse," I pointed toward a small, crocheted bag with a Bakelite handle and a satin bow, "and run. Everything is still here. This wasn't a robbery. First glance," I said, knowing that I had somehow captivated my audience of professional cops, "I'd put money on a passion killing."

"By Valentini's men?"

I waggled my head. No. I stepped back, taking a better look around. "Why would they kill someone who meant so much to their boss?"

I stared down at drag marks and heavily disturbed gouges in the dirt. Not many of them, though. She hadn't struggled much, so maybe it was someone very strong. I looked up the hill to the sidewalk. No drag marks. Did she come down into the lot willingly?

"On his orders," Rollins asked, following my gaze wherever it landed. "He may have set her up during a fight or because he was jealous of some other mug flirting with her. Just because he ordered her killing doesn't mean he was happy that he did. All that blubbering might have been regret."

The logic wasn't bad, though it assumed quite a bit. "This isn't looking good for Valentini. Pretty good news for Somerset. But I'm saying out loud, none of this makes sense to put over on Valentini. But then, when does murder ever make sense?"

"So you say," Rollins grinned. "I think a chat with some of the locals is in order."

Good. He listened. My appreciation for Bennie Rollins was increasing.

The Examiner was coming past me when I stopped him. "Professional opinion, she died between 5 and 9. Got it. But, what's your personal guess?"

"Personal? As in, a guess I can't back up yet? Gut or intuition?"

"Experienced gut or intuition," I added, flattering him a little. Though, it was true, he had some significant experience in the job, in the big city.

"Seven to eight p.m. But you realize I can't officially narrow it down further until I take a long look at the body. Call that estimate my unofficial hunch."

"Would you put money on it?"

"I would." He followed the stretcher up the hill, talking about the case as if it was nothing new. Probably wasn't for him.

Somerset waited on the sidewalk at the top of the hill. "Get that woman out of here," he shouted to the officers. To me, he snarled, "I don't care if you've got a license, there ain't no such thing as a female detective. Go home, little girl. You're lucky I'm not arresting you for interfering with an active investigation. If I see your face or hear your name again, I'll lock you up. You don't belong here; you never have."

I recognize a declaration of war when I hear one. And I was happy to pick up the gauntlet flung at my feet. Of all the rules and laws that apply to my profession, I hadn't broken any of them. Arrest me for doing my legal job; I was ready. I have plenty of lawyers with a beef, only a nickel call away, all of whom wanted to go around or two in court with law-breaking or overly aggressive cops.

But, what job needed to be done? Whose need would be served? Frannie Coventry had been found. That was it. That was all I was hired to do.

Based on the comments of the uniforms and Examiner, they'd already convicted Valentini of being her killer and convicted Frannie of asking for it.

I hated that. I hated the assumption with all my soul. Frannie made bad decisions, but that didn't make her death unworthy of the effort to find the truth. Nobody in their right mind wants to be murdered. Strangulation was an ugly way to go.

Well, hell. Between my confusion over Valentini's behavior, Somerset's blatant disregard for my earned license, and the end of my first case being a disaster with the missing person found dead, I was pissed.

And now I had to tell Lockwood. Everything.

Maybe I'd get lucky and he'd tell me everything.

I couldn't help thinking this wasn't over. I didn't want the case to be over, but deep inside, reason told me it was because of too many reasons, good and bad.

CHAPTER FIFTEEN

Disappointment comes with a laundry list of ailments
and a bill that's due.

-Lou Tanner, P.I., Notes for female Pemberton
Graduates, 1935

The revolving door barely gave in to my push. I pushed hard,
using all my frustration to make the door open to my command. My
face was red, I felt burning on my cheeks and pressure pounding at my
temples. My stride sent out two messages: you don't need to see me
and don't you dare screw with me.

Going upstairs at a swank hotel, with laughter punctuated by
clinking cocktail glasses and silver knives on bone China plates floating
in from the adjacent restaurant, was normally quite pleasant. Not
tonight. This morning. Geez, what time was it?

It was late, and I had only enough brains left to call ahead.
Lockwood wasn't a sap; he knew why I was coming up.

A tall, slender figure sat in the lobby, quickly held a paper high
enough to cover his face. By the mud on his shoes and trousers cuffs,
it was a man who'd pounded some serious pavement. Cheap overcoat.
Déjà vu smacked me hard across the face — like it does.

Anytime, any other time, I believe in demanding answers. Just
not now. I had to stay focused on the Lockwood case.

The big Hotel Detective walked up to me, as I waited for the
elevator. He had his own ideas about me. He wasn't the regular guy.

My guess was he thought I was some bangtail headed upstairs to break a few commandments. I wasn't in the mood for assumptions. I'd had too many of those tonight and not enough Old Forester bourbon.

"Okay, Sweetheart, move along, no business here tonight."

"Only business tonight, big guy. I'm expected."

"Don't get all sassy with me. You may be a high-priced escort but —"

The glare I gave him stopped him cold.

He thought I needed extra persuasion to skedaddle, so he pulled his badge out of his pocket and flagged me with it.

Typical move.

The elevator chimed, its door opened, and I stepped in, turning to face him. From the moment he first approached me, I'd let my fingers dive into my purse. As he opened his mouth and blocked the doors from closing, I held up my badge, about three inches from his schnoz. The expression on his face was beyond price.

"Honest to God?" he asked. "You're a P.I.?"

"Yeah. I'm here see Elliott Lockwood, room 1407 —"

"Oh! You're Lou Tanner?" He interrupted. His whole body changed its expression. "My partner thinks the world of you and your Uncle Joe." He let go of the doors. "You called Mr. Lockwood first?"

"Do I look like a beginner?"

"Well," he shrugged.

Okay, he was right, I do look young for a job filled for the most part by retired cops and former army intelligence.

I couldn't be a creep. He was doing his job. "Have a good night."

The doors closed before I could ask him what he meant, and I felt the sensation of falling upward.

Odd. Well, I sure hoped he had a good night. I wasn't. I'd be a first-class idiot if I thought dealing with murder and lost relatives would be happiness and joy all-the-day long. Uncle Joe was clear on that point; being a detective sometimes stank to high heaven. I accepted that fact. Yet, Frannie's death was bothering me. A lot.

Willkie Valentini was the sore spot in this mess. Had Valentini been indifferent or belligerent, I wouldn't feel the least bit guilty putting this killing in his lap. But he wasn't. I thought for a moment he might try to commit suicide by cop. Hard-core gangsters who off their unwanted human refuse don't cry over it. Not even if they did it by accident or in a fit of rage. Sure, he was human, if pretty low on the food chain, but his life depended on his reputation — and he damaged that, in public no less.

Was he faking? That didn't feel right.

The elevator stopped two floors short of my goal. The doors opened to no one. Figures. Phantom elevator riders.

I knew I had to tell Lockwood about Frannie's death. He'd read about it in the papers anyway, I might as well lay it out and let him decide how he wanted to react.

Why the hell was I making friends with guilt?

"Nobody gets killed and doesn't feel it. I suppose asking if she suffered would be the dumbest question I could ask," he said bluntly. "Not that the policeman who called me would answer if I did ask. They had a suspect but no verifiable motive or proof of opportunity. But that officer, detective, was absolutely certain they had their man."

Elliott Lockwood sat in his hotel living room, on a leather couch, cigarette in his hands, head lowered.

I'd taken the overstuffed chair across from him. I had no idea how he was going to react, and I figured giving him some space might be wise.

"But, I'm asking. Did she?"

I couldn't tell him everything; not the glassy, terrified look on her face, or the garroting marks on her skin. "Not much." I was lying. Nobody gets strangled and doesn't feel it.

Damn it, I had no words to say. *Gosh, sorry about the stepdaughter you don't like, she got slaughtered, and oops, it looks like you actually do care?*

Those words weren't passing out of the lips of Mrs. Tanner's well-bred daughter.

He wouldn't look at me. That was a habit of his. One that I would forgive tonight.

"Mr. Lockwood, I think —"

"Elliott." He corrected, taking a drag, focus still fixated on the carpet.

"Not during this conversation. This is business. You need to know that this isn't over yet. Mr. Lockwood, you have too much to do now. The police will want to talk to you again."

"No, I don't think so." He regarded me after a moment. "Detective Somer - something."

"Somerset. Milton Somerset."

"He's convinced he has the killer locked up. Evidence be damned. All he wanted to do was tell me and ask me when I want to collect the body." His voice warbled a little. Who could blame him? "Irenie, apparently, went into hysterics and is sedated for the immediate future." Another long drag. "I thought I was helping Frannie, maybe find a future – get herself together before she was in too deep with the wrong people. Now I get to bury her."

"I think it's odd that no autopsy is being done. This is clearly a homicide. Cause of death may be obvious at first, but the proper approach is essential. Something could be missed. Mr. Lockwood, please insist they do a full autopsy before releasing her body." *Chapter 39: Bodies, Morgues, and Medical Examinations* came to mind instantly.

He stood up abruptly to go stand by the cabinet radio and a big mirror. He kept trying to decide whether to put out his cigarette or to move the ashtray another four inches to the right, then the left, then center again. Shaking his head, he reached into his coat pocket and pulled out his wallet. "You did very well. You found her. And you did more. You made sure the police had the right girl. I'm not sure how I'd handle a visit to the morgue, to identify someone's corpse."

"First, you go down to the morgue and do what must be done. Then, you go across the street to the Blue Fox and try to drown your sorrows." I checked my nails for a second. "Well, that's what I'd do."

He began to pull bills out of his wallet and I had that deeply unpleasant sensation as though it was money being left on the nightstand after a night of illicit sex.

"Mr. Lockwood. I'll say it again. The job's not done."

"What do you mean?" His eyes flashed.

"I need to find out who —"

"No." he said awfully fast. "No more. I honestly don't think I'm ..." his words fell. "I have all that I want to handle. If the police believe they have the killer, I'm satisfied." He shoved a stack of bills at me. "I don't need an invoice."

"Of course, you do; you're a business man. And, you're overpaying," I said, a little tartly. "This case ..."

"Is done. Before I lose my mind, I need it to be done." Lockwood's voice wobbled a bit and he swallowed hard to maintain control. "I don't want you pushing this any further. It was one thing to ask you to look for Frannie, but it's a police matter when it comes to murder. The case is closed."

"What are you doing, Mr. Lockwood?"

"Living. Going on. Cleaning up this mess and hoping I have better luck next time. Hell, Irenie can have the house and anything she wants. I don't care."

"But you do care."

Blue eyes drilled into my soul. This time, I didn't flutter to pieces, I drilled right back.

"Technically," I started, "the assignment is closed. You asked me to find Frannie and I did."

"You have more questions, don't you?"

"Yes, Mr. Lockwood, I do."

He must have dug in deep for a last bit of righteous energy. "Then stop calling me Mister and call me Elliott," he snapped. "You're not working for me, not anymore. You're free to do whatever you want. Just call me Elliott. And drop this. I want Irenie, Frannie, and ... and ..." I couldn't tell if he wanted to blow up or burst into tears. "... out of my life. No more cases. I want ... I don't want you looking into my life anymore. I can't stand the idea of it any longer"

He still didn't know about the photo album, and under the circumstances, I wouldn't show it to him. Then again, what if he was the photographer?

But I wanted the truth from him. "Alright, Elliott. Why did you hire me in the first place? If Frannie was the wild child everyone says she was, some dame with a badge wouldn't get her to listen. Why me?"

Lockwood walked straight over to the bar and poured a glass from the first bottle he reached. I'm glad he forgot his manners 'cause I would have turned it down. I was sober and was staying that way.

He didn't answer.

"Do you like photography, Mr. Lockwood?"

"As art? I suppose so. What does that have to do with —"

"I mean as a photographer."

I'd thrown him off balance. "Not much. I tried photography once, at Irenie's encouragement but we both agreed I had no talent for it. I gave away the equipment by year's end. Why?"

I felt relief expand from my spine to my shoulders. "Nothing. We need to stay on point. Why did you hire me?"

He started to answer about three times. He sighed and gave in to my question. "You're a union supporter, aren't you?" He wasn't asking — he was making more of a statement. "Of course, you are ... you're too practical not to be."

"I am pro-Union. Wholeheartedly."

"You may not like this."

"Go on."

He was stalling.

That was getting me pretty hot, and I wasn't willing to wait him out. "Frannie was blackmailing you, wasn't she? Like she was blackmailing Harold Harrison and Cab Proctor? That's why the check was there, in her room. That's why you're nervous when you talk about her."

Lockwood watched the smoke curling up from a newly-lit cigarette. "Yes. I presumed she'd slept with Harold and Proctor and threatened to make a scandal out of it. That's what her mother would do."

Nice mommy. "Did she set it up for Frannie?"

"I don't think so. But she taught Frannie everything she knew." He went back to the couch and dropped onto it, hard. "After a while, you couldn't tell them apart without the difference in hair color. Frannie became Irenie."

"I noticed. You mentioned unions. Was there something about your company and unions, and Frannie had that on you?"

He didn't fuss too much when I came to sit by him. "I made a terrible mistake. About ten years ago. Ever heard of the Pier 41 Dockside Strike and the slaughter that ended it?"

I had.

It was a terrible day in union history. Management of an import company called the cops when the dock workers went on strike. It turned into a melee and wholesale massacre. Wait? Wasn't Lockwood the CEO of an import company?

"I thought they were armed, the strikers. I was worried about the boys who crossed the picket lines. Rumors were coming to us about violence and sabotage. It was getting out of hand." He drew heavily on his cigarette. "I called the cops, hoping they would break things up or make them move out of the entrances to the pier. They started shooting seconds after arrival. I asked them not to. I swear I did. Then, they found that the strikers weren't armed, they weren't going after the picket-crossers, and so many of those men are dead now. I hadn't ordered it, I hadn't asked for it. But if I hadn't made that call, if I had left things alone, it wouldn't have happened."

A lump formed in my throat and my mouth went dry. Lockwood was responsible for all those dead men. Or was he? He thought he was.

He swilled the booze for a moment. "I've done everything I can since then. I made sure benefits went to the widows. Got fired for that. Now, with the new company, I hire union and. I get as much work for my employees as I can."

"You try to make up for things."

"I'm not a bad man. Honest to God, I thought that things would go differently ... that the police wouldn't ... I can't live that down. The papers and the police listed the caller as anonymous. No one should have known. So, imagine my surprise when Frannie brought that to me and required her first few payments. From me. Her own — I wouldn't outlive her need for cash."

"What changed?"

"She stopped asking. She even tried to be nice a couple of times after the divorce started. Until Irenie interfered. Then she left. I mean, she left the house."

Accepting his explanation about the union bust wasn't as hard as I thought it might be. He had much to atone for but maybe it was like he said, the situation spiraled out of his control. I had to decide about that later. Frannie was my focus now.

"I'm back to asking, why did you hire me?"

"Because of all the reasons I gave you before." Long drag. "And, because you were new enough not to have secrets of your own. Maybe I liked the idea of a woman who didn't have a past of her own or designs on my future. And honestly, there was no way in Hell I could send a man to deal with Frannie. She had pocket money from me because of my mistake, but others? It was worse, she had terrible secrets. She collected them like dolls."

I nodded slowly. "So, I need to find out exactly what Proctor and Harrison were paying for."

"You don't need to. The case is over."

"Yours is." I took the money from his hands. I'm not stupid. "I'm on a new case now."

He looked mortified and clearly understood what I meant. "You're hiring yourself?"

"Because this case doesn't make sense."

I wanted to ask all sorts of things, like what happened at Irenie's salons, as if I couldn't guess. Who did he think took those racy photos of Frannie? What was their relationship, in truth? I wanted him to confirm he had nothing to do with the Militia. Yeah, they had nothing to do with this case but I needed to understand — for me, for my own sense of comfort. Looking at him, I couldn't do it. Sure, I'd kick myself in the morning, and I was being a sap, but I couldn't bring myself to hammer home those questions.

Tomorrow was a different day. But, not tonight.

Lockwood stood up and looked out of the big picture window toward California Street. "It's not that late."

"It's well past midnight."

"I'm thirsty."

"You're pissed off."

"Not as much as I should be. I'm glad no one, but you, knows my secret. And it is only you, isn't it? Now that Frannie is gone, I don't have to wonder. You'll keep it." After a long break in his thoughts, he added, "Why am I so relieved? Someone's dead?"

"Because the dead body isn't yours and you have escaped their cruelty. Blackmail is cruel, trust me. You can do whatever you want with your life now and they won't ever again show up with their palms out." I didn't mention that there were more than two of us who knew his secret; someone told Frannie.

He didn't move for a bit. "No, I can't. I'll always have to pay for my mistake."

"We all end up paying for mistakes, ours or someone else's." I stood up and retrieved my purse. "I think its best if I go now."

He kept his back to me. "Will I ever see you again?"

The Elliott Lockwood case was over.

"I don't think either of us can answer that question tonight. Let's both get some sleep."

The Frannie Coventry case was only now starting.

CHAPTER SIXTEEN

Some criminals aren't as smart as they think they are
— or want to be. Don't be surprised if his intelligence
score is around his shoe size.

-Lou Tanner, P.I., Notes for female Pemberton
Graduates, 1935

Saturday mornings were great for lolling around in bed, taking coffee at leisure, and thinking about a trip to Ocean Beach. Maybe the Sutro Baths?

Most Saturday mornings — but not today.

Frannie was dead and any attempt at taking a personal day would be nothing short of a betrayal of my newest client, and my sense of right and wrong.

I didn't sleep much. Once I got home, I'd started in on those letters I filched from the Lockwood House. From Frannie's mattress. If I thought Somerset would do a thorough job of investigating yesterday, today I doubted it one hundred percent. I hadn't stolen official evidence as I had the vague permission of the house's owner and I'd taken the letters before Frannie turned up dead. But, I would still need to turn them over to Rollins. I promised to share my findings. But, not until I had a good long look at them.

Love letters. Hokey, genuine, love letters between Frannie and Willkie. He hadn't lied about his relationship with her. Depending on how you viewed them, they either exonerated or condemned Valentini.

I was leaning toward the former, Somerset was blindly determined to accept the latter.

I don't remember when I finally went to bed, exhausted by the feeling I hadn't found anything moving the case in any direction.

I lay in my bed, staring at the ceiling. Too much was raging in my brain box and nothing was lining up. Tired wasn't a strong enough word for how I felt. I picked up my pack of cigarettes, looked at it with disgust, and dropped it back on the nightstand. Everything in my mouth tasted terrible, like the Third Army marched through and not bothered to wipe their feet before entering.

I looked at the pack. The cigarette. The memory was as clear as a martini glass. His lighter, held by those long fingers. His eyes. A Scotch on the rocks and smooth jazz. If it turned out to be my last smoke, the last one locked in a moment of bliss I hadn't known in a long time, well, that was life. What I couldn't live with was the nagging truth of Elliott Lockwood — he of the wilting blue eyes — being late to meet me last night. He was a punctual man. Why had he been late? Why did he arrive at 8:20? Frannie died between 7 and 8 p.m., at least according to the Medical Examiner. Those two notions were adding up to an unpleasant possibility. Was my former client Frannie's killer?

Someone upstairs dropped a glass on their tiled kitchen floor. My nerves froze my body as floods of mental images raced through my head, warning me of what might be dangerous. Memories, such as the zeppelin cable — in the big, far-too-tall building. The rushing winds. Ice cold grasping at my body. Feeling the empty space between me and the ground was immediate and horrible.

I forced myself to take three, long, deep breaths. The cable incident had been nothing but an accident. A zeppelin worker hadn't secured the cable well enough. Accidents happen, don't they? People do dumb things all the time.

Ignoring the rush of cold through my chest, I also forced myself to realistically consider if Elliott Lockwood was Frannie's killer. I sure didn't want him to be, but the truth was the truth. If he did it …

Then of course there was Irenie and her muddy coat, arriving in a panic. She'd been out about the same time as Frannie's murder.

But what kind of mother would kill her daughter? What would drive Irenie to do such a thing? Sure, she was a self-absorbed, gold-digger, but the last time I checked, selfishness wasn't the only motive for murder.

Cab Proctor was being blackmailed and I had to find a way, an excuse, to question him. Blackmail was the oldest trigger for a killing. And there was every possibility that Harold Harrison slipped up, so I'd need to talk to him too, without his wife around to command the discussion.

The man in the window, looking down at Frannie's body, last night? Now there was a question I had an answer to, though it was best I double check. I dragged my copy of D&S Magazine and flipped to the back pages. Yeah. There he was. I was one hundred percent sure now.

Glaring back from the cheap newsprint was Skates Berk, Valentini's right-hand man. Funny he hadn't run to his boss's side last night. The byline under his mug shot was nothing more than his name and last arrest date. As one of Valentini's boys, he had the means to knock Frannie off, either out of loyalty or by command. Good ol' Skates had a face that looked like his biggest problem was having been born at all. Yeah, he was another creep I needed to glean more about — a notion which left my mouth dry. Well, getting to know such delightfully grotesque people comes with the job.

No matter how I rolled it around, Willkie Valentini killing Frannie made no sense. A man doesn't go to all to pieces, and certainly never to cover his own tracks. Still, I wouldn't put it past a man like him to put on a big show, to throw the cops off the scent.

Who was following Frannie the night we'd met? Who was the man in the alleyway I nearly tangled with? The dark Buick outside of Lockwood's house? More than ever, I needed to size up Proctor and Harrison.

My doorbell sounded.

Who the hell was awake and moving at this hour? What hour was it?

I stumbled along, pulling a dressing gown over my sleepwear and forced one eye to focus on the door peep hole. The Louisville Slugger was at my fingertips.

Marley stood there with two greasy sandwiches, a package of aspirin powder, and I hoped to God a pound of coffee beans.

I yanked the door open.

"Good morning, sunshine," she chimed.

"Drop dead."

"Hangover?"

I glared at her. "Nope. Lack o' sleep."

"No hangover? I am disappointed in you." She circumvented me and headed to my kitchenette. "I brought hangover cure anyway," she waved the sandwiches, "and I bet it will do for cigarette withdrawal, too."

Ah, what the hell, she came bearing gifts of grease and caffeine.

"So," she started without taking a breath, "the case is complete. The papers all say the poor girl was killed by her lover, a violent gangster, and he was in custody." She plopped down on my comfy chair. Her red locks easily molded into a series of Marcel waves and were wrapped into a bun at the back of her skull. Rust rayon dress with huge lapels in ivory. Cute little number of a hat she'd dropped on her overcoat on top of my desk.

"'Was' in custody?"

"He had an alibi. They had to let him go last night. Apparently, he left vowing revenge, he was framed, set up, you know, the usual."

The room shook a little.

"Earthquake," she asked, not alarmed in the least. Jaded San Franciscan.

"Nope."

"Zeppelin?" She leaned to look out my window.

"Cable car or full trolley."

"You need to live in a place not built on sand."

"I like my place," I said around one of the sandwiches. Bacon, cheese, and avocado. Grilled in butter. More grease than I had the right to eat. Perfect hangover food, except I wasn't hungover. I'd said no, again, to Elliott Lockwood. He needed a drink. I could have said yes, and let whatever happened next, simply happen. Instead, I told my client to go home and sleep. I planned on getting some much-needed shut-eye too.

Of course, I couldn't. I couldn't be sure of him or anyone. Not yet.

I was sure of Marley, who hadn't stopped talking since she came in. In short bursts between her incessant chatter, I brought her up to date with my worries and ideas.

"You like him, don't you Slim?"

"He's easy on the eyes, but — let's say I tend toward more complex men. And, he's a client first." I couldn't help being honest with her. "Despite all that, for reasons I can't figure out, yes, I like him. Just like. Nothing more."

"Slim, you probably already thought of this, but — Mr. Wonderful sounds like a prime suspect to me."

Nodding, I leaned against the wall. "He was late to meet me. Maybe he grabbed a 'Crawler and made it from Grant and Green to the house on the hill by eight-twenty p.m. He had motive. She was blackmailing him."

I didn't want to think about it, and to her credit, Marley didn't press the issue. But honesty was a tough gal who won't let you ignore her. Elliott was a suspect.

I kept talking. "Irenie was late too, with mud on her shoes and fancy coat, something she could have gotten in a vacant lot. Yet, Frannie was her cash cow, if you'll excuse the phrase. Without Frannie, she has little else to sell or to hold over Lockwood. Valentini's alibi might be nothing more than someone protecting him. But I tell you, that wasn't a performance I watched. He was grieving, honest and for true." I gave her a brief description of Valentini's reaction last night, culminating in several low whistles from Marley. I ran my fingers through my hair, snagging on a couple of curls. "We need to expand our search."

"Oh, Slim, I found a few somethings on that Cab Proctor fellow. Not the kind of man to bring home to Ma, if you get my meaning."

"Anything out of the ordinary for a bored, rich man?"

"Two paternity charges he paid to have hushed up. He's quite the winner. He's been in trouble for inappropriate photographs too."

"I love your lawyer connections."

"Don't forget a few clerks over at the county and federal courthouses."

She handed me her notes and I added them to my little book, whistling as I read about his barroom tiffs, the trail of abandoned women, and interest in expensive automobiles. That notebook of mine was getting thick with details. "Seems like the perfect man to snag in a blackmail scheme."

Marley made a face. "Seems like the perfect man to get killed by some woman's husband."

"It's a damn wonder he hasn't been. Listen, Marley, can you add one more name to your list?"

"Sure thing."

"Skates Berk. According to some crime news, his full name is Leslie Samuel Berk. He's one of Valentini's men, an enforcer, maybe a partner. Caught sight of him at Valentini's arrest last night. See if you can tell me what role he plays, what he's done in the past for Valentini, if he's invested in Valentini's success. The usual routine."

"Okay, boss lady."

My phone started to ring, and I staggered over to answer it. Marley beat me to it, gave me an evil look, and answered. "Miss Tanner's residence."

A voice, I was sure was Elliott's, was substantially loud on the other end of the line.

"Just a moment, Mr. Lockwood." She put the receiver against her thigh. "Are you in?"

"Give me that." I took the phone and gave her evil for all the evil she gave. "I'm not paying overtime." I cleared my morning throat. "Hello Mr. Lockwood. How can I help you?"

144

"I ended up at the house, after last night. My liquor cabinet is still fully stocked."

I gandered his meaning. "How's your head?"

"Pounding. You were the smart one, heading home."

I bet. And I bet Irenie didn't make out any better. "What can I do for you other than offer aspirin powder? I believe you said you were satisfied and your case is closed."

"You didn't believe me."

"True. But I don't —"

He interrupted me. "The cheque is gone. I looked around, even checked places I know it wasn't, and it's gone. Did you say that was a sign of something? If Frannie wasn't alive to cash it, then who did? Irenie? Please tell me Irenie isn't a suspect. I told you I didn't want this case to go on, but if Irenie …" He was in a full panic.

"Alright. Stay where you are, and I'll come over. Can you handle Irenie for a bit?"

"I handled her for a few years, one more hour won't be worse."

"More like two or three hours. You might be better off taking a stroll or getting a bite to eat. I have an errand to run before I look over Frannie's room again. An important errand."

There was a long pause I couldn't quite gauge. "A new case already?" Elliott's voice was plaintive. I wasn't expecting that.

"Something like that. I can meet you outside of the house in three hours. Or, if you'd prefer, we can meet at my office."

Another long pause. "Here at the house. Three hours. If I need to, I can hold off Irenie."

I suspected he was wrong but decided to keep such a thought to myself.

I put on one of my sweeter little dresses and pulled a silk coat out of the closet. Men like Proctor open up easily when he thinks he is safe with a woman of class and breeding, a woman who would keep her mouth shut for the sake of a precious reputation. He'll go into hunting mode, sure everything he likes is willing prey. I wasn't stopping him from taking one look at me and going on the prowl.

I admit it — I was not averse to using a little feminine charm to get something I want out of the Cab Proctor's of the world.

I carried a smaller purse; ladies of society didn't carry big work bags since they don't schlep their job with them, like I did.

Up on the top of the cliff, the clientele was exclusive beyond expense. If you didn't know someone who knows someone, then you needed to look like you did, to the point no one asked you about your connections. That, I had down pat.

Above the Sutro Baths was a cozy, exclusive club. The view was breathtaking. The Pacific Ocean rolled in, a series of waves stretching back to the horizon in even lines. Sea Lions barked at each other, making noises reserved for cheap speakeasies near closing time. In the distance, a misty set of jagged islands rose out of the sea. The Farallon Islands. Fish, sharks, birds, and that was about it. Couldn't see them half the time, fog being what it was. Today, though, I swear my view was all the way to Japan.

Nestled into a cove of pale sand and cliffs waited the tiled structure of The Baths. Glass. Giggles. Swimming suits. Exposed skin and reputations. More than one hustle going down out of sight from the families at play. There was nothing exclusive about the attendees, except their whiteness. The Howie Johnsons of the state weren't allowed. My heart squeezed and sank.

I had a description to work with and Proctor wasn't hard to find. With the rest of the tennis crowd, he leaned against the mahogany bar. Black hair, slicked back, looking as if a rigorous game of tennis hadn't bothered a hair — not that he'd done anything so vigorous. White slacks and shoes. White trousers beneath a plaid decorated sweater. A thin moustache followed the breadth of his thin lips. Tan. Elegant. Using a cigarette holder. A camera hung around his neck. Yeah, a camera. So, Proctor was an amateur photographer.

He took one look at me, watching him, and decided I was fair game. I didn't wait for him to stalk me. I strode up to him. "Cab Proctor?"

"Who?"

"You don't know if you're Charles Proctor?"

"I don't know whose asking. But if you want me to be Proctor, I'm sure we can work something out."

I slyly lowered my chin, looked up at him through my eyelashes, and started my turn to go. "Doesn't work if you aren't the real thing."

"I'm real. I'm very real."

I grinned coyly and started to go.

His grip on my arm was strong. Too strong. I was beginning to wonder if he had early warning I was coming. His fingers crushed through the fabric of my dress, bruising my skin.

CHAPTER SEVENTEEN

```
I recommend you carry a purse. In it keep a gun,
another gun, a bigger gun, and maybe some lipstick.

-Lou Tanner, P.I., Notes for female Pemberton
Graduates, 1935
```

This mug always got his way, no matter what. I tried the lady-like option of glaring at his hand on my arm. When that didn't work, leaned close and whispered, "I've got a very loud, piercing scream. And if you aren't the man I'm looking for …"

He was quite amused. Too much so. I gathered he liked a little push-back when he got rough. "Okay, okay. I'm Cab Proctor. And your name is …"

"Lucille." I gave him the overhanded handshake which approached from such a position that a man might shake in earnest or kiss a girl's knuckles. Yup. He went for it; lips planting a slimy snail's trail across the back of my gloved hand. He squeezed my fingers looking to see if I handled the pain to his satisfaction. Charming.

"So, Lulu, what brings you here, looking for me?"

Lulu? No one calls me Lulu. What a creep. My expression stayed pleasant and engaged while I enjoyed considering how many ways I could get away with ending his future interest in sex.

"Is there a place where we can talk — privately?"
"We're all friends here."

"Including Frannie Coventry?" I whispered.

His face reddened in embarrassment and he took a sudden interest in the sweater-pills on his chest. "Frannie doesn't come here much anymore. You a friend?"

"No. I've only met her once, but I do have some information that might help you with her."

"What makes you think I need help," he snapped while not meeting my gaze. What was it with men. Am I so scary they can't look me in the eyes? "And, how much is this gonna' cost me to learn what you've got?"

"Relax, Honey." I smiled and leaned against his arm. "I don't want much. Now, can we talk in private or are all these people really your friends?"

"Define 'friend.'" He snorted.

"*Touché.*"

"Come on, Lulu. To my office." He motioned for me to follow, not even offering his arm. I didn't mind, I wanted to keep him in front of me, where I could keep an eye on his hands and motions.

Proctor opened a door and I signaled he should go first. As I stepped through, I made sure no one was following me.

Like Harold Harrison? He walked in, dressed in a suit, loosened tie, and no Gem Harrison on his arm – or anywhere nearby. Money down, Gem was kvetching with Irenie over on Vallejo Street. They were likely trying to out-mourn one another. Harold was ordering a drink, when he noticed me. I didn't stay long in his sights and followed Proctor.

The "office" turned out to be the liquor storage room. Pallets and boxes rested along the walls, with the company of empty bottles. An open door to the left appeared to access the basement. A wine cellar?

Stopping in the middle of the room by a tall wooden crate, sure no one would hear us now, Proctor turned on me. "Frannie didn't send you, did she? We were all done, Frannie and me." He walked toward me, shoulders back, hoping his height might be intimidating. "Now, with Frannie not in my life, I do have room for another doll." His eyes wandered up and down my figure. "You look like you want some improved company. And I'm a vast improvement on your average Joe."

I gave him a solid, unmistakable shove back. "Sorry, boyfriend, I don't take scraps off another woman's table. Besides, as you said, Frannie didn't send me."

He glowered at me, folded his arms, and physically dared me to try to tough-guy him again. "So, Irenie sent you? Figures. Stupid bimbo. I told her to calm down and not to worry. I have no intention of …" Maybe it was my expression that confused him, but he stopped mid-sentence, clearly not knowing if he should say more. "Irenie didn't send you, either?"

"No. I came on my own."

"Whatever for?"

"To ask you about a cheque you partially wrote to Frannie. No, don't deny it, I've seen it."

"None of your business, Honey. If you have half a brain, you'll steer clear of that family. They're whacked. Everyone one of them."

"Frannie and her mother are certainly interesting gals."

He huffed. "You've got no idea, Sister. The husband's just as nuts too."

I tried not to get defensive. My cheeks heated, and my first instinctive desire was to pop him one in the beak. But, I needed more from him. I fought my violent urges and grit my teeth. Lockwood deserved better than that from a lowlife like Proctor. Why was I being so emotional about Lockwood? Keep it professional, Lou. "What did you promise Irenie? What does she have over your head?"

"What are you, a private dick?"

"As a matter of fact, I am."

He glared at me, smug as politician. "You? That's rich. Well, Sweetheart, I don't have to answer your questions. You're no copper."

"True." I reached into my purse and pulled out my badge for him. For me, I took the moment to make sure the Savage was ready for my grasp. "But, I'm a lot easier to deal with than the police."

"So what."

"So, you dumb stump, I don't have the habit of dragging people into dark jail cells and beating confessions out of them. Use your brain. You have one, don't you? Tell me why you gave Frannie a cheque, unsigned."

"To keep her mother off her back. I told you, Frannie and I were done."

I nodded, as if I believed him. "Why did you think Irenie sent me? Come on, quit holding back … why did you think Irenie sent me?"

"'Cause Frannie wouldn't. She couldn't." He bit his lower lip and drew back. There it was, he'd said something he thought was too much.

"I know she couldn't."

He looked away from me. "Something happened to her, didn't it?" His voice was pleading and despondent.

"Something permanent."

Proctor sat down hard. "Are you sure? She's dead?"

"I saw her myself."

Was he acting? Of course, he was acting most of the time, leaving anyone to wonder who the real Proctor was. He pinched the bridge of his nose between his fingers and started a kitten-like cry.

"Snap out of it! You already knew she was dead."

Proctor jumped and stared at me. No tears. Not even a little redness around the rims of his eyes. Faker. I glared. He sighed, almost apologetically. "A little bird told me. I can't say I'm surprised. But honestly, the cheque was insurance for Frannie to keep her mother at bay."

"Frannie was blackmailing you. The cops will come find you. Here, very likely …in front of all your friends … arrest you for her murder."

"No! I mean, no, I didn't …"

"That's your best defense?"

He sat with his mouth open.

I tucked my badge back into my purse. "Where were you last night?"

"At the Shanghai Palace over in Chinatown."

"All night?"

"Ah, yes. I think so."

I gave him a look of disgust.

"You're not a cop and I don't have to answer your questions."

"No, Mr. Proctor, you don't, but if you don't, the police are prone to jump to all sorts of conclusions when they fingerprint Frannie's room and find your prints all over it." Folding my arms and looking as immovable as I really was, I asked my question again with the simple imperial lift of an eyebrow. "There's also the question of the photographs."

He put his head in his hands, possibly reacting naturally for the first time all night. "I was at the Shanghai Palace after nine, you can ask the bartender, Frank's his name."

"Dinner?"

"At Carmody's."

"Carmody's, at Grant and Green?" I didn't say where Frannie's body turned up, so it was more than curious he admitted to having dinner right across the street.

"Yes. I left sometime around eight. I think it was eight. Then, I headed up to Frannie's place and sneaked in. I figured she was out. Irenie usually is too. So, I got in."

"Easy enough. You knew where her room was."

"I've been there only once."

Eyebrow up.

"Okay, Miss Tanner, more than once."

"And Irenie Coventry didn't catch you and Frannie during your visits?"

"Who do you think set us up?"

Proctor was twice Frannie's age and already piling up the corpses of dead relationships. My impression of him dropped even further — if that was possible. "So, you went to her room around when?"

"Eight fifteen? Maybe earlier. I don't remember. I never made it to Frannie's room. Irenie's ex showed up. I heard him come in and I didn't stay around."

152

"Why did you think you could go into Frannie's room without Irenie catching you? How did you know they would both be out? I doubt Irenie would give you her schedule if there wasn't something in it for her."

He started fumbling with his cuff-links. "I just knew."

"The cops are gonna' fry you." I started to leave.

"No. Irenie keeps a fairly regular social schedule. I knew she'd be out. You have to know Irenie. She's a gold digger with ambition. She practically sold her daughter to me. Except —"

"Except what, Mr. Proctor?"

"Frannie and I liked each other. Frannie, she wasn't so bad. Irenie didn't have to push her on me, like she did with the others."

My stomach knotted, and my heart pounded its way up to my throat. I had a heater and wanted to use it so bad. So very bad. "Others?"

He messed up his perfect hair, running his fingers through the grease. "It wasn't all Irenie. Frannie knew there was money in it too. Through me and the others, she got access to people who wouldn't give her another glance otherwise."

"You gave her access in addition to money. Let me see if I got this; once you two parted as friends, she still asked for money? So, you made some introductions to get the payments lowered?"

He nodded. "Sort of. It was more of a favor at that point."

"Anyone dangerous?"

He paled and nodded again.

"Like Willkie Valentini?" I had no patience for his stalling. "A known killer, and you handed Frannie over to him! Some friend."

Proctor held up his hands. "No. It wasn't like that."

"You better tell me what it was like or I can't help you with the police."

"You'll help me?"

"I might. Then again, if you killed Frannie, I promise to throw the switch myself."

"Okay, okay." He pulled a cigarette case out and offered me one. I refused it. I refused a cigarette. I was too livid. But that one voice hiding in the back of my head was a little proud at the moment.

"You were saying, Mr. Proctor?"

Letting out a long, smoky breath, he paced and talked, the gripped cigarette between his fingers, using it to punctuate every word. "Frannie had something bigger going. Something she was cutting her mother out of. I gave her one last cheque. It wasn't filled out or signed. It was, I dunno', a promissory note? Irenie would think I was still paying or prepared to and wouldn't ask Frannie questions. Besides, I didn't want Frannie coming back after her big plan fell through, all piss and vinegar, ready to take it out on anyone who abandoned her. Frannie was queer about abandonment. You know what? She wouldn't take it at first. It was free cash for her, and she didn't want it."

"Have I got this straight? She really was into something big. She still accepted your cheque only as a means to keep Irenie from pressuring her to keep blackmailing you?"

He drew long and heavy on the cigarette. I felt a longing, then pushed it out of my head. "Miss Tanner, this sounds absurd …"

I tried not to laugh. Absurd, at this moment, would take on a whole new definition.

"… but I had to talk her into keeping it. Whatever she was into was risky. She said so. But if it worked, she wouldn't have to deal with me, her mother, her stepdad, any of the other guys. None of us. After that, it wasn't hard to convince her to keep it for protection. She needed everything she lay her hands on."

Christ! Who was she working over who would give her so much power? A car pulled up near the closed door, then backed away. Vehicles coming and going was normal. Seagulls squawked and cried outside. Proctor had practically smoked the cigarette up to his fingers.

"Did you see anything when you were at Carmody's on Green?"

"Knew you would ask. Yeah. I saw. I saw plenty. Why should I tell you anything?"

"Look, you miserable …" I pulled out my heater and pointed it straight at his left eye. I took a deep breath, which wasn't easy or pleasant with the cloud of tobacco smoke Proctor left in the air. "Frannie's dead. I don't know what she was into, but I don't like dead people turning up where I should have been finding a live kid. She was a kid — you know, right? You, an adult, were diddling a child. Were you the photographer of a bunch of pornographic shots? That's illegal too."

"Okay, I took some photos, but she was always clothed. Nothing really pornographic. As for Frannie being a kid? Maybe in years, but you didn't know Frannie. She was more like an adult than you'd expect." His voice trembled. I was shaking him up good. His stare never moved from the muzzle of my rod.

"Ever hear of statutory rape? Solicitation? And, you were near the scene of the crime — are you getting the big picture yet?"

Nope he wasn't. He was there, wide-eyed and fish-mouthed.

"Let me add up your score: you did some nasty things with an underage girl, she blackmailed you, and you killed her. You've admitted to being near the scene of the crime. You're strong enough to have overwhelmed her and strangled her. You're the strongest suspect around."

Proctor began shaking a little. "Look, back then, Frannie was, how should I say this? Interested. She wanted me. It's not like I molested her against her will. She wanted it."

"Think any cops will weep if I plug you?"

When I made sure it looked like I'd pull the trigger, he cowered and held up his hands protectively. "I wasn't the only one near where they found Frannie!"

"Spill it or I spill blood."

"Can I have another cigarette?"

"No. Talk!"

He tried to stop shaking. Didn't work. "You're not gonna' like what I have to say."

"I already don't like your stalling. And I definitely don't like you!"

"At Carmody's, there was a whole bunch of people. I'm not narrowing it down like you think I am."

A shadow moved across the window behind him. Someone on their way to the Baths?

"Irenie was on Green Street. And I laid eyes on Elliott Lockwood too, coming out of the 500 G's — Valentini's place on Grant. Most of the time, I wouldn't care, but I don't like Lockwood's connections, what with gangsters and the military."

My breath caught.

Proctor kept going without my prodding. "And another guy."

God, who hadn't been there? "Who?"

"Big guy. Ugly hat. One of those narrow-brimmed things that are cheap or foreign. He seemed more interested in Irenie, though. But, I tell you what, if I didn't know better, I would swear he was —"

The window exploded, glass and bullets flying.

CHAPTER EIGHTEEN

Avoid staring down the barrel of a gun. It's just good practice.

-Lou Tanner, P.I., Notes for female Pemberton Graduates, 1935

Mother of God! A Tommy Gun!

Proctor took no less than three bullets in the back, saving me from the slugs. The spray of metal was frantic and destructive.

If it weren't for the door and distance from the shooter, those slugs would have shredded me for sure.

I seized Proctor by the collar and pulled him down to the floor. He was dead weight on me. The bullets kept ripping everything apart. The door flew open after its lock had been destroyed.

I waited. Heater in hand — heart in mouth.

Proctor wasn't breathing or moving. He was leaking.

The horizontal hail of bullets stopped.

Footsteps ran to a car.

I leaned my head to see out the open door. The shadow was blurry, but I thought I made out a big figure, distinctive gun shape, and the possibility he caught me looking at him.

Heater up, I fired three shots at him. The Savage was a good weapon. I heard a car window break, another slug hit metal, and — hell, I didn't know what happened to the third slug. The shooter didn't cry out, I still might have hit him. I was sure I'd hit him.

My ears were ringing now, and the shadowy shape sped away. Gravel spit out from under the car's tires.

All I thought of was getting Proctor off of me. I needed to see if he needed my help. I needed to see if he was still alive. I needed his weight off me.

Like the latest from that Hammett writer-guy, my best clue was partially served to me by Lady Luck, interrupted by gun-play, and the meal killed. Damn it. I double checked. Proctor might still be alive.

Not a chance. The first two shots went straight through his heart. Or damn close. He'd taken more hits before we'd hit the dirt. No pulse, wrist or neck. His eyes didn't blink, despite all the dust tossed up by the ruckus.

Right about that moment, I felt my left shoulder ache, then sting, then scream at me. I reached up and found blood trickling down my arm.

I don't remember much of the next half hour.

Rollins and a uniformed officer looked me over. I wasn't a pretty sight. Blood was all over me, mostly Proctor's, but some of it was mine. The officer had a first aid kit, which made me laugh. What was he planning to do with that? Surgery?

"Hey, Doll. Welcome back." Rollins crouched down by me.

"Back?"

"Yeah, you've been ducking in and out of consciousness."

"I fainted," I asked sheepishly.

"You got shot. People pass out usually. And, you didn't exactly faint. You got goofy and lost a couple of seconds."

"Shot? No." Brilliant communication on my part, but then, I hurt like hell.

"True. More like grazed. Pretty bad, but there's no slug in you." The officer smiled, pulling a gauze pad and linen bandage out of his box. "You may want to get stitches and some happy pills. You paid your pound of flesh this time." Nice Shakespearean reference.

"Oh, she will," Rollins said, interrupting my protest.

I let out my breath. I wanted a cigarette and I wanted it now. "There goes the strapless look for me," I mouthed off. I don't know why. They say sarcasm was the response of people who ran out of things to say. I had plenty to say, but sarcasm was keeping me from getting cited for indecent language.

Somerset stood behind Rollins, forcing me to look up at him. "They don't let you wear dinner gowns in prison. I told you I'd arrest you if you showed up again." He had the nerve to pull out handcuffs.

For a lovely moment, I thought Rollins might slap him. And yeah, I should have kept my mouth shut, but pain and disorientation don't encourage wise decisions. "Look, Detective. I was talking to a guy. What law did I break in making conversation with a guy?"

"The guy's now a stiff. Murder is a crime."

"Well, I sure as hell didn't shoot him. This splendid change in the décor was the work of a Chicago Typewriter, not a revolver."

"Says you."

We all glared incredulously at Somerset. There were holes in the holes, in the walls and doors. The window glass lay on the floor, shattered into total oblivion. Plaster and wall paper were lying in shredded chaos on the floor.

"Maybe you killed this guy after the attack? Did he owe you money? Were you here to maybe blackmail him. Or do it for your client — whoever that is? You got a permit for that thing," he pointed at the Savage.

"Yes."

"Says you. We'll take it as evidence. We'll need to get everything about your client, your whereabouts, and get your notes."

"Not a chance," I snapped. "You don't have a warrant, do you?"

"Don't I? Says you. I can go clean out your office just 'cause I'm in the mood."

Rollins started to protest, but Somerset shut him down with a look.

"Says you," I quipped, urged on by the throbbing pain. "Want me to site you law and statute as to why you need a warrant? I don't mind a cop that's aggressive, but the law is made for all of us."

I angrily waved him away and let the officer bandage up my arm. My dress was ruined. Oh well. At least I wasn't dead.

Called away, Somerset walked off, but couldn't step off until he'd given me the don't-leave-town speech. I refused Rollins's offer of help to get up. I was no shrinking violet, and I was damned if I was looking helpless in front of all these men. And, I wasn't letting Somerset break the rules on my watch. Neither was Rollins, I gathered from his cramped expression and jerky movements. He was even grumbling under his breath. Bennie was one of those happy-go-lucky guys; he wasn't a grumbler by nature.

They took out Proctor under a sheet. Me, I bumbled along after, clutching my shoulder. *Pemberton's* doesn't tell you how much being shot hurts. I imagined what it would feel like in a more tender place, or if the slug was still under my skin.

After inquiring if I was under arrest, to which Rollins laughed in a strained way and said no, I stopped to make a call. Had to borrow a nickel from the cop since they still had my purse.

I called Marley and had her go to my apartment and mail my notebook to me in the post. It was unlikely the police had my address. Yet, I couldn't take a chance. My notebook was sacred property. It was the story of my journey plus every secret of my client's. Without a warrant, it wasn't anyone's business. I explained to Marley what she was allowed to answer and what she wasn't, if asked. She'd do alright for herself. When in doubt, tell the truth. Besides, if someone was taking odds on a confrontation between Marley and the cops, my money was solidly on Marley.

For the next five hours, I sat in a police department interrogation room, being asked and asked again, how did Proctor figure into my case, what did I want from him, did I shoot him, was I in love with him? I was pretty sure they were stalling while searching my office.

By midnight, they let me go home. Marley helped them locate my gun permit, copies of the paperwork for my P.I. license, and sighted client confidentiality when they produced no warrant. Figured they didn't have one. *I love it when I am right.* With a warrant, I had to turn over everything — that was how things work, properly. But every P.I. and cop can tell you, warrants take time. Rollins was sweet enough about keeping me in the loop. He even offered to drive me home. Of course, that would give him a chance to ask more questions, which he admitted.

"Don't crowd me, Bennie," I said with a slight laugh.

"You still need stitches. Maybe I should call you a doctor." He handed me my purse — thoroughly worse for wear.

"At this hour? Nah, what I need is rest. If it still looks ugly in the morning, I promise to go see a doctor. Promise." I shook his hand.

Bennie glowered. "Despite Somerset, you don't have to prove anything. And if you think that," he pointed to my bandaged shoulder, "is gonna' look alright in the morning, you're higher than a kite."

I must have burst out laughing, because I turned every head in the place. What a sight I must have been. "Bennie, I always have to prove myself. I always have to be twice as good and a hundred times tougher for you boys to think half as well of me. Always will."

"That's not true."

I patted his arm. "Maybe not for you Bennie. You're one in a million. It's everyone else I have to be superhuman for. Look at how Somerset treats me. He hated my guts before I even said hello."

"He hates my guts too. That's just his way."

"Not much fun for a partner."

Rollins shrugged. "He's not much of a partner, but we do our best."

I waved goodbye, glad to be out of the madhouse.

Outside, Marley stood by a hack — a real hack. She kept him there for close to an hour. That was expensive, but God, it was welcome. She took one look at the primitive wrapping on my shoulder and ran to me.

"You're going to a hospital, Slim."

"No chance. People go to hospitals to die. At least take me home to die in my own bed."

She scowled. "Emergency ward it is."

What was with people not listening to me? Well, she worried, and I had to appreciate that. And my bandage looked worse than I did.

Heck, even the cabbie worried and insisted on taking us to an all-night medical facility. There were only a couple in San Francisco and we, yeah all three of us, waited patiently for my turn. I expected to dip into that Allowance to tip this guy. Talk about above and beyond.

I made them promise me they wouldn't leave me in the ward overnight. I was not dying in a germ-infested facility with no privacy and doctors pushing morphine.

According to the cabbie, one Skeeter Jones by name, while I was being damn-near squibbed off, the day produced some interesting news. President Roosevelt laid out his plan for economic recovery this year, Hitler held another rally and some famous American praised him for his exceptional army air corps, Amelia Earhart broke another record for being the first woman to do something. He didn't quite remember what, and stocks in American Telephone and Telegraph went up. He had shares. So did his sister, but she had been reluctant to buy at first. Skeeter told Marley and me the whole story. Every. Single. Detail.

I have to say, this guy going on about this, that, or the other thing was oddly soothing. I should have been irritated or downright angry. But I wasn't. Exhausted. That was the correct word. I was in pain. And pissed off someone tried to kill me. Of course, maybe this was nothing more than me accidentally being in the vicinity, and the killer was after Proctor the whole time. That made me collateral damage, and it felt even worse than being targeted.

The waiting room had a radio, and after a few songs by Cole Porter, Irving Berlin, and Edward Heyman, I was glad for the background noise. I still needed to get a radio for the office.

Every time Skeeter got up to check when we would be seen by a doctor, Marley brought me up to speed on what happened at the office. The bottom line was, it was damn good neither of us had too many personal or sensitive objects in there.

"I mailed off your notebook, like you asked. I'm surprised you left it at home in the first place."

"And no one followed you there when you retrieved it?"

162

"Not a soul. They didn't touch your apartment after all. There was one bright bit of luck. I wonder why they didn't."

"Because I leased under Lillian Collington-Tanner, not Lucille Tanner. I had to have the President of the rail company sign for me, since the landlord wouldn't let a woman sign a contract on her own, and the less Cecil is involved with my life, the happier he is. He signed and didn't look back."

"So, they can't find your address by your name. Clever girl."

"Sure, they can, but not without doing some substantial leg work." I shifted my seat. I was beginning to wonder if I'd ever see a doctor. "Are you okay after all of this?"

Marley waved me off. "Slim, I'm clear on what I've gotten into. Maybe not every detail of what to expect, but I expect to see a cop or two in your office. Don't worry about me."

Skeeter trotted over. I finally took a good look at him. He had to be in his late fifties, maybe early sixties. Short and blocky, like Bennie Rollins, but somehow more huggable. Clean shaven, with a neatly pressed button-down shirt, bow tie, pressed slacks, and new-ish coat. Money down, he married well, and his wife took pride in his appearance. He pulled off his cap to reveal thin, white hair. He looked the way I thought my Dad might look at that age. "Just a couple more minutes."

"Thank you, Mr. Jones." I said, deeply impressed by his attentiveness.

"Skeeter. I'm just Skeeter."

"Did you call Mrs. Skeeter to tell her you'll be late?"

"Nah. The missus knows I work late. Not due home for another hour. Thanks to my job, we keep some odd hours. But then, we're old, we don't sleep as much as we used to."

"All the same," I said. "Please tell her thank you for letting us monopolize your evening and making you late for home. And I'm grateful for a late-night cabbie. You fellas are rare."

He grinned in a tight-lipped way, and his eyes squished up. "For a pair of lovely young ladies with manners, the missus would kick my behind for not taking care of you."

Skeeter hopped up, after valiantly restoring my faith in humanity, and checked one more time.

"Marley, I need more information about Skates Berk, Elliott Lockwood, and anything you can find on Harold Harrison, a VP at some downtown bank."

"Easy. You, of course, will be bedridden, yes?"

It wasn't a question.

"Let's see what the doctor says."

"It may depend on what the police say too."

Yeah, there was that too.

Oh hell, I needed to meet Lockwood.

CHAPTER NINETEEN

Pick your drink and stick to it. Make sure it's
something you can get at any hotel, gin joint, or hole
in the wall. Make sure it can trip off your tongue
with little to no thought.

-Lou Tanner, P.I., Notes for female Pemberton
Graduates, 1935

The stitches hurt as much as the initial wound. I remember that from *Chapter 9: Preventing Injury*. Of course, *Pemberton's* was referring to tripping while on surveillance or paper cuts on police forms. Strangely, they didn't give much attention to the process of being shot. Maybe because they didn't want to entirely discourage future detectives. Of course, they discussed the nature of gunshots, but always in terms of someone else. God, it hurt.

With everything that had gone on, plus a shot of pain killer in my arm, I was fairly disoriented. My sarcasm level rose, but from my friends' reactions, I was at least funny. My head was cloudy but still on straight. I wasn't too far gone. Still – I appreciated the help. My shoulder was twice the size of the other side and they'd put my arm in a sling, so I was effectively single handed.

Marley got me home. Skeeter drove, and when I'd paid him a princely sum for his efforts, which he attempted to refuse, of course, he gave me his dispatch number and cab registry designation. Being able to call for a cab by number and name in San Francisco was worth a pile of gold.

He made sure Marley got home too. Her place was on the other side of the Park, in the Richmond.

After they'd left me, with a small pile of pills I promised — I would take — I lied, I pulled out my cigarette case, bottle of Old Forrester, and a glass. I skipped the pills. I didn't need to be fuzzy and disconnected. My painkiller was the bourbon and the nicotine. It worked okay.

I left a message for Lockwood at his hotel. I had no idea how to tell him about what happened. I simply apologized for not making it. That was all I had the energy to do.

In the meantime, I was starting to connect a few dots. Cab Proctor said Irenie had been near the crime scene, with some fellow. Or some fellow was interested in Irenie. And of course, he never got a chance to tell me what he and Irenie agreed to. Christ. The fellow had been at the crime scene before approaching Irenie. Then he'd said something I'd avoided thinking about all night. Elliott Lockwood had not only been at the crime scene, but he'd been seen coming out of Willkie Valentini's club. I didn't like it. Elliott hadn't said anything about it and he had plenty of opportunity to do so. And what was that crack about the military and Lockwood?

The third swallow of bourbon was at my lips when someone banged on my door. No, they did't knock, they banged.

No one should be at my door unless it was Marley, my landlord, or a neighbor. Who was up at three a.m? The landlord was an older gal who couldn't pound too hard. She would announce herself as well. I tip-toed to the door, snagging up my Louisville Slugger. None of my neighbors would keep pounding on my door like it was a brothel.

I was either stupid from the injury and booze, or I was much too angry. I silently unlocked the door with my fingers sticking out of the sling, shoulder burning, listened for the knock again, meaning the person was close with one hand occupied ,and whipped it open. Making myself as big as possible, I blocked the door with my fuming expression, Louisville Slugger held at the ready.

Cheap hat and overcoat. Good shirt, trousers, and shoes. Jaw dropping his mouth into a big "O."

No longer hidden by the shadows, I filled in the blanks pretty damn quick. This was the man I'd seen watching Lockwood the first night of the case. He was the man who had slipped me the note. He was the man I bought a drink for at Stan's.

His green eyes widened and slowly he raised his hands in a warding gesture.

We didn't speak.

He stared from my menacing face, to arm-sling, and back again.

I did a fast assessment. He was taller than me by about five inches. Salt and peppered brown hair. Five o'clock shadow. Clean hands. His face was completed with a wicked, square jaw and deep lines carved into his skin by time and weather. About forty-years old, well-worn and startlingly fit. He was a kind of handsome that got called "craggy" and "well-defined." Between his posture, his expression, and his glaring eyes, I gathered he'd been around the block of life. And, to add to the description, he had a box, a device, some sort of dingus slung over his shoulder I had never seen before.

"What happened," he demanded.

"What do you mean? Who are you? And, keep your hands where I can see them, or I'll pound some common sense into you."

He pointed, his hands still raised, at my arm. "What happened? Are you badly injured? I've been trying to find you all night."

"Who the hell are you?"

"You talk to your Grandmother with that mouth?" He smiled, a little sheepishly. "I'm your guardian angel."

"You're running late, Saint Michael. I could have used you about eight hours ago."

"That's about when I lost you. Can I put my hands down?"

"No."

"I'm putting my hands down."

"No."

"I'm reaching for my identification."

"What part of 'no' don't you recognize?"

"Oh, the part Agent Jim Mason told us to ignore."

Mason? Oh for the love of God.

I dropped the Slugger into the gap where it resides and slammed the door in his face. Where's my bourbon?

Apparently, I hadn't sufficiently closed the door, because Green-eyed G-man invited himself in.

"You do realize I've got a heater I can plug you with, if I get a mood?" I growled.

"You do realize shooting a Federal agent is a felony?" He carefully, wise to my cranky nature and potentially armed status, removed his badge and showed me. I didn't read it. It had all the basics even my blurry brain recognized.

Just because I only produced a rude reaction, I looked him over and sarcastically added, "They need to pay you boys better. That's the ugliest fogger I've ever seen." There. I felt better.

Green-eyes looked down at his cheap overcoat. "Sometimes it's better to look a little shabby, especially when you're tailing someone."

He wasn't wrong. "And you're tailing me, Agent?"

He nodded.

"Why the note?"

"'Cause I'm not the only one watching you."

I mumbled something about nice handwriting. "What was the name again?"

"Christopher Hayes. War Department."

I sat down in my easy chair and didn't offer him a seat, but he took the opposite chair without my say-so. Figured he would. "Any chance you're telling me why you tailed me tonight, Agent C. Hayes, War Department? And don't be surprised if you get thrown out. Landlady's rules, no visitors after eight p.m."

"Nine p.m," he corrected.

I reached for my glass of sanity. It was out of grasp, so I started to get up. Hayes popped out of the chair with the ease of a healthy man and snagged the glass for me. Pouring a little more, he handed it to me.

"Thanks."

"What happened," he asked, sitting down again.

"Police think I shot myself and a man standing near me with a Tommy Gun."

Scowling, he shook his head. "You don't own a Tommy Gun."

"How do you know?"

"I'm your guardian angel, remember."

I sipped the bourbon. I wanted to knock it back, all tough and the like, but for some reason I didn't. He watched me with those green eyes.

"Look, I'm tired, a doctor just carved a bullet out of me," that got his attention, "and I want to go to bed. Do you have a point, or can we meet up tomorrow when I find what I did with my manners? They might be in my sock drawer but I don't feel like looking for them right at the moment."

"It's a little appalling when you don't use them."

"I'm horrified by their absence. Now, if you don't have a bedtime story for me ..."

He leaned back. "Isn't this where you tell me to kiss you and make it a love story? That's what you told Jim, when you two first met, right?"

I did, didn't I? "No, this is where you don't kiss me. And I was being smug with Mason. I wouldn't ever want to kiss him."

Oh, he wasn't letting me off the hook. "Here, let me tell you my story and if you nod off, I'll come by your office in the morning and repeat it. Deal?"

I lifted my glass in acquiescence. Come on, liquor, do your stuff — I need this goof to brush off.

"You may not like this, but the Department is a bit worried about you."

"Treasury or War?"

"Both. Me. My Director."

My shoulder started to throb. "If you really want to impress me, go have a chat with Agent Mason about leaving me alone. And is it okay if I'm grateful tomorrow?"

"I heard about what he pulled." He smiled broadly, with nice white, straight teeth. "He still has the black eyes to prove you're not to be trifled with. Gave us some song and dance, but we figured it out. All the same, I'm sorry. You can swear out a complaint."

My skin crawled. As if I wasn't already physically uncomfortable, chasing a complaint through the legal maze of the government made me decidedly unwell.

"You went to the Pointe, didn't you, on Jim's orders?" He tried to sound lighthearted and failed. "Yeah, you did, doing one of his little errands. Me, I'd rather avoid the place but I don't always get a choice in these things. I don't have a good feeling about the Militia."

My skin wanted to escape my body. "So, let's not talk about it. I have a case to solve that doesn't include any government boogey-men or whiz-bang toys."

"But, you got on and off the Militia base —"

I held my hand up in an angry, warding gesture. "That's a story I don't want to tell. If I can pretend it never happened, maybe others can too. Why don't you give it a try?"

"I have. Didn't pull it off like you did. Got officially … um … uninvited permanent-like."

"I don't need this."

"Can't say as I blame you for wanting to walk away, but, if it helps, you impressed some folks at the War Department. You can help us in the future, too. You have potential as a detective. Good investigators are in short supply."

"And the minute I stop giving you free services, you'll snuff me out like a cheap cigar?"

The Agent looked sincerely insulted. "Not a chance. And you are getting paid if we employ your services. No freebies for us. You're a good investment. You're good at what you do."

I struggled to my feet and he watched me struggle.

"Have you ever thought of becoming a federal agent?"

I must have given him one hell of a look.

He laughed. "Yeah, yeah. We haven't exactly impressed you at this juncture, thanks to Jim Mason. I'm going out on a limb here and say you're not interested in international politics, weapons, and spying."

"Good guess." I pushed my drink glass aside. "Look, I'm a Shamus. That's it. Just a Shamus. I'm pretty darned good at it. I'd rather find missing cats than work on big secret projects."

"You've got your feet solidly on the ground."

"Up to my ankles in muck, you mean." I drained that glass with every ounce of awkward grace I had in me. But damn if I can't milk the helpless drunken damsel in distress for long before the P.I. in me busts through. "So, what's your beef with the Point? I don't like them because they make noise all night, keep secrets, and treat my city like a common prostitute." Okay, Green-eyes, give me something.

"What's not to love? Former soldiers who won't give up their base and probably have dirty photos of congressional big wigs who let it happen? A bunch of unchecked war mongers who have too much cash and too much time on their hands? Bullies who like to build bigger and better machines to bully with? No beef — nah, not me. I should add noise to the list too."

"I suppose I can commiserate with you then. I hate bullies. Why are you here again?"

"I'm checking to make sure you're okay and ..." he stopped and nodded at my arm. "Well, I lost track of you near the Sutro Baths, and then there were cops all over the place. I heard on the wire there'd been a shooting. You didn't go back to your office or come here, not for a long time. I guess I added it up. Look, I mean it, we want to keep you safe. You did us a favor, now we want to do the same."

I put my fingers lightly on my shoulder. "I guess I owe you one for at least checking. Don't suppose you know who shot up the Seal Rock Club?"

I didn't like it when he shook his head.

"Call me myopic, but I have a case to solve. I need to concentrate on it. It's important. It's a plain, simple murder. Well, maybe not simple. But if I do solve it —"

"When you do," he corrected.

Nice touch. "Okay, okay, when I solve it, then I'll think about coming out to play with you boys."

"I can take you at your word?"

"What is that over your shoulder?"

Green-eyes, happy for the change of subject, petted it like a cat — which reminded me I would have to feed Not My Cat sooner rather than later. The whole unit was strapped over his shoulder and across his chest. On the back was a large, rectangular pack, and on the front was what looked like the mouthpiece of a telephone. A single sided set of earphones was resting around his neck. He puffed up a bit with pride. "Personal, two-way radio. Battery operated. I can reach anyone at any time. As long as they have a receiver. Don't have to stop and look for a phone booth to call in reports or to call for backup."

"I want one," I grumbled.

"Arrangeable. It's not precisely top secret these days." He stood up, to take his leave. "I'd ask you if you if you wouldn't mind my keeping my eye on you, Sweetheart, but I'm not asking, and you wouldn't say yes anyway." With that said, he nodded politely, ordered me to get some sleep, and headed out the door.

Out in the hallway, Mrs. McCarthy confronted the agent. Green-eyes had his badge out before she told him, "no male visitors in the building after nine p.m." She looked inside my place and noted my arm in a sling, and decided we weren't doing anything indecently horizontal. Poor Green-eyes, he took a serious scolding as he walked down the stairs to the lobby.

I sat back down to rest my eyes for a moment or two, having filled another glass with hooch; I fell asleep, I don't remember when. I was sorting and filing everything in my brain, which was a useless effort. I wasn't in a place to do much that was logical. I woke up, drooling a tad, still dressed, having spilt the dregs of my glass of bourbon on my skirt.

Today, I decided with the firm hand of the owner of Tanner Investigations, was my day off.

I took off my dress, slip, girdle, and stockings, none of which was easy with only one hand. Crawling into bed, the building shook. I didn't care if it was from above or below; I was going to sleep through it.

As I drifted off, I realized my command decision was pointless. It was Sunday. Though, does a Private Detective ever have a day off? Or weekends?

The sheets felt cool on my shoulder, and for a moment they felt like a gentle touch. Had I made the right decisions in life? I could have been properly married, with a loving husband and kids by now. No, I'd taken the right path for me. Mother had wanted so much for me to be the perfect socialite daughter, but I wanted so much more.

Besides, I'd ruined everything by spending my free days with Uncle Joe. He taught me everything I needed to be a good detective. He was fatherly, never a threat. He never treated me as anything but an enthusiastic brat. I just remember he was there when my own father wasn't. The downside to being the king of railroad design was that Daddy didn't get home often. Mom was making sure there was a home and a social place for us to exist. Yeah, Uncle Joe, with his tales of gangsters, rum running, murders solved, and private investigator's heroism kept me enthralled.

When I told him I was following in his shoes, he didn't laugh at me. Instead, he sat me down and began telling me the truth about detecting, with stories showing there were consequences for what PI's do. He talked about crushed lives, broken hearts, and dead bodies. I always thought he was just trying to scare me off. I didn't run, and he didn't abandon me when I still said I wanted to be a detective like him.

Joe Parnaski had more ethics than most rich men had dollars. And, in the end, it got him killed.

My eyes watered.

I was there when it happen. It hadn't been a deep graze in the shoulder. Point blank range, two professional plugs to the heart then the head. I'd stayed hidden as Joe had told me to, I was still a girl and that wouldn't be enough to save me if they found me. The killers never knew I was there until I was testifying against them. Fat lot of good that did.

They got away with it.

I got sent to finishing school in upstate New York.

Joe got buried in a veteran's cemetery.

Things went on, as if nothing had happened.

I cried out frustration, pain, loneliness, and rage into my pillow. It was cathartic.

My caseload doesn't come with vacation.

There was no rest for the wicked.

At this point, I was off the clock. Giving it away for free. But hell, the real case wasn't solved. Everything I did from now on out would be part and parcel of my reputation the one I built with my heart.

Outside the window, steam locomotives sounded off each time they traversed a street crossing. Fog horns bellowed from the bridges. And in the cacophony of their harmonic collision was a comfortable melody that lulled me away from the bad memories.

Sometime after my eyes and my nose stopped running, I fell asleep. No dreams. No lucid memories after all. Just dead sleep.

CHAPTER TWENTY

They say a woman is old after age thirty. Yeah, "they" say a lot of stupid things.

-Lou Tanner, P.I., Notes for female Pemberton Graduates, 1935

An hour and a half later, I rolled up to Irenie's place in Skeeter's hack and took note of the black crepe — everywhere.

I felt no pity. This batch of folks lied to me by word or omission; Frannie was a thing, a pawn, and little more. Irenie prostituted her own daughter and I'd had more than I was willing to take.

My arm hurt.

Signs of death were everywhere, wrapped in morbidity like Queen Victoria after Prince Albert died, the place drowned in mourning, right down to sand poured on the street to keep the sound of horse's hooves from interrupting the bereavement going on inside. This street never had horses up here, ever. Weren't any houses up here until that impossibly steep road made it possible. Aero-drop Services delivered the coal, so the sand nonsense was only for show. Black cloth draped around the small fence, and all the curtains remained closed.

Taking a deep breath, I knocked on the door. Lockwood himself answered. He'd put on a suit of black. It was a little out of fashion, but I didn't expect him to go out and purchase something new. It was tasteful. He looked good, and I held back the urge to wrap my arms, arm, around him, to promise everything would be okay. But it wasn't okay.

"Miss Tanner?"

"Mr. Lockwood. I need to come in."

"The case is over." He sounded nervous.

"No, it isn't. May I come in?"

Every thought played out on his face: worry, confusion, resignation. He opened the door wider and stepped aside. "I don't think you should follow up on this anymore …"

His eyes fell on my enlarged shoulder and sling. "What happened?"

Before I leaned into my explanation, the bereaved mother conducted herself into the room from the second story balcony.

Irenie was amazing, and I had to think about closing my mouth. High collar to floor, she dressed in a bias-cut, rayon black gown that dragged behind her as she took each step. I understood one wore unrelieved black crepe when in mourning, but that wasn't the way of the modern creature. Against Victorian rigorous mourning practices, she sported a pair of glistening black earrings and a dazzling necklace to complete her costume. My Grandmother would have found it vulgar. Irenie came down the stairs slowly, deliberately stopping with each step and blotting tears with a black-edged handkerchief. Quite a show.

Memories of Frannie's body, laying on the ground in an empty lot, her fear from the cab-incident — it all burned in my cheeks.

"Oh, Miss Tanner. How kind of you to come." She was droning and enunciating with all the drama of a Shakespearean actor. "We are needing all your help in this hour of our sorrow."

"I'm not a social secretary."

"No, but being Mr. Lockwood's friend, with connections, I thought you … Under the circumstances, we can use help, even from his friends."

So, I hadn't entirely put the thought of my being a new gal for Elliott out of her mind. As if I was Cinderella being blockaded from attending the ball by a wicked stepmother, Irenie started in with a list of chores for Elliott's assumed new lover to do. "First, we'll need to set up the reception. And of course, Mr. Lockwood can take care of any expenses …"

"He already has. Retainer and expenses." I'd had about as much of Irenie as I wanted.

Irenie's demeanor changed faster than a snake shedding its skin. "I don't understand."

"I'm not surprised." I headed for the stairs.

She blocked me. "What?"

"I'm not a writer. I don't work for San Francisco Magazine. I'm not his girlfriend, either. Now move it or I'll move you, Sister."

She glared at Lockwood who had no idea what I was up to. I pushed by and started up the stairs.

"Elliott, who is she," Irenie demanded?

"I'm a private investigator and I'm off to Frannie's room."

Irenie wheeled on Elliott with complete indignation. "An investigator? I doubt it."

"She is," he announced almost nonchalantly.

"How could you! Did you hire her to spy on me?"

I didn't stay for the fight breaking out. Elliott knew how to handle himself. He'd allowed Irenie to walk all over him like an old doormat and I was willing to bet he was done with her nonsense too. I overheard something to the effect of, "Irenie, just shut up. This isn't about you."

Good man.

With quiet but quick care, I rummaged around Frannie's girly room, a fact of which still bothered me. A lot. Lockwood had been right. No sign of the cheque. Irenie might have taken it, but could she forge her daughter's signature? Or Proctor's? I doubted it. So, who took the cheque?

I wanted to learn the real reason why Cab Proctor gave Frannie an unsigned cheque. I needed to learn it. I was desperate to know if he killed her. He might be dead, but that didn't mean he hadn't done the deed. Then of course, Elliott and Irenie were both suspects. My whole body seized-up. Yes, Elliott too.

Coming back downstairs, I took my sweet time.

"Just what were you looking for in my house?" Irenie snapped.

"My house," Lockwood corrected.

"That's the business of my client," I shot back at her point blank.

"Well, I consider it my business too. Have you no respect? We're in mourning here."

"I can tell," I said with arguably too much sarcasm while looking her up and down. Irenie reacted by clutching her black necklace, sticking her nose in the air, and trying to high hat us.

"Elliott." She turned a cold shoulder to Lockwood and barely looked at him. "How could you do this to me? My beloved child is dead. My heart is broken. I'm in shock. And you, you bring this bimbo into my home. I don't care if you signed the papers, it's mine. I live here. And this," she swung her hand carelessly in my direction, "This is beyond the pale. If you have to have a mistress, I think it's cruel to bring her here to insult me."

Lockwood got up on his hind legs and his face reddened under his five-o'clock shadow. "All about you, isn't it? For the last time, and I mean it, the last, this lady is a private investigator." He leaned in and all of a sudden, my pride in his backbone faded under the deliberate cruelty I didn't realize he had in him. Lowering his voice, he spoke about three inches from her nose. "I hired her because I expected you were using Frannie and I wanted to rescue that girl from you and your conniving. I don't care about your feelings. I don't care if this inconveniences you from your salons. I stopped caring about you and your dirty needs a long time ago, when I learned what you really are. Nothing but a gold-digging, manipulative bitch."

Irenie burst into crocodile tears, let out something shrill that sounded like a protest or a challenge to the validity of Lockwood's parentage, and ran over to the bench on the other side of the room to wail into her handkerchief.

Lockwood looked frustrated, embarrassed, and fresh out of compassion to give away.

The Harrisons arrived with their usual timing. Gem was in full mourning dress and full dramatic performance. She took one look at Lockwood, pathetically called him names offensive only to an eight-year-old, and rushed to Irenie's aid, dragging a waft of overpowering perfume behind her. Harold Harrison stood in the doorway, wearing a black pin-striped suit and an exasperated expression. He looked to Lockwood who was surprisingly unsympathetic to his fellow put-upon husband.

In fact, he was giving off an air of hostility toward Harrison. The banker picked up on the signal, nodded, and shuffled over toward the pair of divas trying to out-do each other in pitifulness. My arm started throbbing.

"You're truly awful, Elliott Lockwood," Gem shouted.

Harrison might have read the inside of his own skull with that roll of his eyes. "Gem, cut it out. Everyone is upset, including Elliott." An oddly insightful of Harrison. "Frannie was a good girl. You bawling over it won't bring her back."

Well, that was the back-crushing straw of lore, breaking the camel's back, because Gem's eyes filled with fury and her face contorted into rage. "Don't you dare say anything," Gem hissed.

Lockwood, Harrison, and I all involuntarily backed up a step. Gem was a slip-of-a-thing, but in the moment, she might as well have been eight feet tall with claws the size of a grizzly bear.

"Don't you dare talk. Just shut up. Shut up! After what you did."

"Gem!"

"Not another word or I swear to God I'll divorce you. And the lawyers will come away with every single penny." She turned back to Irenie, who I swear smirked for just a moment, before the two of them fell to great lamenting, teeth gnashing. Yeah, the whole works. One hell of a performance. I got the impression it had been done before. Or maybe rehearsed. "You probably killed her to keep her quiet!" Gem hissed.

Oh my, that came from out of the blue.

I looked at Harrison, who was too used to being verbally, maybe physically, slapped. So, he had some sort of tryst with Frannie. Great, I was hoping to reduce the number of potential suspects, not increase it. And there I stood, my arm in a sling from being squibbed, in a room with a bunch of folks who all wanted to kill Frannie.

I was never so happy to be armed. Having a heater within reach sometimes makes people a little too confident, but what the hell, I was no exception. "What about Cab Proctor?" I asked a bit too nonchalantly. "I thought he was the one with a relationship with Frannie."

"Cab only courted Frannie when I told him no," Irenie said through her handkerchief. "He wanted me. But I was being faithful to a faithless man," she shot at Lockwood, "and I told Cab no. Why? Why would you ask?"

"He's dead." Nah, I wasn't too nonchalant.

The room stopped cold.

Irenie glared out into space, as if someone just stabbed her.

Gem wasn't nearly so charitable. "Serves him right. Probably shot by one of his numerous girlfriends."

God, what nice people. I suppose they come with the job, and I'll worry about my sanity when they no longer surprise me. "Not unless any of them own Tommy Guns."

"Damn shame," Harrison said, risking his well-being. "I saw you with him, Miss Tanner. At the Seal Rock." Gem gave him a crusty look. He glowered over at her. "I was meeting with Frank before going to Pacifica for a few holes. Want to call him? He'd vouch for me."

So, he recognized me when I went to see Proctor. "I would have stopped to say hello, but someone interrupted things with gunfire. I'm surprised you weren't aware of the excitement, Mr. Harrison. Whoever shot up the club's back room turned heel and fled. After, of course, killing Proctor. The police were all over the building."

He shrugged. "Frank and I left a minute after you saw us. We weren't there. And," he turned again to Gem, who wasn't having any of him, "and I haven't been back since."

I wanted out of that place so badly. But, I had a job to do. Unfortunately, all I got were more wild and unbelievable accusations, tears, and plenty of nothing. Irenie and Gem fled to the back of the house, Harrison went to find the liquor cabinet, and Lockwood opted to chase after the women. So, basically, I left, but only because no one was around to talk to.

Poor Elliott, stuck with Irenie. Not that anything she would do surprised him anymore. Still, I felt like a heel leaving him with her. What a night. One surprise after another, and yet ... none of them should have been a surprise considering the players involved.

The real surprise of the evening was finding Marley standing at the curb, leaning on a big burgundy Studebaker, and indicating Bennie Rollins inside.

I walked up, unsure. Did they find another body?

"He called right after you left. He's got something he wants you to see."

"And you came along?"

"I had to give him directions, Slim."

"He can use a map."

She just batted her eyelashes.

I sidled past her and leaned in the window. "Okay, Bennie, Whatcha got?"

"Ever been to a morgue, Sweetheart?"

CHAPTER TWENTY-ONE

The only thing the Dead have over Liars is that the Dead don't keep trying to make up for being dead by dying more.

-Lou Tanner, P.I., Notes for female Pemberton Graduates, 1935

Morgues are not pretty places. Clean, but not pretty. And the smell is enough to send a sane person running out of the building. They also have the added dimension of housing bodies whose ghosts had every reason to be mad as hell. Everything echoed off the polished stainless steel. Even the little floor cleaning 'Bots were silver metal, I guess so they can be hosed off after cleaning up an autopsy. Or worse.

Marley, wisely, waited out in the lobby.

They drew out Frannie's tray from the cooler, with her body shrouded in white cloth discolored with pink and yellow stains near key mortem locations.

"Bennie? Any reason you want me here, ready to cough up this morning's breakfast?"

"Yeah," he said with a depressed sigh. The Medical Examiner lifted her arm out from under the sheet. I was grateful he hadn't revealed the whole body. It had been a couple of days, and the aroma told me Frannie's corpse was already going through au natural decomposition.

The arm was dark bluish grey in several spots near the elbow and wrist.

I couldn't help myself, I saw the pronounced shapes. I shifted to stand facing her and held out my hand to demonstrate how the bruise appeared to be someone gripping her from the front. "They tried to hold her arms," I commented, "it looks like someone held her wrists.

"That's what we concluded," the Examiner said flatly. "The bruises weren't apparent when we first did the autopsy, but in time, they appeared. It happens."

I looked up at Rollins. "So, we have more than one killer to contend with. Someone held her from the front, while another strangled her from behind?" I turned to the white-lab-coated coroner, asking, "Did she have marks on her hands indicating she tried to prevent the strangulation?"

"No."

Then two killers had been involved. Strong killers. Two men? Oh God, what if it was Lockwood and the man Proctor couldn't identify for me? As if my stomach wasn't already trying to escape through my throat.

"But," the Coroner added. I hate that word sometimes. "There are other marks on her hands." He turned her hand, palm up. Long, blue lines slashed across her skin.

"She was cut."

Rollins stuck his hands deep in his pockets. "Defensive wounds."

My eyes squinted, as if that helped. "So, she was attacked with a knife, but ultimately strangled. Did any other cuts show up?"

The Coroner nodded.

"Any of those potentially the cause of death."

"No." Short and easy answers.

Sliced up, and when that didn't do the trick, strangled while someone held her. This was no accident, no kidding, as if I'd ever thought otherwise, but I admit it was disappointing to have reinforcement of the truth.

The Coroner covered her up again, indicated we should be quiet, and pointed to the door. I heard nothing, but I didn't work there. The man in the white coat recognized every sound and he heard something he shouldn't.

Frannie was quickly put back on ice, and Rollins escorted me from the building, checking around corners as we went. We snagged Marley, and met up out back, in an alley. It didn't smell any better than the Morgue and was less clean.

Dr. White-coat made sure we exited the joint and whispered to Rollins. Well, it wasn't much of a whisper, I overheard what he said. "Bennie, you like her, but you can't be bringing women around here."

"Relax. She's a licensed Gumheel. Ain't that sweet?"

"I know, but — she's a — she." My guess, the Coroner didn't think it was so sweet.

"Well I can't go over the case with him. He's got his mind made up and besides, I think he …" Rollins looked at me and realized I was overhearing them. "Thanks again, Chuck."

"Sure." He nodded and slammed the big metal door closed.

Marley caught all he "whispered" too but waited for me to say something.

"'Him.' Your partner, Somerset. He's determined to nail Valentini, isn't he?"

"In ways you'll never understand. Look, Honey, keep that to yourself for now. And no mentioning what we did here. Chuck'll keep it close to the vest, too."

"Why?" I asked kindly. I needed an answer, but Rollins had been taking a risk bringing me in.

"I want to snag the right killer. Killers," he corrected himself. "I don't care who did it, I just want to catch 'em. And I'm not getting what you would call support from my partner."

"Fair enough. You helped me out. There may be some support I can give you, within the rules and regs of P.I.'s. Thank you, Bennie."

He nodded, knowing I couldn't give away my client, pulled his hat down and headed off.

Marley and I looked at each other, realizing at the same time, we were two well-dressed ladies standing in a creepy alley for no good reason.

"Delightful perfume, this place has. What's next, Slim?"

I understood and accepted what I had to do, but there was something I needed to glean first. What was Somerset's beef with Valentini? It was too personal, too intense. I explained it to Marley as we walked out of the alley, trying our best to be casual.

"Old papers are in storage at the library. It's closed today, but I can stop by early in the morning. Plus, I'd bet some of the gals from the police secretarial pool grasp a few details off the numerous reports." She adjusted her pork-pie hat on her pile of red braids.

"I'm seeing what some of the employees in the neighborhood have picked up about the family."

She stopped me as we approached the corner. With an expression that said, listen to me. "Including Mr. Wonderful."

"Most especially Mr. Wonderful."

"Doesn't feel good, does it?"

"It doesn't," I replied, "but he may be involved. The gist of this little visit was to confirm there are two people involved in this crime. We're looking for two."

"Something else bugging you?"

She appreciated me and my detecting style. "I haven't figured out why Frannie was over in the Bayview area. That's where I first ran into her."

A shadow loomed over us, and a zeppelin blotted out the sun overhead. It turned toward the Montgomery Station. The glass of the tower caught a glint of sunlight. It was interesting, as far as buildings go, but impossibly high. Never mind it had to be.

"Miss that place yet," I asked, jerking my thumb in the direction of her former office.

"What place?" She smirked, drew out a cigarette case, and offered to light one for me. I didn't refuse. "Oh, that place? See, I'm gainfully employed elsewhere now. Don't have time to think about the past."

"You had to manage a gang of coppers coming to look my office over."

"Easy-peasy." She waved her cigarette in the air. "You don't have enough in there for them to work over. They made a little mess. Nothing I couldn't clean up in ten minutes. Distracted them too." She pulled playfully on her skirt. *She definitely has good gams and uses them well.*

We were both laughing, but the truth was, she'd just stepped into a world I'd had fair warning about.

"What?"

I shrugged my right shoulder. "I guess I keep thinking of this job as a solo performance. But it isn't. You're involved. Heck, even Skeeter is involved, to a degree. Mom always said the hardest part of being married to my Dad was that she had to teach him how to think as a unit, not a single."

"Ha! I suppose having a proto-partner is like being married. Well, Slim, I can handle it."

I stopped her and stared her straight in the eyes. "You armed, right now?"

"Yes."

"And?"

"Just waiting for *Pemberton* to send me my first package of coursework. Then I'll start studying."

Not the answer I was expecting, but good enough. I couldn't decide if that made me happy or more worried. She was determined. Well, so had been little Lucille Tanner. If Uncle Joe was open and patient with me, I couldn't do any less for Marley O'Brien. "I expect your homework to be turned in on time. Say, want to hear my latest adventure, after you dropped me off? About the man with the green eyes?"

She just blew some smoke at me and grinned.

CHAPTER TWENTY-TWO

Most of the time, all I want in the morning is quiet
and coffee. Yards of coffee. Coffee that can take rust
off of iron. Unadulterated, hot, black coffee.

-Lou Tanner, P.I., Notes for female Pemberton
Graduates, 1935

Six days later, and nothing new appeared in the papers. They
had one story and they were sticking with it. The gangster killed his
moll. Open and shut case.

I didn't buy it. And I wasn't sitting around accepting it, either.
A quick call to Marley sent her off on a quest to find out all that was
knowable about Willkie Valentini's businesses. I was following the
money. Who would benefit if there wasn't a Mrs. Valentini around? I
had some ideas, but I needed facts.

I also needed more facts about Elliott Lockwood. Was there
some aspect of his business that was affected? I'd done a cursory
background on him, but after what he'd told me about the union
business, I realized I needed more. Was someone in his company
involved with Frannie or Irenie? The military connection? He was
more of a mystery and I confess I wanted to be sure my infatuation
wasn't misguided.

I wasn't too surprised, but employees around Irenie's residence
had nothing new and juicy to share. Just the stuff I'd already found.
No one thought Irenie belonged there.

The overall silence was impressive. I guess nobody wanted to lose their job, not till the economic welfare of the country improved.

There had been one exception, a chef hired on to supervise a Friday afternoon soiree, across the street and two houses down. He was the type that supervised more than cooked. Tall. Clad in white with the soufflé hat on his close-cropped hair. He barked orders with military precision and a thick Parisian accent. Cakes, boxes of Champagne, and trays of colorful hors d'oeuvres were being loaded in through the servant's entrance.

I dressed for optimal success. Crisp suit of brown and crème wool. Not too feminine. Brown shoes, brown gloves, and a fedora in brown felt — Uncle Joe's fedora. Overcoat of tan. And the unthinkable, no sling. I didn't need to play the weakness card.

Frenchy the Chef didn't even look at me when he told me to blow off, he had enough help. When I didn't move, he tried turning his ire on me. Didn't work. I flashed my badge with gusto. "Only in America," he snarled, returning his attention to a crate of dead chickens, "can a dame get a dick's license." He obviously had learned some slang words though not how to use them, so I suspected he'd been here in the states at least a little a while.

"Yeah. Let's hear it for the red, white, and blue, which are your colors too, by the way. I can make this easy and quick."

"Why should I yap to you?"

"It's me or the police. Your call."

He slammed the lid down on the future coq au vin. "Fine. Make it quick."

"Have you ever catered a salon up at the house at 1021 Vallejo Street?"

His eyes narrowed until I was sure he couldn't see. His cheeks were red and his arms stiff. "You whacked? There is not enough lettuce to make me sling grease at that place!"

I tried not laughing at his ironic choice of idioms. "Why?"

"What are you, some dumb bunny? The dame of that creep house is a prime round heel. And a real pro. Those salons, nuthin' but sex. Indecent, if you're quizzing me. We all know the stories. She used her daughter like a bangtail when she got too old to get her own johnnie boys. The goose looked the other way until he finally moved out. Daisy. A dumb palooka. He married pretty Janes. What a rube. He got a ball-n-chain who's jealous of her own child. Americans," he spit out. "Those people up there need to croak each other or just drift off. That's the crop. I cater to a respectable crowd."

"I can tell by your superior command of the English language, you're used to a better clientele." All that slang he spewed, with a French accent too.

"Make tracks, broad." He then realized he'd accidentally slammed the wing of one chicken in the lid. "Merde. Look, is that all you want?"

"That's it. You've been very helpful."

"That's a house that gonna' need fumigated when they're gone. Everyone be screwing everyone else."

My heart pounded. "Husband too?"

Frenchy stopped to think for a moment. "No. But their friends are always taking advantage. I think the girl said no. Bet one of the Johnnie's knocked her off."

"That's interesting."

Now he was mad, and really, I tried to compliment his deductive reasoning. "That's what happens when you cater to people from the other side of the Hill." He waved in the direction of the Mark Hopkins Hotel and the Church. On the other side was a less expensive version of Nob Hill. "Now, go away. I have to get this properly prepared for respectable people."

I didn't argue.

He gave me what I wanted. I bet the Harrisons savvied more than they were sharing.

I didn't have time to organize my thoughts when a sweet, silver sedan pulled up and out popped two goons. Needless to say, they were blocking my way.

The back window rolled down.

A man with a worn face and practiced sneer leaned forward for me to see.

Skates Berk.

"What's a dame like you doing in a place like this?"

"Avoiding clichéd come-ons from drive-by gangsters." God my shoulder hurt, and I was not in the mood to kick some fella's ass, but I had a bad feeling I just might have too.

Bruno One was my height, a little heavy in the middle, and not carrying his heat under his arm. His knees bowed a little. Hit him in the knee cap, make it bend the wrong way, and he'd go down. A solid kick was my best move.

Bruno Two was big. Really big. I wouldn't be able to take him down. I noticed his shoulder holster bulk. If he wanted his heater, he had to pull it through an overcoat and a jacket. That would give me time to pull my rod and point it at Berk.

I hoped none of these were necessary options, but I came prepared.

"Wise ass bimbo. I like it. Bet you're smart too."

"So the rumors say."

"Smart enough to take some free advice."

I folded my arms. "My mother always said advice is only worth what you pay for it. But, I can hear you out anyway."

"Back off. Mr. Valentini don't need no help from a Broad."

Well, there's a lie. Straight up. His face was a book. Too calm. Possibly assisted by booze. His eye pupils were big. Yeah, he was on something.

"Now, why would he turn down free help?"

"He don't want it." Skates was getting annoyed.

"So, if I ask him, he'd be in complete agreement with you?"

"Him and me, we think like Siamese twins."

"And of course, if he's out of the picture, you'll take care of all his business while he's in jail? You're a true friend. Just like a brother."

Berk sneered. "Business ain't none of yours."

"I don't suppose you inherit his business in case of his sad and heartbreaking demise? Being his twin, and all."

Bruno Two started to move and my hand slipped into my purse. I felt the Savage at my fingertips.

Suddenly, Berk broke into laughter. "Not bad. A bimbo with brains. Only, you got it all wrong. I like being in the background, in the dark, where no one can see me. Valentini is my golden goose. I got a thing for eggs. Sometimes it's better to be the friend of the kingpin than the man himself."

True. Berk would always blend in and make his coin, without ever being the focus of police investigations and gangland take-overs. Still, I wasn't exactly having a cool, nice conversation here.

One and Two made huffing noises at me and crawled back into the goon-mobile. Two stopped and rubbed his arm, gave me a dirty look for seeing it, and squeezed in next to Skate.

"So long, Toots. You best be smart enough to never want us to talk again." The window rolled up.

Never wanted to talk to you in the first place.

He was giving me his official policy. One he was betting both our lives on.

Saturday, late afternoon. For some reason, the weather wasn't so lovely, and neither was the City. Sure, it was a Saturday, but I was going into the office. To be cricket with myself, I didn't have anything else to do and I was too wound up in the case to want to do anything else.

Choosing to leave off my sling hadn't been a bright idea. I hurt. Bad. So, I pulled it out of my bag and wrestled it back on.

There were notes waiting on my desk. Marley to the rescue! According to two legal secretaries, names to be withheld, Valentini's above-board businesses were slated to be split with Skates Berk and some other mug I didn't recognize. I'd need to learn about him, but his residence was in Chicago. Long way to come to kill off a block to an inheritance. Skates had a closer motive. He got the businesses, or at least half, should something untoward happen to Valentini. Frannie

191

marrying Valentini, and a change in his Will, would mean she would inherit all the businesses and money.

So, if Skates was the killer, why not knock off Valentini at the same time? It might be a harder trick to pull off, but also, there was the inheritance split. If Valentini was alive and in prison, assuming they didn't fry him for killing Frannie, then someone had to run the businesses. And that would fall to Skates.

Made him suspect number one at the moment. A little Machiavellian but still … yeah, he was number one for now.

Not My Cat and I sat, sharing the boss's chair, with me providing the warmth of my lap. I finally figured out how he got in and out. There was a hole in wall under the coffee station. From watching him come and go, I discovered a hole that lead to the interior of the building structure and then out to the second floor near the mail shoot. For the time being, I wasn't complaining to the building superintendent — it was handy. Not My Cat came upstairs for meals and quiet, then took his business outside. I didn't need to come up with a toilet solution for him.

Marley was off to the picture show with some fella she'd taken a liking to. Sweet guy: glasses, thin moustache, well kept, a little shy of hair on top, but darling. And, he was well mannered, hard-working, so she told me, and had a weakness for pets. Former Army medic. He'd come by last night to pick her up at the office. I was happy for her. She deserved a man who was good to her.

Although, if they turned their relationship to something more than movies and drinks, would he want his wife to be a Shamus? Marley had her heart set on getting a P.I. license. Well, no point in putting the cart before the horse. They were only seeing a movie.

Howie was still in his spot, finishing the sports section from the evening edition. His black eyes narrowed as I approached. "Hey, Lady Galahad, you want to stay out of the papers? I hear it's healthier."

I took the paper he offered, stuffed it into my arm-sling, and pulled out my nickel. "So, what do they say?"

"Oh, the morning after the killing of that gal from Nob Hill, the Chronicle was stunned that a woman got between the police and a notorious gangster. They mentioned a rumor that a woman was an investigator but didn't give your name."

My smile squished to one side of my mouth. "I guess that's not too bad. I can only imagine what would happen if my name got popularized too much."

"And then there was," he pointed to my arm, "the shooting over at the Seal Rock Club. It frustrated the Examiner that you couldn't be found for an interview. But they did deduce that the woman at the crime scene and the shooting were the same woman. Are they right? You haven't dropped by in a few days, but I can see you're injured."

"It wasn't nuthin'," I said with a bit of swagger.

Howie crossed his arms. "Look Miss Tanner, I'm not your mother or father, so I don't have a dog in this fight. But, I'm telling you, you got lucky. Most folks eatin' brass don't get up and walk away."

"The man I was with didn't."

"See what I mean."

I closed my eyes and sighed. "I appreciate what you are saying."

He waited for me to say more.

I didn't.

"How do you feel?"

"Like I've been shot."

"They have to dig anything out?" Before I answered, he pushed his sleeve up a bit further. In his deep brown skin were two pucker marks. He gave me the stink-eye and let his sleeve down.

"War or post-war," I asked.

"Flanders. 1917. I was going home the next day. The Huns pushed on our trench and most of us collected bullets. The twins there, on the arm, they've got brothers and sisters." He patted his chest. "I'm told it's a miracle I survived. Sometimes it feels like they're right, sometimes it doesn't."

I got his message. "Too bad it isn't like it is in the novels or the moving pictures; take a couple of plugs and move along like nothing happened."

"Nothin' further from the truth," he added.

A cold breeze pushed down Market and two Trolleys clanged their bells at each other.   A sports-style auto sped through the intersection.

Beyond being held to impossible standards while treated as second class citizens, now Howie Johnson and I had something else in common. I liked that. "I got a deep graze. Got lucky as you said, no one had to go fishing for brass. They just carved it off the surface and stitched it up."

He nodded, approvingly, if I wasn't mistaken. "I suspect you learned your lesson about when to duck? 'Course, I don't tell you anything —"

"Because you're not my mother or father?" I smiled at his kindness.

"Yeah. Say, where are your folks, if you don't mind my asking?"

The sides of my face dropped, dragging my mouth into a frown.

For a moment, Howie looked mortified.

Of course, he didn't know the whole story. I don't go around talking about it. But, I'd been wanting to let it out of my system for a long time. Marley had the basic story, but we'd never really gone over the tale, blow by blow. "I don't mind. They reside at the Jewish Cemetery in Colma.   Mom was Jewish, Daddy was Undefined Protestant."

Two men shoved in, took papers, and I swear one didn't pay enough. Howie's eyes followed them. He didn't waste too much time on them. What would be the point? "I'm sorry. Recent?"

"Yeah. Car accident up on Highway One. It wasn't pretty. Not something that should be." I swallowed too hard. I wanted to say something out loud. Howie was sympathetic and confidential. Why hadn't I said anything to Marley or any number of friends? "I — I don't believe it was an accident, but the case is closed."

He leaned back, said nothing, and listened.

"Best folks you could ever ask for. Dad was brilliant. He designed a high-speed locomotive with overhead rails and started a whole company. Looked after me to the bitter last."

"Who looks after you now?"

"Other than you, Mr. Johnson, no one else, just little 'ole me."

"Well, if you don't mind my sayin', little 'ole you needs to go out more. Life isn't all work and no play."

He had a point. And frankly, I've already decided just where I need to go. Socializing and work, at the same time. It wasn't what he meant, but it was a compromise I liked.

It was high time I learned about San Francisco's night life, especially if it involved Skates Berk.

CHAPTER TWENTY-THREE

You can always find men like that. Just look for the
guy who doesn't know that the Spring Thaw has
already happened.

-Lou Tanner, P.I., Notes for female Pemberton
Graduates, 1935

Outside, it was dull, wet, and dirty. People rushed by, keeping
their heads down and hands in pockets or under arms. In this secretive
shadow world, a series of bright swashes of light told you where to go
for the action.

Once you passed through the Gates of Heaven, the club's
arched doorway, you were in a new world of artifice and fantasy.

The Shanghai Emporium was one of the better nightclubs in
Chinatown. It looked like everything you expected from an exotic,
themed joint. I was pretty sure the pagoda decorations, paper lanterns,
and red-painted woodwork weren't representative of the real Shanghai,
let alone China, but for club-goers, accuracy was unimportant.

Sure, I was working, but I needed to fit in. I'd pulled a blue,
boat-neck gown with a draped back, and long sleeves that covered most
of my wound dressing, out of my unpacked steamer trunk. My sling
matched the deep, dark color. Fearing I might take a tumble or need
to be ready to run, I chose low heel pumps. Mrs. McCarthy helped me
put my hair up. It was classy but practical. The matching coat with

feathers sat on my shoulders and I'd figured out how to tie a scarf over my head to protect my hair from the spitting fog and rain.

The glare and rage of music were overwhelming at first. It was hot inside — smoky and wild.

The chinoiserie doors of the Shanghai opened to a short flight of stairs down to the main dance floor. Across the back of the startlingly large room was the bandstand filled with two rows of white tuxedoed musicians. The band was heavy on clarinets and brass. The leader was bouncing on heels in rhythm with the rag-time piece they were piping. An oriental woman, in a sleek, silver lame gown waited by the microphone stand.

Behind the band was a modernized rendition of a moon-bridge cut into the wall. Every detail screamed out that this was China. And yet it wasn't.

Red lanterns sat on each table. Waiters in short-waisted coats ducked and dodged past each other in a chaotic dance to serve tray after tray of brightly decorated cocktails. Some of the drinks were in fancy glasses, some in plain.

A pall of smoke hung over the tables aligned around the perimeter of the hardwood floor. Well-dressed couples and teams of friends sat at round tables covered in red satin cloths. Many a cigarette was lit for a lady as part of a tacit flirtation. Heads leaned too close. Hands were doing things unseen behind the protection of the tables. Diamonds, real or faux, glistened from the central floor, where dancers intertwined provocatively.

A cigarette girl walked in front of me, her short skirt showing off her selling assets regardless of what awaited in the box held waist-level by a pair of thin suspenders.

I handed my coat to the Hat Check 'Ton. Someone had offensively painted slanted eyes onto the metal creature. It took my coat, swiveled at the midsection to hand it off to another 'Ton, then swiveled back to me. A ticket jerked through a slot in its hand, from a roll kept deep in its arm, and I took it.

Despite the faux-Chinese paint job, I found myself thinking that this was my idea of a 'Ton: helpful and small.

A man in full tuxedo walked up to me as I strolled down the steps. He was squeezing his eyes into narrow lines and smiling with all teeth. "You welcome," he said in a dramatic, over-the-top Asian accident. "Come, sit here. You likee a drink? Wong is your server tonight. You number one guest. I get you drink."

"Gene?" I looked at him again. With the eye squeezing and funny talk, I wasn't sure I recognized who he was at first.

Eugene Wong stood up straighter. "Lou?" His eyes opened up, the smile became natural, and his normal voice welcomed me. "Haven't seen you for ages. How are you?"

"Alive. Say, what's with the 'likee a drink' business?"

"Oh, you follow usual trail." He leaned in while pointing at some tables away from the wild crowd for me to pick from. "Rich people want a certain experience when they come in here. They don't come here for the real Chinatown. They're here to be amused by the exotic." He conducted me to a nice table for two and pulled the chair out for me. "Hey, what's with the arm?"

"I got shot."

"No kidding?"

"No kidding."

"Geez, I think I may stick to medical school. Less dangerous. Whatcha' drinking, Lou?"

"Bourbon. Neat. Thanks."

"Coming up." He was about to place my order, when a large, middle-aged woman waved him over by shouting, as if Gene couldn't understand her without the volume up. He smiled at me, winked, put on his fake-face, and headed over.

With a cigarette in my hand, I stopped to think about it; I was lucky in so many ways. I didn't have to play such a fake character to earn tips to pay my way through school. And yet, many was a time I had to be the sweet, demure daughter at company functions, where I think my Mom was shopping for a husband for me. She meant well but I wouldn't have been happy married off to some social climber's son. Unless the guy was different, special, it would never work. All the same, I had my college paid for and cash flow for a little while. I'd lucked out. My future was all mine for the earning, but yes, I'd lucked out with a gentle childhood. Mostly.

A nice glass of amber liquid arrived in front of me, and the band launched into something jivy. The canary up on stage sang along with the well-known tune, in Chinese. It was interesting. She made it work. Lovely voice.

A lighter descended to my cigarette. Elliott Lockwood, in a black suit with black tie leaned over.

"What are you doing here?" I said, feeling a bit territorial. Lockwood dressed himself very well, but not as one might expect for a nightclub on Saturday evening.

"I'm having a little talk with Willkie Valentini."

Cold washed over my whole body. "No, you're not," I snapped. "Sit down."

He narrowed those beautiful blue eyes at me. "I have to. Someone has to."

"And, I am."

Watching me with suspicion, he sat down. "You're not on this case anymore."

"Yes, I am," I said, putting my unlit cigarette down. "I've been hired by the most foolish client of all — me."

Putting away his lighter, he scowled. "This isn't your problem anymore."

"You made it my problem."

"I shouldn't have. Really, I mean it. You shouldn't keep on a closed case."

"You worried now? That horse is out of the corral."

He took a deep breath. "Yes, I'm worried. I never should have hired a woman to do a man's job. You aren't strong enough for the job. It was a mistake."

On the balcony to the left of us, Valentini, the man I thought was a lawyer from the other night, and two other Brunos, stepped out. Lockwood and I eyed the scene intently. The gangster didn't puff up, check his suit, or act otherwise blustery.

Lockwood glared at him at first, then at me.

"I can handle this." I put my hand on his shoulder.

"You can't. You're just a girl."

I took a long, slow drink of bourbon, not once taking my eyes off him. In that time, he went from trying to look angry and stern, to concern that he'd hurt my feelings. Good hearted wimp. Yup, he's looking away. His fallback position.

"Now that you got that lie out of your system, I'm telling you it won't work for you to go talk to Valentini."

"I meant it."

"Yeah, right. Sorry, but I'm the detective here and I can read you like a book. You're not talking to a notorious gangster who may be in deep mourning and jittery. He doesn't know you. He does remember me. Let me give you another prediction. You've got a roscoe on you."

"A what?"

I really tried not to roll my eyes. "A roscoe, also known in polite society as a gun. Or do I quote Mae West about that bulge in your coat?"

Sheepishly, Lockwood squirmed in his seat and tried to make his gun less apparent.

"Shanghai's owner is getting lax if they let a guy come in here packing heat. Of course, you don't look like some sort of gunsel. And I don't think you are. Want to tell me your whole, doomed plan?"

He folded his arms, almost childishly. "You're the detective."

As if I hadn't predicted he'd say that. Right. "Okay, Mr. Lockwood. You came here to make him confess. You planned to show yourself to Valentini, then pull your gun on him and either shoot him or make him promise to go to the police with a confession."

His mouth opened slightly.

"Mr. Lockwood, I don't have the first idea of how to run an import/export company, certainly not one that survives in these troubled times. Pretty much a miracle, if you ask me. But, as much as I don't comprehend how to do your job, you don't appreciate how to do mine."

He shut his mouth.

The song changed to Cheek to Cheek, one of my favorites. I took that as a sign from heaven that I had some extranormal approval. I held out my cigarette again, and he lit it with some reluctance. I drew in the nicotine and exhaled away from him. No need to be rude. "See the skinny guy next to Valentini."

Lockwood did.

"That's Skates Berk. He got that nickname from his habit of skating past every charge the police have leveled at him. That includes running some dirty business behind the scenes of a series of clubs his boss owns."

"This one?"

"Gold star to you Mr. Lockwood. Yes. This one. There are rooms out back for gambling, prostitution, and until the last few years, illegal liquor sales. I point him out because Skates is also one of Valentini's closest friends, if you can call that friendship. He will cut you down in seconds if he thinks you're after his source of income. You'll come out of it looking like bloody Swiss cheese, before you even make the top step. Get the picture?"

The light wasn't great, but I was still sure I saw Lockwood pale a bit. He certainly had a dry mouth all of a sudden. He waved for Gene, who dropped the fake-for-the-tourists-face and delivered his scotch.

"The other guy? Wide as he is big? You might never even make it to Skates before that guy pulls your arms out of your sockets."

"How do you know all this?"

"I read. I read a lot. Not knowing the players gets one into trouble. These guys mean business."

"So do I."

"Why?"

It took Lockwood two minutes and two swallows of his scotch before he answered. I had time. I waited.

"Lou, he killed Frannie. What kind of man am I if I don't do something? The police let him go. Frannie is an afterthought to them, as if she never existed."

"They let him go, Elliott, because he didn't kill her. He loved her. I can find you proof, but he genuinely loved her. My women's intuition is screaming at me along with the facts. He didn't do it. So, if I let you go up there, you're killed and I'm blamed for not stopping you. Somerset, you've met him, well, he's looking for any excuse to lock me up."

Well, that got his attention.

I knocked back the last of my bourbon. "Stay here." Then, I added, for the sake of his manhood, "I would like to use you as a backup." I was scrambling for anything to keep him in his seat. "Knowing you're here can help me."

"What are you, what's the term, 'packing heat?'"

"In this dress? Nothing. They'd take away any heater if I had one, so what's the point? Just stay in sight range. At least you're here. Don't jump to any conclusions. And for the love of God, don't wave that heater around."

Gene walked up when I stood. I ordered another scotch and bourbon for us, then whispered in his ear. I thought Gene might pass out, but good man, he nodded and headed over to the base of the steps to the balcony.

I was hot on his heels.

Every man, including Valentini, stared down at me. My arm hurt. My ears rang, from being too close to the trumpet section. My heart was trying to climb up to my teeth and my stomach was right behind.

Who did I think I was? These guys kill people for just looking at them funny. Who was still around that would mourn me if they knocked me off? Very few.

Gene marched down the stairs with a look on his face that said, "Are you out of your mind?" Damn, if I didn't think I was.

In this light, Skates's face looked more worn out and pock-marked than the gopher-riddled Kaiser Sports Field near Golden Gate Park. His mouth was a lipless line turned downward. The Big Guy squared off his shoulders and sized me up, concluding I wasn't a challenge and huffing a bit in disgust. He started rubbing his arm. I had a funny feeling about where my third bullet, the one I shot at the Seal Rock Club, went. I was at the point of mentally wagering that Big Guy sprayed Proctor and me with Tommy Gun fuel. Couldn't prove it – yet. I smirked a little and Big Guy snarled in my direction.

Nothing to do about it except hope he hurt as much as I did.

Valentini was not so quick to judgement. I hoped that expression said he remembered me.

Before I reached the top step, Skates stepped in front of me. "We're busy, honey. Nobody up here wants your business." Skates's mouth turned up then back down. His eyes were small and his face long.

"Sure you do. You just don't recognize what business I'm offering. Might not be what you think."

"You're in the business of getting hurt, that's what."

I believed him

I didn't move.

CHAPTER TWENTY-FOUR

Folks will always tell you all sorts of things – free advice, every time. Value their advice based on how much you actually paid for it.

-Lou Tanner, P.I., Notes for female Pemberton Graduates, 1935

"Beat it, bimbo."

"Not until Mr. Valentini says so." I planted my feet, grateful for the low heels. Yet I wasn't in a place of strength. My back was to the stairs.

"I say so. I told you earlier; Mr. Valentini left me in charge of pests like you."

I decided I hadn't gone to the trouble of dressing to the nines, leaving off the pain killer that fogged my logic, and dragging myself to this place to have a chit-chat with the likes of Skates Berk. I turned my whole attention to Valentini, who was taking a seat but watching me. "You remember me, don't you?"

Skates and Big Guy looked to the boss. Valentini's eyes narrowed.

I stepped forward, so he had a better gander at me. "The other night, in the lot?"

With that, Valentini's eyes widened with remembrances. I was taking a chance he didn't want to remember anything of that night, let alone me.

"I'll ditch the broad ..." Skates started. "She thinks she's a Shamus. Delusions, you think?"

"No." Valentini stood up and signaled for me to sit with him.

Skates moved in behind me and whispered, "You do anything I don't like, I'll have Mikey here take you out back and give you a lesson you won't live long enough to remember."

Oh no, he wasn't getting away with his little tactic. I turned on him and loudly announced, "Don't you threaten me. I'm here to help. Frannie Valentini is a murder victim and the police are chasing the lead they want to be guilty, not the one that is. Isn't that right, Mr. Valentini?"

Skates didn't like being talked back to. Good. I didn't like his being on this planet. He tried to correct me, "Frannie Coventry."

"I didn't kill her!" Valentini blurted out dropping his forehead onto his fingers, resting his elbows on the table.

I lowered my voice. "I understand that. You wouldn't have killed her."

"Cops say otherwise," Skates sneered.

"The cops are wrong." I never stopped looking at Valentini.

Valentini looked up. "Skates, we need drinks."

"What? Willkie ..."

"Just some drinks, I'm okay."

With a wave of his hand, suddenly I was alone with the gangster. I sat down, and he followed suit.

"What's with the arm?"

"Got shot."

"Keep mouthing off to Skates and he might add a few holes of his own."

"He wasn't being helpful, so I mentioned it." Valentini's face would tell me everything. He had a healthy amount of girth around his whole body, and yet his tuxedo fit him to perfection. Bespoke. Nice. His eyes were red around the edges and the irritation was around his nostrils too. To show some respect, I took out my badge, while letting him see that there wasn't a rod in there with the lipstick and showing him proof I was who I said I was.

"The world's changed. Now we've got lady dicks."

"We're handier than you think."

"You askin' for a job?"

I shook my head. "I'm on the level. I'm always on the level. You operate under your own conditions, so, working in this racket isn't my cup of tea."

"How'd you wind up mixed in this?" He took out a big cigar and lighter.

I pulled a cigarette out of my case and held it for him to light. "I'm a licensed P.I.. I was hired to find Frannie."

He huffed. "Her family hire you? That'd be a joke."

"And not a very funny one. Mr. Valentini, I'd like to put my cards on the table."

He took about a minute before he nodded in agreement. Downstairs, a woman's laugh burst out above the jazz band. He cringed a bit.

"Did you and Frannie tie the knot?"

He shook his head and drew heavily on the cigar. It stank, but it was giving him some comfort, so I kept my yap shut. "It was supposed to be, she wanted it, over at the church today."

"I'm sorry. Genuinely sorry."

It was Gene who delivered the drinks. Skates and Big Guy Mikey kept back, unwilling to soil their hands with menial delivery service.

"Mr. Valentini, I ran into Frannie two nights before she died. I had no idea who she was. I was on the job the next day, looking for her, still not knowing that she was the same woman I'd met. We were in the Bayview area, she was being followed — I think. I never got to ask her. She took my hack and left me in the rain, alone with whoever was on her heels."

That made Valentini bark out a laugh. "That was Frannie. She survived like no other. Her mother taught her that much."

"What else did her mother teach her? I'm not asking to disparage her character. I need the facts, even if they aren't complimentary."

"That makes sense." Heavy drag on the cigar. "Irenie is one of those women who is past her prime and she understands it. All the things she's ever wanted but didn't achieve, she made Frannie do or achieve for her. You get my drift?"

"Sadly, I do. That's pretty much the story on the street too. But that didn't bother you, did it? You fell in love." I wanted him talking about the romance. It was happier and would give me plenty without making him shut up — people either share their pain, or they don't, and Valentini didn't strike me as a man who wanted to share his pain. I was a reminder of a moment when he let his guard down.

He looked at me, his eyes watery but not about to cry. "What wasn't to love? To me, she was a dream. Sure, she had a past, but she never lied to me about it. She was even doing some business, I think with her father. She didn't talk about it, so I can't say for sure."

Interesting.

"And when I asked her to stop, she did. When I gave her the ring, she said yes. When I promised to sell off the businesses, she believed me. To a man in my business, that's pure gold."

"When did you ask her to stop doing her mother's bidding? I ask because I'd like to understand the timing. Again, I'm not disparaging Frannie's memory."

"She was no angel. But, she was honest with me." He smoked for a long time. "You think you can find out who did this?"

"I want to."

Another long pause. "She accepted my proposal last week. We agreed to lay off our businesses."

"You were getting out of the club and other ... business ventures?"

"Selling or leaving, right down to the last brick."

That would be impressive. Who had the kind of coin to pick up what he was walking away from? I couldn't and wouldn't help myself; I asked him.

"No takers yet." He smiled, satisfied.

"Not even Berk, over there?"

Valentini burst out laughing. "Skates? He can't afford it. None of 'em can. It'll likely be someone from outa' town. But, you'll work that out whenever it happens."

"Probably." This place was jumping, and I started to think I couldn't guess how many zeroes would be needed on a cheque to buy this joint . "If I were to say, knock you off, right here and now…"

He raised an eyebrow.

"Hypothetically. I'm not packing. Who inherits this joint?"

No answer, but Valentini's eyes shifted over to Skates' position. Interesting.

I set my cigarette down in the ashtray. "I'm sorry to ask this, but I have to; but who do you think did it?"

"Her family. Her former lovers. Her blackmail victims. Hell, maybe even the cops killed her to set me up."

"Can you vouch for Skates and the Big Guy over there?"

"Them? They know better than to touch Frannie. Nah, they didn't do her in. I gave 'em orders to keep off."

Yeah, and soldiers always follow orders, sure. "Do you recognize someone named Cab Proctor?"

He shook his head thoughtfully. "Lover or victim?"

"Both. But it looks like she let him off the hook about a week ago. He gave her a cheque for payment, but she held it without getting it filled out or cashed. She was holding up her side of the bargain you two had. You keep saying, 'her family.' As far as I can tell, that's Irenie." I hoped he wouldn't identify Elliott.

"Her stepfather too."

Damn.

"How do you know him? Or do you?"

He put down his cigar, noticed the upbeat clarinet solo going on downstairs, and took a swallow of his drink. "That sap came by to warn me off the girl. All fatherly. I told him about our engagement and sent him packing."

"He knew you'd proposed?" That was something Elliott hadn't told me.

"Sure. Frannie said she was gonna' run home and show everyone the rock I'd given her. She was so proud. And happy..." his voice dropped off. "She said she was gonna' to wave it under the nose of her mother, stepfather, even those two squabbling friends of her mothers."

I raised an imperial eyebrow. "Have you met Gem and Harold Harrison?"

"That's them. He's a regular here. The wife sometimes comes in to catch him doing something she doesn't like. We usually end up throwing both out."

Oh, that was interesting. "Was Harold one of Frannie's former lovers?" I wanted confirmation. This was such an odd conversation. Valentini was completely comfortable with the subject. Well, if Frannie confessed and then left the business, why not? Men like Valentini aren't predisposed to forgiveness often in matters of intimacy. He was a surprise in many ways.

"I think so. She managed a couple of loans from his bank and I'm pretty sure she couldn't have done it unless she had a grip on him."

I sipped a bit more of my drink and put out my cigarette. "Mr. Valentini, thank you for your candidness."

"You gonna' find her killer?"

"Like I said, that's my goal."

"Find him." That was an order.

I couldn't come up with anything snazzy to say, so I nodded sharply.

As I turned to walk way, to the lingering crooning tones of I'll Be Blue, in Chinese, Valentini called after me, "Maybe a woman flatfoot is a good thing after all. That was the easiest grilling I've ever had."

I looked over my bandaged shoulder, replying, "It was the most informative grilling I've ever conducted. By the way, do you own a dark blue Buick, with some damage on the right front?"

"No."

"Skates?"

Again, a laugh. "I don't know."

"I thought Skates was your friend." I was being coy now.

Shaking his head, rather than wagging a finger at me like I deserved, Valentini asked, "What friend? I got no friends."

"You got me, until I find Frannie's killer."

"Who shot you? If you find out, leave it to me to take care of things."

"Thanks. But I want my reputation to be built on my taking care of things. I still appreciate the offer." And with that, I descended the stairs to the dance floor, maneuvered around a few moving couples, and past Skates. I couldn't help myself — I batted my eyelashes at him. "Thanks for the drinks."

Pretty sure that screeching sound was Skates clenching up. I didn't look to see.

I had my eyes on Lockwood, who got credit for staying put as ordered, but we needed to have a long talk. A real long talk.

"Let's go," I commanded to his face, as a cleaning 'Bot skittered behind me to work on a shattered glass from the table ahead of us. I didn't wait for his reply, picked up my coat check ticket and headed up the stairs.

He followed behind me, glancing often toward the balcony. I turned to see Valentini's concerned face staring down at us. I nodded again.

Three long strides away from the Shanghai entrance, I turned on Elliott Lockwood. "You haven't told me the truth. From the very start, you've withheld information that makes a difference. Two people are dead, and I've been shot. Isn't that enough for you, or do you want more violence before you tell me everything?"

"Lou ..."

"Let's start with the simple questions from the case. How did you know Frannie and Valentini had anything in common, let alone a relationship? You said you didn't move in her social circles. Did she tell you? I ask because it doesn't strike me that you and your step-daughter had that close a relationship. To quote you, you didn't really like her. She wasn't blackmailing you, was she? Or was she, and it wasn't over a union incident?" I was in too much pain to let level-headedness trip up my anger. "Let's try another question. Why were

CHAPTER TWENTY-FIVE

Decide right now that you're not dying because of some
idiot. Adopt it as your motto. Have a tattoo of it on
your leg – they can use it to identify your body in
case you're wrong.

-Lou Tanner, P.I., Notes for female Pemberton
Graduates, 1935

By the time Elliott tossed coins into the 'Crawler's meter box,
even the Fox Theater had shut off its big sign and locked its doors for
the night. Market Street was dark, wet and unfriendly. God, I looked
forward to spring.

Elliott wrapped his arms around my arms, holding tight as if I
might slip out of his grasp to be lost forever. He didn't need to.
Frankly, the rhythm section pounding my nerves took a smoke break
from my head during the ride over. I was fine, and I kept saying so.
Elliott wasn't listening. Pig-headed dope! And I was still furious with
him, albeit, distracted at the moment.

Inside the elevator, he slammed the gate closed and hit the
button for third floor.

"Mr. Lockwood?"

"I'm an idiot."

"Well, since you already paid me off, I'm not afraid of
agreeing."

He looked at me with a pained expression.

"Can you to be straight with me, 'cause I'm getting tired of asking. And please, please don't stare at your shoes. They aren't interesting enough and I doubt you do that in board meetings."

He huffed a half-laugh. "No, but I do it with my secretaries."

Secretaries? Plural. Sure, why not, he was a President after all. It explained a great deal: women made him nervous. Great. "Let's start at the top and end up with the Militia out at the Pointe. Then you can tell me how you were aware of Frannie's relationship with Valentini? Last, what were you doing there at Valentini's the same night and exact same time she was killed?"

"You, you don't think I killed her? I hired you to find her. Why would I do it and then kill her?"

I sighed until my lungs ran out of air. Maybe we both needed to be truthful to ourselves tonight. "No, you hired a woman detective with what you assumed was limited experience and likely limited contacts. Remember, you walked into my office, asking me if I was 'Miss Tanner.' The sign says, 'Lou Tanner.' Everyone else in the world thinks I'm just another man. You already knew I was a dame."

"They'd be wrong to think you're just another anyone. You've got a good memory."

"I do indeed. Were you banking on me not being the tops in the field of detection? You were, weren't you? You needed me to be a piece of fluff. Why else did you come to see me, already aware I'm a woman, and so late in the evening. You didn't want Frannie found as much as you wanted to assure yourself you did something about it. Even if you thought any effort would fail. Is that right?" It hurt to say it. Reality was a very cruel mistress to the unenlightened and distracted, I wanted so bad for him to be more than he obviously was. But Mistress Reality always tells you, the obvious and simplest answer was usually the right one.

Well, at least he didn't stare at the floor this time. But I read him like a proverbial book. I'd plugged his fakery with the truth and he was bleeding out his embarrassment. "It's important to you to be seen doing the right things, isn't it, Elliott?"

"Not only seen," he softly protested. "I've done some awful things, I told you so already. I don't like making mistakes and, well, the Coventry family was a big one."

"And your business with the Militia might go south if you appear untrustworthy?"

"They don't have a good reputation to begin with, the last thing they want is to do business with a man and his family who will cause embarrassment."

"Most people have no idea what the Militia is up to. I think you should re-think the strategy of doing business with them."

We stared at each other for a while, having little to say. Good thing this was the world's slowest elevator. I can climb up three floors faster than this thing crawled up one. My intuition told me he wasn't a danger, even if, God forbid, he killed Frannie, he wasn't after me.

"You're right, Lou. I'm not a liar, but, I left things out on purpose." This he said to me, looking me dead in the eyes. "I — I followed Frannie a couple of weeks ago."

"Why?"

He took a very deep breath. "I thought she had been arrested by the police."

I reached over and flipped the switch to the elevator off. We stopped. "Go ahead."

"A business associate saw her picked up by the police. He promised to keep it quiet. But disagreeable news, when we're trying to pull in new business with profitable clients?" He annoyingly took an interest in the ironwork of the elevator cage. Damn it.

"Such as the Militia?" I was squeezing as much blood as I could out of that turnip.

"They are respectable and have government funds. I decided, right or wrong, to put my company in front of my own family and spied on Frannie. If she was sleeping around — oh God, if she was selling herself or letting Irenie do so — my whole company would be destroyed by the scandal."

I nodded, appreciating his fear wasn't unrealistic. Besides, I was getting the real story now. "Did you actually see her with Willkie Valentini?"

Lockwood nodded. "Worse — I saw him give her a ring. I thought he was giving her a present. You know, the kind of expensive gifts men give to their favorite mistresses. What do they call a gangster's woman?"

"A moll."

"Right."

"Why did you go over to his club, the night Frannie's died?"

"To ask him to stop seeing her. I offered him money. He laughed at me. I was ready to do anything."

"Because the scandal would ruin your business?"

He only nodded. After about a mile between his thoughts, he added, "a scandal would ruin me. I already have a divorce finalizing, an ex-wife who holds orgies she euphemistically calls Salons, and an ex-daughter who — well …"

I chewed on the inside of my mouth, partially as a bad habit I had when I think and partially to distract myself from the throbbing in my arm. "You didn't realize it was an engagement ring?"

I floored him with that one. His lips parted, and he stared at the elevator gate, then back to me. Slowly, his head bobbed and he moistened his lips. "Now it makes sense. He laughed at me, said things would change for the better. I thought he was suggesting he might take over my business, take my house. I was foolish to believe that. It didn't occur to me. Engagement? Are you sure?"

"Yes. They were getting married. He was leaving his bigger businesses behind and taking her away from the life she'd been living. I think you understand what's entailed?" For a moment, I thought he was relieved, as his shoulders dropped and his hands unclenched. Was I misreading him? "What?"

"I don't know why, Lou, but I think I'm glad. Not because she was murdered, of course not, but that she found, well, someone who loved her. She never got that from Irenie. I sure failed on that account.

Valentini? I suppose even a gangster ... And he was ..." His words faded off.

Outside, a trolley rolled by and clanged its bell. It was a normalizing sound. I started the elevator moving again.

"Do you think Irenie learned the truth?" I asked.

"You better believe it. Just because I didn't know ... you have to realize Irenie kept a watch on Frannie. You don't think Valentini killed her, do you?"

I shook my head. "I saw him when they found her body. Valentini was not the man who'd killed the woman in front of him."

"Well then, who?" His face contorted. "Oh God, I damn near killed him."

"I don't think you would have done it."

His eyes widened. "I wanted to. I went there to kill him."

"Like I told you, it wouldn't have happened. Sorry, but I think you were in over your head tonight. I suspect your heart was in the right place, but your head wasn't. Willkie Valentini is no one to mess with."

We passed the second floor.

"How about you tell me about your relationship with the militia?"

Elliott pulled off his fogger and shoved most of it under his arm. That's no way to treat an expensive overcoat. "I can't tell you much, or, at least I don't think I can. We imported iron and fittings for them, once. I've heard rumors about the Tin Man Project and other crazy plans, but I never believed them.."

I did. I wouldn't put it past the boys at the Pointe.

"My turn, Lou. Why did you go to visit Valentini tonight if you thought he was innocent?"

There was a quick change of topic. "Because, I am still involved in this case. I've already given up my pound of flesh, so now it's personal. I played my female card from the deck and took whole the hand." I hoped he'd recognize my Bridge analogy as we finally exited on my floor.

"You are that."

"A handful?"

"A woman." He said, stopping in the middle of the corridor. The floor was shiny — the janitor must have come through earlier with a floor polishing 'Bot.

The elevator headed back down to the ground floor.

I opened the door of my office and ordered him to stay put on the couch. My skin tingled. I was vulnerable. Me, with no rod, in a body-forming gown, and dance shoes — low heeled or not. My skin wanted coverage. Armor.

I only had a pair of trousers needing pressing and a once-worn mock turtle-neck sweater in my desk. I don't remember when I put them there or why. I kept my eye on the gap in my office door and worried Lockwood might look through as I changed.

Maybe, I didn't worry too much.

Peering down at the sling I'd left on the desk while changing, my sore arm throbbed up a warning tune, assisted by a drum section in my brain. This was no time to appear weak. I tossed the sling down on my chair.

I loaded up my overcoat with the only things I needed: my badge, cigarette case, and rod. Dusty but practical shoes gave me back the confidence of a rookie cop on his first stake out. And last — I pulled Uncle Joe's fedora down onto my head.

It was time for that honored chapeau to be worn again — by someone about to make some serious rookie moves. Gotta start practical learning sometime.

Lockwood only raised an eyebrow as I signaled for him to step out into the hallway. I couldn't help but wonder if he'd sneaked a look at me when I was changing.

For only a second, I noticed the scent of cleaner. Only a second. Sound, smell, visual details, they all wandered out of my head. All I had was Elliott and his wonderful blue eyes. Hadn't I had enough of those lying blues?

The universe was against me. Even the rhythm section in my brain took a smoke break.

"You changed clothes," he noted, "I take it you feel better?"

"I feel sore, but yes, better than earlier. The pain has passed. For the most part."

He walked up to me. Close to me. Very close. Too close. "Does pain ever pass? Do we ever recover from the pain?"

"Are we still talking about my shoulder?"

"I don't — are we?"

There was one thing about romance, it had the bad habit of making people babble incoherently about one thing or another — and who wants to spend the effort on logical conversation when the touch of a man's fingers on the arm sends fire and thrills up and down the body?

A bang downstairs said someone was in the elevator. They were probably someone heading home after working late.

Elliott put his over coat over his arm and drew me in. "We don't have to leave yet, do we?"

This was wrong, and I knew it.

He held me close, avoiding tugging on my injured arm. Very gentlemanly.

Was it wrong? He wasn't my client anymore. I understood his weaknesses better.

The idiot here was me. And I stupidly enjoyed the kiss he gave me. Warm. Dry. Lingering. Entirely repeatable. I lost track of how long we stood there. Yes, his kiss bore repeating. And he kissed me again while I tried to remember to breathe.

He wasn't my client anymore.

His fingers slid through my hair. I let my hand lay on his chest.

He was right here and now. How the hell was he doing it? He had me in an embrace and I wasn't fighting. The kiss was long and luxurious. His arm gripped me tighter and time disappeared.

The case was still open.

He kissed me another time, after I caught my breath, and there was more than a little urgency to it.

Mr. Wonderful was a dead woman's relative in an open murder case.

God, that kiss was good.

He remains a suspect!

I pulled back.

I guess I confused him.

"Listen." I had to step away. "Elliott, I can't do this. No, please let me explain. I like your attentions, especially the kissing part. A girl could get used to this. It's been a long time and, and I want this to go on. But it can't. This case is still open. Maybe not for you, but for me. This is no good if I can't finish the road you yourself started me on. It's not right. Damn it, Elliott, you're still a suspect."

I might as well have slapped him right across the mouth he'd kissed me with. He looked stunned.

"Elliott, you had time, motive, and presence. You were at Valentini's around the same time Frannie was killed, you were late meeting me at the Vallejo Street house, and she was blackmailing you at one time. I can't let my emotions foul up the investigation."

He shook his head. "I couldn't … I'd never …"

"Then it's my job to find proof, but not if I'm over the moon about …" I couldn't finish the sentence.

Someone coughed.

Somerset was standing with Rollins at the elevator, cigarette barely held between his teeth. "If you're done fraternizing with a killer, Honey, we'll take it from here."

Elliott turned to face them. "I didn't," was all he said. He looked at me, with those pleading blue eyes.

"Sure, you didn't. Elliott Lockwood, you're under arrest for the murders of Francis Coventry and Charles Proctor." He pulled out a pair of handcuffs.

What the hell was going on? "Bennie?" Sure, I turned to the one sane guy in the bunch.

Rollins shrugged. "You said it, Honey. Means, time, motive."

"Don't try to stop this, Honey. I'll gladly take you in, too, as an accessory after the fact." Somerset pulled back his overcoat to reveal a hip holster for his .45 and a long case for one hell of a knife. He prepared for every contingency.

"Got a warrant," I blurted out in desperation.

"Yeah, I do. Stay out or I'll ..."

Rollins took the cuffs out of Somerset's hands. "Leave her alone, Milt. She 'ain't asking for nothin' that isn't legal." He looked at me after ordering Elliott to put his hands out and slapping the cuffs on his wrists. "All the paperwork is signed. He'll be downtown."

"Wait."

Somerset almost reached for his heater. I took Elliott's fogger and slipped over his hands.

"What's that for?" Somerset stared at me.

"Why embarrass a man until you have him red-handed. Means, time, and motive are nothing without evidence."

"Nobody's out there to gawk at us."

"I don't care."

Somerset leaned in close to my face and, cigarettes and booze lingered over my nose. "You ain't got time to care."

I looked past him to Elliott. "Mr. Lockwood, I can call your lawyer."

Elliott's expression slid from shock to hopeless. "You don't need to." He wasn't giving up, was he?

"You need a lawyer, Mr. Lockwood."

"No. I'm fine ... it's ... I'm sorry." Elliott stared at me sadly and I prayed it didn't mean he was giving up. Or confessing.

"Sorry? No! Who's your lawyer? Give me his name."

All I got from Somerset was a snort of laughter as he took Elliott to the elevator. Rollins looked like a puppy someone kicked. I waited while they made their descent.

When I couldn't see Elliott any more, my logical brain kicked past the pain and started working. I had to reason things out. Elliott Lockwood's life was on the line. If they convicted him of two murders, he'd hang for sure. Cab's killing was a gangland style dust off. Unless they put a Tommy Gun, a particular Tommy Gun, into his hands, they couldn't pin the Club House attack on him. Besides, I had a good idea who did it. But Frannie's murder? Yeah, I was still stumped.

I heard the elevator reaching the bottom. Slowest damn, time-wasting elevator and yet I was wasting time standing there like a jerk.

A couple of other ideas were starting to creep into my brain. I didn't like them one bit, but if I called myself a detective, and one who deserved to wear Joe Parnaski's fedora in public, I had to face those ideas.

I didn't have time to stand around like a helpless damsel in distress, making dewy eyes at a lover, like one sees in every picture show. I turned on my heel, opened my office again and rushed in.

"Operator? Appian 48675." My lawyer would do in a pinch.

"Connecting you," the brass recording said. Had 'Bots taking over everything? It was taking forever. Plenty of voices coming from the various exchange operators were audible as they connected my call from Klondike to Appian. I sure hoped that dear, old shyster was awake.

"Hey, Bimbo?"

Skates Berk put his finger down on the phone cradle, cutting off my call. He had three men behind him. Dressed in all black suits I thought were far too close to what the Nazis were wearing in those newspaper photographs I'd seen. I guess I said so and Skates landed one hell of a left on me. I don't remember anything beyond swirling colors for a couple of minutes.

"And here I thought he wasn't gonna' keep his promise. But he did."

Movement, I remember it. Something sharp and stinging, stabbed into my neck. A bumpy wrestling match getting me down the stairs. Someone's kneecap was down for the count, and I planned on more, until my muscles stopped cooperating.

A big car. A dark Buick, pulling away from the curb, and my ride was a big, grey, ugly Ford. Didn't they know Ford stands for Found-On-Road-Dead? Who buys one of those, except a fool with no style sense? I was delirious. That too must have come out of my mouth, because the Militia Sergeant smacked me again.

Whatever they shot me up with, it was doing a doozy of a job. I'd never even been drunk like this.

A guy in a cheap hat and coat came out of nowhere. From there, I remember being knocked around and stuffed in the Ford. I didn't see what happened to the cheap hat and coat. Pretty sure he got bounced.

I didn't see that coming.

I didn't see *anything* after that.

CHAPTER TWENTY-SIX

What I want is a nice house, a good husband, and a
successful career. Based on my desire for the third
item, I wasn't banking on the first two.

-Personal diary, Lou Tanner

Being slapped a couple of times got my circulation going but
not my brain. It was someone's thumb shoving my shoulder wound
waking me up. I yelped. Who wouldn't.

Son of a bitch.

Skates emptied his lungs into my face.

"He was wrong. You are tougher than you look," he said. He
thought about something, long and hard, but never did explain.

My brain was turning somersaults in my skull. Lockwood?

No. That didn't work right. It wasn't Elliott Lockwood
throwing me under the trolly. My brain was fuzzy but I tried something,
albeit weak, to trick Skates into giving me information. "So, Mason
ratted me out."

"I ask the questions."

"It was Mason, wasn't it," I choked out.

He shook his head and his lips twisted into a smile.

As my brain cleared, I got a better look at my situation, and it
was grim. Cold seeped into my chest and worked its way down to my
hands. I was tied into a chair, four of Skates' Brunos were snickering
from the other side of the room, and Skates, himself, had already

threatened me. I had every right to believe — this was it. That twinge of shame squeezing your ribs, the one only someone who'd blundered into their own death could feel? My ribs were telegraphing an emergency warning to my brain.

"Let us start again, Dollface. What do you have on Willkie and me and business."

If this was it, I wasn't dying until I learned all the who and why. Was Mason the rat? He had to be. "What would I have, I'm just a dumb bimbo, remember?" That got me slapped hard. My teeth hurt. God, did anything not hurt? Still, hurt equals alive. And I wanted to live.

He picked up the cigar again, enjoying the hell out of it. Taking a moment to savor the situation, he grinned for the threesome playing cards and commenting under their collective breath.

I tried to shift. My heart rate was trying to break speed records. I wanted to live!

"Spit it out. Whatja' got on me?"

"Why aren't you asking Mason? He's the guy with all the answers."

The more I thought about it, the less my screaming brain believed in a Mason and Skates alignment. Who knows, maybe if I kept pressing Skates — getting him to talk and to keep talking — he might say something useful.

And, maybe I could use the time to figure out how to escape here. Where the hell was here?

He brought his cigar dangerously near my face. I could feel the ember trying to sizzle a hole in my skin. "You're all full of questions, but that isn't how this works. Here, you ain't a detective. You're invisible. You don't exist." The glowing cherry was right in front of my left eye. "I dunno who this Mason is. Who is he? Ex-lover?"

I hate it when I'm right. "A mug who might make you rethink what you're doing." Or not. I was fighting off visions of my life, which was only three minutes from start to end, by my guess.

"Detective Somerset, now he was helpful." Skates offered.

Somerset? I opened my mouth to ask how it was Somerset was speaking to Skates.

I stopped.

Damn.

Oh, I'm such a sap sometimes.

He laid one across my face and for once, I didn't care. And in those moments that lingered while the pain across my mouth faded, I understood what I'd been missing. He must have knocked my intelligence back into place.

Escape wasn't just for my own life now.

I had one shot at this. "You're a Patsy, Skates. A big, dumb-as-a-stump Patsy, and you're about to lose everything."

His expression went stony and he raised his hand again. I stuck my jaw out in his direction daring him to smack me around some more. "Go ahead. Slap me. You're lucky I'm stuck in this chair, otherwise I'd slap you back."

The sides of his mouth turned up for half a second. "I believe you. So, how am I a Patsy?"

"You made certain you can't be allowed to live after tonight. Your boys, too." The mumbling in the corner stopped. "You caught on to too much. I just haven't decided which way they'll take you out."

"What are you talking about?"

"Ride with me on this." I lowered my chin. "I'm an idiot ... a sap."

"I'm not arguing."

I chuffed a bit. "Me neither. But, I'm not stupid, you said so yourself. That's the catch. I'm not the Patsy this time."

"Sure you ain't."

"Here's your ticket, board this train or you'll be left behind at the station. And you know why you should?"

"No."

"Because you're a bigger sap than me and you're gonna' be taking the fall all by your lonesome, since I doubt your Brunos, over there, will fall on their swords to save you. Still, they might be taken out as collateral damage. Oopsie. Maybe they should play it safe and take off — now while they can."

That bothered him. He gave his thugs a sharp look they seemed to understand.

"You got used, Skates. You're gonna' be blamed."

He drew on that stinker, but this time, directed his smoke away from me. I had his attention now.

"Mind if I stretch?" I nodded chair I was tied to.

"How have I been used?"

"Stretch first. I'll explain why you're a sucker in a minute. Promise. Trust me. Telling you every little teeny-weeny detail is my pleasure. Then, watching it all come true when you don't believe me ..."

He gave one of his boys a sharp nod, the Bruno released me, and I got to move a few frozen muscles. These guys had no respect for a dame. Not that I expected them to. I leaned back in the chair but folded my arms. I made damn sure I looked like I had no interest in going anywhere. And for a bizarre few seconds, I didn't.

"So, here's how I see it," I started. "You aided and abetted a kidnapping and maybe a murder. Such things don't bother you, under the usual circumstances. You think Somerset sent you to pick me up because he likes you? He needs you to dust me off. You're doing his dirty work. Hell, I won't waste your time with the age-old promise, 'if you let me go, I won't tell the cops.'" I barked an awkward laugh. "Problem is, you were set up by a cop and he's making sure you are caught, taking you out of the picture, and wiping out the whole business."

The cigar bounced at his lips anxiously, and I counted the inhales increasing. Skates gripped the stinker nearly to the point of crushing it.

But Skates wasn't stupid, so I had to make sure the parts of the story fit. My problem was I was putting the puzzle together while talking. "Before, though, he used you to set up Valentini from the inside and banked on playing it either way — whether he got Valentini himself or you did. He expected you'd be too greedy to let a chance to take over all of Valentini's businesses slip by. He calculated how far you'd go, and he played you."

That would piss off Skates, but I still had his attention, which was all I wanted. I got the clear impression he was a user who didn't like being used. Imagine that.

"And, yeah there's more, the cork in the Genie's bottle's pulled out. An innocent man is going to turn up dead, with signs of you littered all over the crime scene, leaving you holding the bag on two murders which Somerset will accuse you of committing." I didn't expect him to care.

"Innocent man? Right. How about, I don't care."

Nope, he didn't, and I didn't expect him to.

"Besides," Skates added, sounding so very pleased he was outwitting me, "no crime scene here."

"Not here. Back in my Market Street office. Why do you think Somerset had you come pick me up there? So you would be seen, leave prints, or ..." I let Skates fill in the blanks.

"You ain't dead — yet — and I don't have some poor Schmoe in here to whack, so nobody's got nuthin' on me."

"'Yet.' But that man is good at his job. He knows how to set up a crime scene, how to leave clues, how to say the right thing. He'll have you set up before the day is out."

"It'll be our word against his."

I tried not to laugh. "Somerset is a long-time cop, in good standing with his community. I'm new. But you guys?" I let him boil that for a minute.

"How do you savvy he ain't on the take, and I ain't the one controlling him?"

Nice try. My eyes narrowed. "Somerset? On the take?"

"Yeah. Once. Something small-fry. Rumor had him looking the other way for a bag o' silver." He began to frown. "Other than that, no."

"Looking the other way is a far cry from being a gangster's right-hand man." I slowed my speech and made him lean forward to keep eye contact with me. "He's obsessed beyond obsession with your boss."

"That's putting it mildly," a Bruno from the corner said too loud.

"Assume Frannie doesn't control Valentini's empire as his wife or widow, because she's, oh, I don't know, dead? And Valentini, himself, is out of the way — in prison, perhaps? Or dead. Ever wonder what happens once Valentini is gone and you — as his second in command — are the only one left with all that lovely money and business? You think Somerset's obsession with Valentini ends after this? No, Skates, he'll find someone new to obsess over."

Tightening his jaw and squinting his eyes, Skates repeated, "I don't care. It ain't like that. Me and the cop, I pay a little, he protects a little. See? I don't care what theories you got."

"So, Somerset told you he'd keep looking the other way. Only, he won't. You'll give him cash and he'll save it as evidence. You'll just become the Valentini substitute he hates now and obsesses over, and he might as well arrest you for murder and bribery, sooner rather than later."

"Cops," he snarled.

"If your hands are clean, you've got wiggle room. But kill me, or blamed for another murder about to happen, then you become Somerset's perfect Patsy. Oh, and you have another problem."

"I don't care." Oh, but he did care.

"Maybe not, until I turn up dead at your hands and the War Department asks why." I didn't know eyes could grow that big, especially on a rat-faced bastard like Skates. "You'll care a lot, because Somerset can't and won't protect you from them. Sweetie, it's all tied together. On top of everything else, you pissed in the War Department's cereal bowl and that's gonna' cost you."

Oh yeah, that got his attention. I was snaking around the explanation but appreciated where the fang-end was and how to use it.

I kept going. "The guy you bounced tonight, thinking he was a nobody? Cheap hat and coat. He wears them as a disguise, and it worked. Sure fooled you boys. Cheap-hat-and-coat-guy is a federal agent whose been assigned to follow me. I'm pretty sure you couldn't care less about some G-man, but the War Department? If I go missing or turn up dead, Somerset will point his finger at you, and you'll go from an annoying, second-rate thug trying to grab his boss's dough to a top tier, anti-American, war criminal and potential traitor. You can handle some territory disputes and local power grabs, but are you prepared to take on the whole U.S. War Department — all by your little 'ole self? Not quite what you had in mind, is it?"

He was following my logic. He waved off the Brunos who were taking too much of an interest in what I was saying, and in a move, I doubted was truly gracious, offered me a cigarette. Maybe to stop me talking for a minute.

I declined, politely. Yeah, even in the worst situations, I'm still Mrs. Collington-Tanner's daughter, and she didn't raise a simpleton. Leaning, painfully, over toward his desk, I pulled my coat closer to me and took out my own case. When he lifted an eyebrow, I explained I didn't like what might be in his tobacco and besides, I smoked a better brand anyway.

Skates was trying to be cool, but I could hear the strain in his voice. "Why is the War Department following you?"

"Something happened last year, and important people want me to be aware they're worried about me."

All the color in Skate's skin faded to terrified white.

"Welcome to the War Department's cross hairs," I noted. I let him light my cigarette. God, it felt good to take a deep drag. At least it also kept my hands busy, so I could hide the fact they were shaking. Hell, I had no idea if any of this was working. I didn't care if this made sense all the way through to the end, but I had to go with it. There was nothing else I could do.

"Hey, sit back and enjoy the scenery for a moment. You need the front-end details. I first met Francis Coventry, the future Mrs. Valentini and step-daughter of Elliott Lockwood, the night I did a little errand for Treasury. Don't ask."

"About her ..." he started, but I waved him off.

"Look, Skates, before you tell me you couldn't care less about the Coventry murder, let me finish the story and show you why you should."

"I didn't whack her."

"I understand."

"You do?"

"I do indeed."

He leaned forward, listening, like his life might depend on it — and it did.

My Scheherazade Maneuver had no guarantee of success, but I wasn't getting beaten or killed without solving this case. It was my first true case and damn it, if this was all the time I had, I would finish it.

Go slow, Lou. Don't stumble on your own tongue.

"I didn't know who Frannie was at the time I bumped into her. I thought she was some gal in trouble. She was being followed by a man with a knife. A big knife. He hadn't cut her up. So, I saw to her safety and I wrote it off as another crazy incident in the City."

"What's that got to do with me?"

"Don't get ahead of things." My brain was slipping on its rail and more steam wasn't making it work any better. Slow and easy. Just like Daddy and Joe always taught me. "Frannie was blackmailing some former lovers who didn't want it known they'd been diddling an underage girl. Turns out, her mother set it up."

"Yeah, Irenie. What a piece of work."

"Don't you know it? Well, turns out Frannie got introduced to a big name in the racket business. You savvy this part of the story, don't you? They went and did the unthinkable. They fell in love. Both of them were ready to skip town, ditch their old lives, and go live happily-ever-after. This didn't sit so well with you, as Valentini would then sell off or trade off the clubs and you'd lose out. Frannie had to go."

"I told you, I didn't —"

"Slow down, I'm not saying you offed Frannie. The man with the knife had the real reason to kill her. So, first he tried to catch her the night I met her, then he tried to cut her up the next night — but she got away both times. It took two murderers to put her down."

"It wasn't me or my boys," he protested.

"No, it wasn't. You're clear on that point. Nobody is saying otherwise. Not even Somerset. He's laying it on Elliott Lockwood, since he couldn't prove Valentini killed her."

"Ha!" Skates barked and started laughing. "That cop is gonna' find Lockwood has too many friends over at the Pointe to do anything to him. The Militia and he are tight."

My heart sank, dragging chills down my skin with it. I hate it when I'm right.

"Skates, you could help me here, and I promise, I won't forget it. You know parts of this story I don't. Look, if you help me, I will explain everything I've found …"

I also hate it when the universe plays with me.

My luck was something spectacular. Cab Proctor died before he told me who killed Frannie but managed to shield me from a hail of bullets. Elliott and I kept being interrupted and allowing me to use my brain and see what I was dealing with.

And now?

Spectacular luck!

The door flew open and in walked Green-eyed G-Man, Hayes. Badge out, hat on, and ticked-off expression burning up his face.

The Brunos had no idea what was happening.

Damn, my luck was on a roll.

"This is private property," Skates protested.

"Private? Sure. That would make bringing this woman here against her will and without a warrant an act of kidnapping. A federal crime. Kinda' thing that gets a guy the Chair."

"You got a warrant?"

Good question by Skates.

"Don't need one. The victim is sitting right here."

Touché. Though, I didn't like him referring to me as a victim. And where the hell was Hayes's back up? Oh, no — he wasn't trying to do this alone?

A PlACE Of fOG AnD mUhDEh

I shook my head and drew in on the last of my cigarette.

"Maybe she came here on her own." Skates tried. "Maybe she wants to be here. Maybe she's helping my boss and we're chatting like old friends?" He was pretty proud of himself. "You don't know the dame or me. You don't got nuthin'. Maybe I'm being a good guy and helping her with —"

"Uh, Skates," I interrupted, "I don't want to ruin your perfect set of maybe's, but I'd like to introduce you to the man you tossed around tonight."

Skates sneered at Hayes, the revelation creeping up his already creepy features.

Green-eyes moved his coat aside, showing a nice piece — a Westinghouse 4-21 Lightning Gun. Never saw one for real before. Murmurs from the other side of the room said the Brunos were impressed. Frankly, I was impressed. The electric gun was slick, big, and from rumors, able to fire more rounds than your average six-shooter. Oh — that was why he wasn't worried about coming in here without back up. It was still a stupid, but courageous, move.

"Ask her," Skates blurted out, giving me a look I couldn't decide was warning or if he was begging me for help.

Okay, now that the boys remembered I was here and able to speak for myself, I decided to run a risky gambit. I put my cigarette out in the ashtray. "Now, gentlemen, this whole thing can be resolved if you, Skates, are willing to own up the dirt you gave me on Somerset's crusade against Valentini, only if necessary, then I'll tell Agent Hayes here I came of my own free will to discuss things …"

I thought for a moment Green-eyes was about to have kittens.

"… and we'll leave it right there, since we're working on a more pressing issue. No kidnapping, no threats, no slapping me around and Skates here just owes me later."

Skates wasn't done with me yet. "Maybe my boys over there don't like the idea of my owing nobody. Hey, G-man, you can count, right? You can count more of us than you?"

233

"So can I," I shot back before Hayes could answer. "I count three smart fellows who are smarter than to challenge the War Department."

The Brunos exchanged looks and appeared to be less enthusiastic about getting into a brawl.

"Good. Now, I need to go. I'd like to see if I can still save my client's life. You might want me to go too, if for no other reason than I can keep you from becoming an accessory to murder, at least a murder you don't want to be accused of. I might be able to keep you out of the papers. Isn't it worth a little gossip and a get-out-of-jail-free card?"

Skates opened his mouth, thought better of saying anything on the spur of the moment and shut up. He said nothing as I collected my overcoat and Uncle Joe's hat.

They had my heater.

Damn. My brain was swimming in the ocean. Whatever they used to KO me was still slopping around my grey matter. I was higher than a proverbial kite and scared my plan was a failure. I had to escape. We had to escape. I gripped Hayes's arm. Correction, I used the G-man as a crutch. I hurt like hell. I wasn't walking straight, and every move reminded me I'd been worked over by a Louisville Slugger.

After giving Skates, and Brunos, a glare that should have reduced all of them to ashes, Green-eyes lead me out of the office.

I think the last fifty yards were the longest I've ever walked. I took the available time to give Hayes my hypothesis on the Coventry Murder. I think he turned a little greener than his eyes and moved along a lot faster.

"Sweetheart, you're in over your head. Let me drag us out of here before we both drown."

CHAPTER TWENTY-SEVEN

Try to stay alive ... if you can ...

The radio squawked, and the strength of the signal — and clarity — surprised me. Seemed no one else was trying to use the same frequencies. The War Department had all the dough, and they were putting it to their own good use. People were starving in the streets, but hey, at least we had the latest way to kill our enemies. No, I couldn't be that shrill. The same War Department just saved my life.

And my brain was still not working right. All I could focus on was the Coventry murder, Valentini, and my client.

We were in a warehouse section but I didn't recognize it. The joint was dirty, boxed in, and spooky. Scrap, containers, and debris piled up along the sides of the window-less buildings. Cars, I assumed belonged to Skates and his boys, were neatly parked in a row.

We climbed into Green-eyes' car, smooth leather seats and the bouquet of a recent oil change greeting us. Hey, and Olds.

Hayes ripped a personal radio off his neck and shoulder and flung it into the backseat. I guess they do have enough coin to make superior toys and then toss them around.

I promised myself I wouldn't complain. Besides, weren't we in a rush? Every second was time enough for Skates to change his mind about letting me go — logic be damned.

Hayes gunned the engine and grabbed a shaft protruding from the steering wheel column. Wrenching the shaft upward, he twisted his body to look out the back window. We jolted in reverse until he aligned the vehicle to make a quick exit out the front gate.

I started noticing more than I should. Rule number one of being afraid was you stop noticing details. It's all about the big picture show. But rule one gets tossed when your head was still fighting off a knock-out dope of undetermined origin.

The riveted grill of his Oldsmobile immediately reminded me of those re-enforced Pony-trucks on the front of locomotives. Leftovers from the days of having cow catchers. Hayes jammed the shaft downward and I tensed to the grinding gears. Gear shift? There wasn't a shaft or knob sticking out of the floorboard. His gear shift was on the steering column? I leaned forward to look, because I'm a nosy little thing and still slightly high, and I feared he had only one forward gear to run the engine on.

"Relax, Sweetheart, this is a little love gift from General Motors. A Hydro-Matic transmission ..."

A pair of Brunos, not the fellows from inside, stepped into the road in front of us. Hayes swerved around them. We hit a canister, I think, then veered back onto the asphalt. He floored it and I flew back into the seat.

"We need to go faster than first gear," I shouted over the roar of the engine. V-8 if ever I heard one, but more, much more power. This was no average automobile.

All Hayes did was grin. His foot didn't let up from the accelerator pedal, even when the car shifted gears on its own.

I want one.

After we're out of here. After we find Somerset, Rollins, and my client.

"I want one."

The Oldsmobile streaked toward the open entry gate. Lights turned on us from in front. Someone shouted into a bullhorn. If Hayes didn't care, neither did I. More Brunos, stationed at the gate, prepared for us. If they got between us and the gate, we were dead. "Why aren't they letting us go?" I shook my head, I needed the dope to clear out.

"Better to kill us for trespassing. Then it's legitimate. Hold on!"

The gate itself was closing.

"It'll be easier if we hit it while it's still partially open!" I shouted.

"I'm already aware"

Wait a minute. The 'Brunos' at the gate weren't Brunos. They were in uniforms. "We're at the Pointe?"

"Smart girl."

"We're at the Pointe!"

"Tada! The problem, in a nutshell."

"Then drive faster! My grandmother did better than this with two horses and a buggy. Change gears."

"Not how this works, Sweetheart."

The gate was getting closer.

Loud clangs hit the side of the car.

I didn't scream as much as I shouted furious, frightened curses. "You didn't tell me its bullet proof?"

"Did I mention GM loves us?"

"The windows aren't," I started to say. He grabbed my head with his hand, and shoved me low into the seat, knocking Uncle Joe's hat to the floor. The windows cracked in spider web patterns. All. The. Windows. Front, side, and back. Damn it, who wasn't shooting at us?

The G-man curled in tight to the steering wheel as the windows worsened and the clanging of bullets on our vehicle increased.

Ahead, the uniforms began to line up. Were they villains like Skates or four men happy to have a job with the Militia? I didn't want to kill them. I didn't want to kill anybody.

The Oldsmobile kept increasing in speed. So did my heartrate.

Maybe out of guilt, but I reached up and held down the horn. We were coming at them, blaring and speeding.

When we hit the front gate, the whole vehicle lurched, and I became a ball inside an arcade game, banging around the interior. The windshield buckled and sprayed glass. The metal gate ripped aside, and our car slid with it.

We spun on the tires, giving off the stench of burnt rubber. Hayes struggled to control the Olds, skidding and sliding, until he straightened it out.

The Oldsmobile, missing front and driver side windows, spun its tires, spraying four militiamen running up behind us with gravel.

I didn't have to guess at why Hayes turned off the lights as we sped down one Bayview alley after another.

I didn't ask. I assumed he needed me watching our rear while he drove. The deeper into the City we went, the more likely we were to find pedestrians who had no idea what just happened.

Nothing. No one behind us.

"Good," he said breathlessly when I told him.

"Correct me if I'm wrong, but that was too easy." I said between deep breaths.

"We caught them off guard."

That made weird sense. "Did they really want to kill us or was it all for show?"

"I only know they really wanted to kill you at one point."

"Thanks."

Once we got down to the Embarcadero and the even numbered piers, he pulled over and turned off the engine. We both frantically checked to see what or who was behind us.

Still, no one. Nothing.

Green-eyes kept glancing back and forth. He shrugged, more than a little confused, by the look on his face. Personally, our good luck was amazing and I was grateful. All the excitement was clearing my head too.

The car started to cool in the January fog and bay-shore winds. The metal popped and creaked. The engine hood had more than a few holes and smoke or steam, I hoped, flowing out of them. Glancing at each other and then our surroundings one more time, we took stock.

It was damn lucky. Very damn lucky we were still alive. A memory of a photograph from the newspaper flashed on my brain. The infamous Bonnie and Clyde got themselves obliterated last summer. "Obliterated" being the operative word for what happened. Their decimated car looked like this. I was part scared, part intrigued, thinking I ought to see if Hayes's car looked the same.

He unlocked his fingers from the wheel. His knuckles and face were white. I didn't doubt his bravery. Hell, he'd come into the place to rescue me, with no back up, but he appeared more than stunned by what happened. I was shaking — so was Green-eyes.

"Are you alright?" he whispered, cleared his throat, trying to sound more grounded and macho.

"Sure. I do this every night. A bunch of us P.I.'s get together and crash a car or two through somebody's fence."

He laughed awkwardly, but honestly. "You've got the kind of sarcasm I could get used to." He checked his hands to make sure they still worked. "You've got balls, I mean, brass, Sweetheart."

"I bet my breasts are bigger than anyone's balls, every time." Okay, it was crude, but I'd survived a potential massacre — mine!

Hayes shook his head and laughed. "I give you the point." He dug around in the back and pulled his radio box up front, shaking off a layer of glass as he did. I dug Uncle Joe's hat out of the glass debris, on the floor, shook it, and put it back on my head.

"BluJay to Nest," he called into the mouth piece. "BluJay to Nest."

"Nest." The voice on the other end was scratchy.

"BluJay stuck in tree." He looked over at the nearest pier. "Number 6. Need wings. Urgent."

"BluJay, do you have the Twig?"

I was "the Twig?" It took nothing to guess all this silly code, though I would have suggested his eyes were closer to Parrot green.

"Yes."

"BluJay. Nest on way. Return with Twig."

Return with Twig? Oh no they don't! "I have to find —"

He cut me off. "Affirmative," he replied into the mouth piece. "We have to find Lockwood. He's the key to this whole thing."

"The police have him, he's safe."

"No, you aren't getting it. He is not safe. And we need to go save him."

"He's at police headquarters, down on Drumm Street."

"Are you sure? Guaranteed? Go ahead. If my client is there, I'll go with you, no argument."

I sure didn't like the expression on his face. He'd assumed … I knew it and he knew it. I grabbed the mouth piece and held it away from his grasp. "Twig to Nest. Urgent."

There was a long pause. "Nest."

I remembered they didn't speak in first person, so I tried my best to copy the style. "Nest. Reach out to Drumm Street Police HQ. Urgent. Location of," I whispered to Hayes, "you were tailing him, what was Lockwood's code name?"

With a wicked grin, he took the mouth piece from me. "Nest. Identify location of Milquetoast."

"That's cruel," I snarled.

"Stand by," the radio squawked.

He lowered the mouth piece to his lap, almost daring me to try to take it again. "Since I'm in for a reaming for your little maneuver, I'd like to understand what you're worried over."

"I know who killed Frannie Coventry."

The personal radio squawked again. "Nest to BluJay."

"BluJay."

"Milquetoast not in police custody."

I stared at Hayes, whose eyes were getting big.

"Understood. BluJay out."

"Stand by," the voice demanded.

We waited while screeches and buzzes filled the radio's output. Then it went silent.

"Nest to BluJay. Return with Twig. Repeat. Return with Twig. Do not attempt further flight."

I started to shake my head. Hayes glared at me and then blankly out toward the street. A couple of late shift factory workers walked by, staring at the bullet riddled car. They quickly picked up their pace and hurried away without comment.

A pair of headlamps came up behind us. The G-man saw them but didn't panic. The lights went out and I could see it was an olive-drab painted vehicle, 1920-something model. A man in Army uniform, a captain if I wasn't mistaken, walked over to the driver's side of the car, tisking, and shaking his head. He pushed back his flat brimmed, heavy bever-felt hat. "Damn, Chris. Wasn't this one new? That makes three cars you've trashed this year."

My humor fled me, and I pulled Hayes's coat open. The weapon under his arm was easy pickings. I had it in hand before either could react.

It was a Lightning Gun. I'd never handled one. It was elegant, weighted well for the hand, and potentially more dangerous for the wielder than the target.

Slick silver-colored metal barrel, longer than your average target pistol. Where a cylinder normally sat, an oval container of something blue with wires rested above the grip. A thick pair of cords descended from the blue oval and plugged back into the base of the grip. The grip itself was thicker than usual, which made it impossible for my small hands to grasp. Yet, someone designed special areas for the fingers, for ease. The trigger was a button under the guard. It was a beautiful piece.

And it saved Hayes and me, by its very presence.

"I can use this in either hand, just as well," I snapped, switching the zapper to my left and opening my door with the right. I had to put my shoulder into it to force it open. The two boys kept looking from me, to the futuristic rod, to each other. It was a damn impressive piece of hardware. I did them the professional courtesy of not pointing it at them. "Stay put. I won't kill either of you, but I can put your career on medical leave. You, Captain, thanks for showing up but I'm taking your car —"

"That's Army property," the captain protested. I couldn't tell if he was more worried about the car or the zapper.

"It's a rescue vehicle now. You can have all of this back. But I have to be somewhere before an innocent man is killed."

"Sweetheart, don't do this," Hayes added his voice to the protest.

"I ought to plug you for calling me 'Sweetheart.' But, there's no time."

"You're not sure Lockwood is in danger."

"Yes, I am. I'm a detective, it's my job to know. I've put the pieces together, and it's a lousy fit, but it's the only way they all work together. Now, you stay put — Mr. BluJay. Captain, go over onto the sidewalk."

While the captain moved, Hayes got out of the busted-up Oldsmobile. "Give me the gun."

"No."

"I'm serious, Sweetheart."

"And I'm not? Look, Shnookums, Honey-pie, Dreamboat; I've got a job to do."

The Captain stifled a laugh.

I ignored him. Holding the heater in my left was causing my injured shoulder to burn. "You have to start taking me seriously, because I damn well am. You don't have my permission to write me off because I'm a woman." I pulled on the olive-drab auto's door handle. "My hunches are based on facts. And my gut is right."

"Yeah, yeah. Your breasts are bigger than my balls."

The Captain made a low whistle and took a sudden, uncomfortable interest in the pier behind him.

I closed the door behind me and started the engine. There was no more time to play word games with this Schmoe.

Hayes darted around the front of the Army auto and jumped into the passenger side. "Then drive. You're in the driver's seat. Go!"

I peeled out from the curb, leaving the captain in a billow of exhaust.

While I drove far too fast, happy for a regular gear shift, I started ordering Hayes to watch out the back, look for gangsters and militiamen, stop looking at me, and make the damn radio work.

With more good nature than I offered him, Green-eyes did as demanded. Fiddling with the radio knob, he found the local police frequencies.

I heard it. Loud. Unmistakable.

My heart squeezed.

Police officers Somerset and Rollins pursuing Willkie Valentini. Off radio. Last location near the Pier 39 Amusement Park. Last report in, ten minutes prior.

"They could be anywhere in the City in ten minutes." My heart tried to leap out of my throat. My face was swelling where I'd been hit, and I'd stop coming up with colorful descriptions on behalf of my gunshot shoulder.

"Then we had better move."

"We'll start at 39. The place is huge. Perfect for doing their private business."

When Hayes started to talk, I yapped right over him. I had too much to tell. I brought him up to date on what I learned, why, and what I thought was about to happen. I also admitted I'd made some serious mistakes in personality judgement. I guess I said it more for my own sake than for Green-eye's edification. I'd damn near blown it, but there was time to make things right.

CHAPTER TWENTY-EIGHT

Try to stay alive ... if you can ...
and if you can't ...

The salty fog blanketing the amusement park at Pier 39 left the joint dark and uninviting. As I turned off the Embarcadero, into the lot in front of the Pier, I shut off the lights and gingerly applied the brakes. The engine was loud, too loud, giving us away if I didn't shut it off as fast as humanly possible. My fingers lifted off the steering wheel as though my very touch would make the car creak or groan or cry out. I don't think Green-eyes or I drew breath for a full minute.

Instead, we stared at the amorphous, black hole of space before us. None of the shops, amusements, or rides had lights on. The diminished city glow failed to crack through the fog or down into the amusement park, leaving only enough illumination to encourage the imagination. Tree tops blended with roof tops and it was impossible to guess how long the park pier was. I knew from experience it stretched out into the bay, a little over half a mile. That was twice the distance they intended but the pier kept getting longer the bigger the amusement park got, the more territory it demanded, the needier the hunger for mindless escapism became.

The Golden Gate fog horns greeted us. The sound of boats bumping into their docks, on-board bells clanging, and fabric whipping in the wind surrounded us. Sea lions barked and grunted occasionally.

His voice wasn't as assured as before. "You're the detective —— where do we start?"

Good question. "Not up front. Killing needs privacy. They'll have to get as far away from prying eyes as possible."

Hayes opened the glove compartment and dug around for a moment. "You are sure about this?"

"One hundred percent."

His facial expression was a cornucopia of experienced disbelief. I didn't buy it either since nothing was ever one hundred percent. I guess he didn't deal with gals who were confident. I only wish I really was, and not faking it for his sake. And for mine. I was only seventy percent sure and feeling the percentage points blowing away with each gust of wind.

Until I spotted the Blue Buick ditched, its tail fender showing from the shadows of the first row of shops. I gave the information in a whisper to Hayes, as if I knew it all along, and he nodded in agreement. There was another car there too, I thought, but I wouldn't say until I got closer.

There wasn't enough room to drive on the Pier, which forced everyone out onto foot.

Green-eyes found what he was looking for in the glove box. A rod. A big gun. No Police Special for him — this was a heater made to knock someone down. Hard.

I didn't know if I was better or worse off with the zapper, but I kept it in my left hand. It was about all my arm was good for. With my other hand, I pulled down on Uncle Joe's fedora. I wasn't going into battle without it.

The amusement park was simple in its planning and confusing in its execution. The Pier was long and straight, and during the daytime, visitors sashayed down the center. On either side were three stories of shops selling about anything you could imagine. A lingering fetor of hot dogs, decaying fruit, and something fried hovered near the food stalls.

Every step came with the anxious thought that the wood planking would creak. We didn't stop.

I sneaked over to the Buick and looked in the window. Nothing. Someone kept their car too tidy. I laid my hand down on the hood — warm. The other vehicle was popping in the cool air and its hood was hot. Whoever drove it, just got here.

Hayes signaled me to start moving into the structures. The aroma of popped corn and sugar drifted over from the closed-up stalls closest to the front. A piece of paper peeled up from where it stuck to the boardwalk and flapped into the air.

Further down, the Pier widened into a courtyard with an enormous carousel, made up of mammals on the middle tier, fantastic birds on the upper tier, and aquatic creatures on the bottom. In the dark, the sharks, tigers, and eagles looked terrifying. The steady ocean-fed wind rocked some of the animals, making it impossible to tell if they were swaying or moving on their own.

The wood beneath our feet creaked. Waves splashed against the pilings under our feet. A sea lion barked.

I listened for human sounds. Nothing.

We approached the carousel, guns at the ready. Hayes placed each step and rolled into the next, maintaining balance and silence. I moved more like the awkward, pre-teen ballerina I tried to be all those years ago.

Sound filled the courtyard. Sea lion or a man? I looked for Hayes but couldn't see him very well. He was intent on slinking his way around the right side of the carousel. He hadn't spoken. That much I was sure of.

I listened again, while carefully placing each foot and screwing up my face each time I produced a squeak in the wood.

A bark of sound. Human.

My eyes adjusted to the darkness. I made out more shapes to be anxious about. One looked out of place. Something protruded from the base of the ride. Legs? A seated figure.

As I came nearer, I could see it was a man, leaning up against the base of the carousel. Not moving. Not waiting in anticipation.

Zapper out and stomach contents in, I faced the man.

Rollins.

Bennie Rollins.

He sat there, eyes closed, hands dropped to his sides. I stood there. It was like Uncle Joe. Same final repose. The memory — of Joe. Of his killers. Of being helpless. It all came crashing down on my head. All the smells and sounds dragging memories up from the buried past. I was in New York again. My best friend in the world stared out at me with blank eyes. I never said good bye. I didn't save him. He was dead. Dead ...

This wasn't Joe. This was someone I could still save.

I shook my head hard, to get the memories to abandon ship. I reached out to Bennie's face. Yeah. Wet. Same as Joe. I felt for a pulse, terrified I'd find stillness.

There was something. Slight. I felt for it a second time. Yeah — Bennie had all the luck. Maybe his killer couldn't see any better than the rest of us and left him for dead.

Hayes was at my side. "Is he?" his whisper caught in his throat.

"No. Lucky him. Can you call for backup or at least a corpsman or ambulance?"

He shook my shoulder in affirmation, slid off his overcoat and draped it on Bennie. Out here, in this cold and damp, plus in his circumstances, Bennie was likely in shock. I covered Bennie's legs with my coat and made sure his hands were underneath.

The plaintive whine of the fog horn at the Gate cut through the air.

Hayes pushed off my shoulder, apologized before I could tell him to stop in ungracious terms, and used his strange radio dingus. Damn. He couldn't get a signal. He came back, pointed toward the front of the pier. I knew what he meant. He had to get away from the fortress of shops to get his message out. He then pointed decidedly to me and then the ground. Stay put. It wasn't a bad idea.

I watched the shadow figure of Hayes hurry toward the park entrance.

Alone. Wasn't this whole mess started the same way? Me, alone, somewhere I didn't belong? This time, I did belong here. I listened to the bark of a seal, while wind whistled through the carousel, shaking it and the animals. Staying with Bennie wasn't a bad idea except it left me with two options; leave Bennie or sit there accomplishing nothing to solve the case.

Bennie took a deeper breath. I checked his puls. No, it wasn't a death rattle. He was breathing a bit better, yet, he wasn't moving. I should have been here sooner. But 'shoulds' were useless to investigators. Help was coming for Bennie. In the meantime, I was the help that was coming for my client. Bennie would understand, or so I hoped when I picked up the zapper and set out, deciding where to go from here.

A shot rang out and left my every nerve tingling.

Cold rushed up and down my arms.

My client? Elliott?

I couldn't see if Hayes was returning.

It was only me on the case.

And that would be enough.

Apologizing to Bennie, I took up my zapper and plunged forward toward the shot. Using the buildings as my only guide, I found my way to the end of the pier.

Nothing.

The space was open. Sometimes they let women from a local ladies' club come here and do interpretive dance. Or local choirs. Or other pass-the-hatters trying to make a buck off of their art. I could see enough to know no one was here. Nor were there any bodies.

One shot. Why only one?

Edging to the back of the pier-end shops, my skin was getting wet and cold.

Who shot whom?

I pushed up against the wall of the cut-through to the back boardwalk.

Someone was moving. I could hear feet shuffling. Moving toward or away from the victim? From me? How many were there, alive or dead?

The fog horn wailed, louder than ever.

The end of the pier faced out to the middle of the Bay, Alcatraz, and Angel Island. Big waves crashed against the pilings and the breakwater about 50 yards away. Wind raced and howled between boats and signs, causing brass bells to clang and sail cloth to snap. Seated on the breakwater was a lighthouse supplied with enough power to provide a reasonable glow across the sailboat harbor and a painfully bright navigation beam. The beam swept the end of the pier, giving me enough extra light to confirm what I didn't really want to know. Lifting my zapper up to eye-level, I didn't shout, but neither did I whisper. "Is he dead? That's Willkie Valentini isn't it?"

On the plank boardwalk lay a figure. Large. One shoe sticking out from the pile of coat, hat, and body. A nicely polished shoe caught the tiniest flicker of light. I didn't need to guess who it was.

The figure standing over Valentini didn't move more than his head. He nodded. A second figure, bouncing and anxious, kept backing up.

I started the sentence a couple of times before it came out confidently. "It's over. You don't have to kill anyone else. Damn sure Skates Berk, over there, agrees. Won't you, Skates?"

The calm figure kept nodding, though my guess was he was doing it more out of reactive habit than providing an answer.

Skates stepped further into the harbor glow. "I didn't kill Valentini!"

"No, you didn't. You set him up though." I turned to the calm figure, staring down at the body. "Put your gun down. That's the only right move."

The figure started to laugh.

His arm raised, pointing his heater at me.

We all waited.

"You won't shoot me." I said while my feet pressed against the ocean worn boardwalk, ready to run.

"You sure?" the figure asked.

"Yeah, I'm sure. This is where you were planning to ruin my career while committing suicide-by-private-dick, isn't it? Maybe taking Skates out at the same time? No thanks. That's a job I don't want."

"You're too smart for your own good, Honey."

"And you've been a cop too long. Come on, Detective, you know this isn't going the way you wanted."

Somerset looked up at the sky, and then at me. He actually chuckled. "Where the hell did you get a rod like that?"

"Friend of a friend."

Skates stared at my zapper, eyes wide, jaw slack.

Shuffling to my right drew my attention over to my worst fear. Lockwood sat on the boards, hands cuffed behind his back and something stuffed in his mouth.

"Mr. Lockwood, it's alright."

"it isn't alright," Somerset asked. "I have to finish this, you know."

"Can't let you do that." I shifted a bit closer to the prone body. "Besides — you got your man."

Somerset nodded robotically again. I guess finally getting what he'd obsessed over for years hadn't satisfied him as he'd hoped. Never does.

Skates had a heater too, but he wasn't as sure with it as I'd expected. Some gangster. He couldn't decide who to point it at. He had three targets. Breathing hard and bobbing his head up and down like a puppet — I guess he'd made up his mind — he pointed it at me. "This is real simple. Valentini took Lockwood away from them, killed the other cop, and then killed Lockwood. Somerset here caught him and plugged him. Me? I ain't even here." He licked his lips. "Keep your yap shut, Honey, and this can work out for you."

"Your plan won't work, Skates. Lockwood isn't dead, and I won't let you shoot him." I looked to Somerset, who slowly glanced my way. "Bennie isn't dead either. I guess you couldn't kill your partner, even if you didn't like him. Even if he figured out what happened and confronted you. Bennie is a good man. He knew your obsession with Valentini was out of control. You'd do anything to take him down. Perhaps kill Frannie and try to frame Valentini for it. Or, maybe frame Skates, now he's getting the business empire and has plans to keep you in line."

Skates went rigid and nervously started pointing his heater around.

I needed Somerset on my side. Come on, Milt.

Somerset began to half laugh, half cry. "My partner, Bennie Rollins? He tried to stop me. My partner — and he tried to protect this animal." He pointed to the pile of clothing that had once been Valentini. "A man should be able to count on his partner. No matter what. He should stand by him. That's what men do."

"And that's what you need to do now," I was pleading with a madman. "Bennie is still alive. You were the good partner. You couldn't kill him. He was looking out for you, not Valentini." Somerset shook his head but I knew I was getting through to him. "He didn't want you ruining your name. And he was willing to stand by you,. That's why he came here. Now you can do one more good thing for him — help him to stay alive. Help yourself by ending this mess now. Lockwood comes with me."

"He ain't clean."

"Yeah I know." I avoided making eye contact with Elliott. Yeah, I knew. I knew a lot of things I never really wanted rolling around in my brain, but none of it mattered now. I didn't need all the details of how Somerset got Valentini out to the pier. My guess was it had something to do with Lockwood, as Frannie's only viable kin. It burned me up inside to think it.

Regardless of who capped who over what, the killing had to end. Valentini wasn't a good man, but I had good dealings with him and I couldn't help feeling sorry. He died for the one crime he didn't commit. Lockwood was my problem. And I didn't give a rat's ass about Skates so long as he didn't start shooting.

I kept my zapper pointed at Somerset. While he hadn't dropped his gun, at least he was moving it away from Lockwood. Okay. Maybe he wasn't determined to kill my client. Skates was another story, which meant I had to keep prodding Somerset's honor to get him on my side. "You're not a very good murderer, Milt. Maybe because you're a good cop?"

"This ain't murder. Do you know what this animal has done? He's the murderer with all the killing, all the money laundering, all the …" He choked on his words. "He had to die. I couldn't let him get away. Not again."

Where the hell was Hayes?

"Milt, did Skates tell you Valentini was quitting the business?" I nodded toward Skates. "You did tell him, right?"

"Of course I did." Skates was starting to rub his head and face, a little too much.

Somerset's bitter laugh echoed in my ears. "He told me — he and Frannie were sailing off into the sunset, leaving everything behind? You're a sap, Honey, if you believe it."

"Yeah, maybe I am a sap. I like a good love story, but in this case, they were leaving it all behind. Weren't they, Skates?" I kept my voice calm, even-toned, and non-threatening, which was a miracle to accomplish as I stood there trying my best to contain the shakes, from the cold night air and everything else unnerving me. Uncle Joe warned me. He didn't warn me enough.

Skates bounced his head in a sort-of agreement, lacking so much confidence I expected his next move was to swoon.

When I heard boards creak, I couldn't tell if it was my imagination or maybe …

The fog horn sounded, making me shiver involuntarily.

Somerset's voice cracked a bit. "He was going to escape. No justice. No paying for what he'd done." Somerset pointed his heater at the body.

For a hot moment I thought he'd shoot Valentini's corpse out of insane spite. "This has gone too far. You need to make things right, even if you have to take the fall. What you do next matters."

"Nothing else matters. It never mattered. Nothing but taking this goon out and I did it. I did it. I finally did it. All that's left is cleaning up the mess."

Now there was a line of thinking I didn't like. I definitely didn't like the question it raised about my future health as well as my client's.

Somerset turned his head toward Skates.

"You can't pin this on me," Skates shouted at Somerset.

"And he won't, Skates," I said, losing my calm control over voice. "Detective, what now? You have the option of letting Mr. Lockwood go, but if you were counting on Valentini taking the fall for all the other killings, it can't happen. It won't line up. I know you don't think much of me, but if I figured it out, you can bet your last dime on others putting the puzzle together."

Quiet suffocated the boardwalk.

The wind muffled its rage.

The waves crashed somewhere else.

I thought I could hear Somerset breathe.

"What does a man do when he has had one purpose in the whole world, and has now achieved it?" He looked in my direction. "And yet, there ain't the satisfaction he wanted."

"Because he didn't come by his achievement the right way," I said for him.

"The end ... the means?"

"If he's an honorable man," oh please let this work, "then he doesn't make things worse and faces the consequences of what he has done."

"You think I'm an honorable man?"

"Actually, yes. Single-minded, but yes, honorable."

He spoke to the fog, "You have no idea what I've done or what I am."

Talk fast Lou. Skates was getting twitchy too.

"I think I do. When you learned Frannie was running off with Valentini, and he would be out of your reach, you had to do something to get him to stay long enough for you to finally catch him. You chased Frannie into the Bayview area, tipped off she was there for business. That's when you and I first met. You were the man in the alley, with that knife of yours." I indicated the knife case on his hip.

"You were wearing a disguise, took me while to figure out who you were."

"Why you kept trying to keep me out of the case."

He shrugged.

Deep breath. Cleared throat. "As for you, you killed Frannie to frame Valentini. But you were seen, by Cab Proctor, who knew he might get framed because he was being blackmailed over an album of illegal photographs. That's a good motive for murder and one folks will believe long before they buy into a cop committing murder to frame a gangster. So, Proctor tried to kick the Coventry joint. He broke into the house to steal the photos Frannie held over him, to make sure there was no connection between him and the dead woman. Word got out, mostly because Proctor was a drinker and a bragger, that there had been a witness. Proctor had to be silenced. For that, you needed muscle."

Somerset chuffed a bit. "Honey, you don't know the half of it."

"I do know the other half of the hit squad was Irenie. I know she throws parties that should have landed her in the slammer. It required a Vice Cop on the take to keep her out of jail. She was extraordinarily jealous of Frannie and wouldn't want to lose control over her. Irenie wouldn't blink at killing her own daughter or making you do it. Was she forcing you to comply because it would help you frame Valentini or because it would end your career if anyone learned you had been protecting her Salons from the law?"

"Yeah, maybe you do know a thing or two." He took another, lingering stare at the sky. "You going to keep going?"

"You gonna' put that heater down?"

Somerset lowered but didn't drop his gun. "Go ahead. Let's see what brains you got."

Admittedly, I was half showing off and half stalling for time. Skates was rock still now, intensely listening to my story, though probably to see where he fit in. For the moment, it couldn't hurt to keep yapping. "Tonight, you used Mr. Lockwood to trick Valentini into coming out here. Not sure specifically how. Maybe you had my client tell Valentini he could have the engagement ring back? Valentini was a surprising romantic when it came to Frannie. I could picture him wanting the ring."

"Not bad. With all the moving parts of this ugly machine, I wasn't sure anyone would keep track."

"Always get the program guide. You can't tell the players without it."

"This game is done. All done."

"Not quite; your partner in Frannie's murder needs to be brought in, don't you think?"

When he didn't answer, I filled in the blank. "Irenie was the one who strangled her own daughter while you held Frannie. Bruises on her wrists showed up post mortem. You really didn't want to kill Frannie, did you? You did a half-assed job of cutting her up but when it came to the final deed, you couldn't."

"Irenie did it without a sweat. She has no heart. She did it like there was nothin' to it. Any other evening in the City."

Skates barked out a laugh easily mistaken for a sea lion. "I told you I didn't whack her. Jesus, her own mother did it?"

Yeah, I wasn't letting this goon get away, and I think I smiled at Skates while feeling the throbbing pain in my face and shoulder. "There's one killing we need to account for. Proctor could never be relied on to keep his mouth shut, and it was Valentini's second, Skates here, who thought up having him killed. Damn near got me at the same time. You know, Detective, you don't have to take that fall alone."

I turned my zapper on Skates. "Skates is your man for the Cab Proctor murder. He gave the order. You can at least arrest a big guy who works for him. Can't miss him, I apparently landed a slug in his arm."

"You bitch! What is it with dames these days? You shoulda' kept your nose out of my business!"

On my last words, Skates pointed his rod at me and shot.

I dropped to my left while Somerset fired. Skates flew backward, caught in the head by a .45 slug.

The boardwalk was silent again.

Why hadn't I fired?

I had a zapper for Christ's sake. I started to stand up.

Somerset then turned on me.

"Detective?"

"The whole mess has to be cleaned up."

255

Oh hell. "Detective, you saved my life. You can stop now. It's all over."

"No. I want it to be done. Lockwood ... you ... me. Yeah, me ... we're the last pieces."

"Detective," I lowered my voice and held up my free hand. "Think about this. It is all done."

He shook his head and aimed his gun at me, at the same time I pointed the zapper at him.

"Milt," I pleaded, like we were old friends.

Didn't work. I thought I could see tears on his face.

I grasped the zapper with both hands. Please God ...

He moved.

A ball of light exploded out of my zapper and Somerset stumbled. He looked at me and then the hole forming in his abdomen. The tunnel bore I'd shot through his torso grew bigger by the second.

He screamed and took one more step forward.

A second shot rang out.

By the way that Somerset fell, I knew it wasn't a bullet from his rod. He fell forward and flopped across the body of Valentini. The shot came from beside him.

Hayes and two government-looking types rushed forward to see what had been achieved. In another moment, they were putting away weapons and getting on their radios. Green-eyes reached down to help me up. My ears rang, all I could see was the smoldering coat on Somerset's back. I thought someone was shouting. People moving. And Hayes's arm around my shoulder, dragging me back to reality.

"Still with us?"

"Did you hear all of it?" I asked, forgetting to breathe. "Please tell me you heard all."

"Every word."

I waved him off, or something, I wasn't sure. Damn it. I stared at Somerset.

I'd killed a man.

No small thing.

Hayes walked over to Lockwood who sat glaring wide-eyed at all this. It took a bit to get the cuffs off, yet with his mouth free, he had nothing to say. Shock.

Hayes came back and stared into my eyes.

I looked at the Agent. "Some ... Somebody needs to go pick up Irenie Coventry. And possibly a big goon with a bullet wound who worked for Skates Berk." I pointed to what was once Skates Berk.

Nodding to me and wandering closer to the end of the pier, for a better signal, he called it all in on that marvelous personal radio he had. More policemen arrived, a fire department boat cruised near, the ambulance departed, and a coroner's van took over most of the courtyard inside the pier.

Lights started coming on, illuminating the slick boardwalk and the spraying ocean mist. I guess someone woke up the amusement park manager or found the right switches.

I stared at Lockwood.

"Lou?" He said while crossing his arms tightly and twisting his lips. I could bet he was trying to make sense of what happened. "He planned to kill me. I can't thank you ..." He reached out to me.

I held up a hand. "No."

There was a shattering sound I swear came from my heart. I am such a sap. I walked into this hurt with my eyes open, thinking I was ready. Thinking I was oh, so clever. Hey, so he's not innocent, I can handle it, right?

"Of course, I should thank you."

I felt the heat rising off my cheeks, despite the cold. "I said, no. I don't want your thanks. You've been lucky at best, and you're going to have to face the consequences of what you've done."

"Lou, I don't understand."

I understood. I understood all too well.

And ... I'd killed a man.

CHAPTER TWENTY-NINE

Try to stay alive ... if you can ...
and if you can't ...
Take the bastards down with you.

Lou Tanner, P.I. - 1935

Lockwood's laugh was forced and uncomfortable. "Lou, what are you saying?"

I took a deep breath. This wouldn't be easy. "You threw me under the train. You set me up. Yeah, I know, you didn't have a lot of choices, but you did it. One of your choices could have been telling the truth and standing by it."

Hayes and Lockwood exchanged glances. Green-eyes heard me and decided he needed to listen in. Good.

"A stray fact keeps bothering me. I've never been able to figure out why Frannie was in the Bayview neighborhood when I met her. She didn't belong there anymore than I did. But that spot is close to the Pointe."

Elliott started to pale, or so I thought. Lights on didn't help too much. Shadows were close, reaching out for us if we were foolish enough to turn our backs on them. The place looked older than it actually was, and the resulting sensation was cold, damp, and ugly.

"You may want to listen in on this, Agent Hayes."

Green-eyes positioned himself at the corridor leading away from the murder site.

Valentini was still waiting under a sheet to be moved off to the morgue on Drumm Street. Somerset had been pulled off of him and lined up beside him. Two men locked together in mutual hate and now all they had was each other in death.

I'd killed a man. I wasn't a sap anymore.

I took another deep breath. My insides and outsides raged at the brutal treatment they took on behalf of my gullibility. But nothing like the hammering my heart was about to take. And to give.

"You and your company, Mr. Lockwood, worked a sweet deal with the Militia over at the Pointe. You've supplied them for a while with raw materials. Is it better refined metals and batteries nowadays? Or more, if what I saw on Gilbert Halliday's desk is any indicator? Your cousin, Gilbert, you remember him?" I was being snide because I could. "All in all, not illegal though a little untidy morality-wise. Probably helped the War Department looked the other way." Hayes stifled a cough. "Frannie found out and in her practiced medium of blackmail, ingratiated herself into what was becoming a lucrative business. She became your partner, didn't she, in selling the Militia whatever they need and want?"

He kept staring, an unusual practice for Lockwood. I guess he didn't need to look away while facing the truth. No point in hiding.

Finally.

He agreed in the silence of shame.

"I don't know if you meant to or not, I'm choosing to believe you didn't but you set up Frannie by telling Irenie what was going on and where Frannie would be. You either told her outright or let it slip that Frannie was handling some business for you. Irenie of course told Somerset and sent him to kill Frannie. Somerset agreed to the opportunity to frame up Willkie Valentini. Irenie had simple needs — her daughter either home and under her control, or dead. As luck would have it, Frannie ran into me that night. Then she stole my cab."

Hayes and I watched Lockwood's face fall into exhausted relief.

"While I choose to believe you didn't fully understand the danger you put your stepdaughter in, you're still not off the hook yet, Mr. Lockwood. You've known all the players all along. You made friends with Somerset some time ago, meeting him through Irenie and helping her foot the bill to pay him off. All you wanted was to keep the cops at bay and to keep the Coventry girls from embarrassing you. Even if you didn't know Frannie was set up for murder, once you were in the middle of it all, Somerset had you by the short hairs. He made you set me up to be kidnapped and killed by Skates."

"No. Lou, I didn't." He reached out and touched my arm. A pitiful, pathetic electricity raced through me. This time I ignored it.

"Yeah, you did. Somerset came to arrest you at my office, but you expected the cop to let you go. Remember, you wouldn't give me your lawyer's name. Why? Because you were certain you wouldn't be under arrest for very long."

God he was pretty, but his eyes were betraying him. Those beautiful blue eyes. Sad. Frightened, as he glanced at Hayes every few seconds. Caught in the act. What a weakling, and I almost fell for him. Not "almost." I had. But I came to my senses.

He heaved a sigh. "Somerset said nothing would happen to you. He wanted you out of the way for a bit." Lockwood looked away. Damn it. There it was, the one lie I'd hoped he wouldn't tell.

My good will deflated — the only word I could think of. I had so hoped he would be more than a gentleman: he'd be honorable. "They drugged me and beat the hell out of me. They had every intention of killing me!" My voice ended on a shrill, higher note. "You aren't stupid, Mr. Lockwood. You knew what was at stake. Men like Skates Berk kill people. Somerset was dealing a dirty hand. You put your needs and profit ahead of everything, including me."

He pulled me in by the waist. "I tried to keep you out of the whole business." He wanted to be forgiven. "I told you to stop. I paid you off …"

I wanted none of this. I pushed him away, with every bruise, cut, and bullet hole screaming at me. "Five people are dead. And I killed one of them. Self-defense be damned, I killed a man." My heart shriveled up with every word. Even Uncle Joe hadn't killed anyone outside of a war zone.

Hayes stopped leaning against the wall. His hand dropped down on Lockwood's shoulder and gripped him hard. "We're going to want to ask you several questions, Mr. Lockwood. You'll need to come with me."

Lockwood glared at me, helpless, pleading for me to intervene.

"No, Mr. Lockwood." I could never call him Elliott again. "You need to go with him. I don't know if you broke any laws directly, but you have answers to give. And all the negative publicity you've been trying to avoid? I think the rabbit is out of the hat now and everyone knows how the trick was done. I'm sorry, but this is bigger than a murder or two. This is, oh hell, I don't know what to say to you anymore. Do yourself a favor and be honest for the first time this year. Maybe the first time in your whole life."

His face contorted in confusion, making me wonder what it was I ever saw in it, and maybe I was a bit relieved as Hayes handed him off to another agent, who took him down a corridor out past the carousel.

Me? I stood there, torn between calling myself a complete idiot and feeling pride in solving my first case. Yet, I couldn't get past the image of Somerset dying. His smoldering coat, his listless body draped over Valentini in some Shakespearean lover's embrace of death — because of me. He'd saved my life. Why? Why had he turned on me after saving me? I wasn't getting an answer. He was dead. It didn't matter to me that Hayes shot him in the head, Somerset was dying before that.

I heard you never forget your first kill. Do you ever get over it? Uncle Joe didn't offer any words of wisdom for this in his journal. The empty spot where my heart once pumped waited silent and frozen.

Hayes chewed on the inside of his lip, then announced to me, "Let me take the heat for Somerset."

I shook my head, not really listening to what he was saying.

Grabbing me by the shoulders, Hayes stared straight into my eyes — hell, into my soul. "I took down Somerset. My Lightning Gun, my take down. Do you hear me?"

"Don't lie for me," I whispered. "I didn't get into this business without knowing this could happen."

"Don't be naïve …"

I didn't hear the rest of what he said. I clung to "naïve" and felt my skin start to flame. "I won't take the fall for someone else, but I sure as hell won't let someone take it for me. I'm a grown woman. I'm a good P.I. You can't have my glory and you can't have my failures. Those are mine to have. All of them. Do you understand me?"

I watched as he shifted his weight away from me. My voice had been low, solid, and unwelcoming to critique. Uncle Joe once told me he only worried about me when I got quiet.

"Okay, Lou. They may ask a lot of uncomfortable questions. You may be giving depositions for days. But, you know that already, don't you?"

"Yeah. I know it. It comes with the territory."

"So does killing."

"It shouldn't. But it does. I better get used to it and quick. No one honest wants …" I stopped, letting the words fall away with the thought. I was explaining it to myself with Hayes as my audience. He already knew what I wanted to say. "Look, Agent Hayes." I took in a deep breath. "Thank you. I appreciate the gesture."

He opened his mouth, heaven only knew what he was planning to argue, what he was trying to convince me of. Damn glad he didn't. I didn't need him talking me out of my responsibilities.

I killed a man. I stared into his eyes and seen his life disappear into the ether. *Pemberton's* manual didn't talk about such topics in any conclusive detail. No one did. It was a dark secret left to carve a void in one's soul. All those doughboys coming back from the Great War? Yeah, I understood them now. How the killing of another human being left you not right with the world.

Would I get over it — recover my senses? Sure. Happens every day for a professional in this business, right, but the first kill was hard, while the next one gets easier and it keeps on getting easier. God help me, I never want it to be easy.

Behind me, the fog horns howled with laughter and I still wasn't sure if I got the joke.

Stan's place. I needed a drink, a pack of cigarettes, and some Billie Holliday on the radio.

I needed to cry too. But such matters were nowhere in the P.I. training manual.

END

ABOUT THE AUTHOR

T.E. MacArthur is a *New York Times* best-selling author – okay, that's <u>*not true*</u>, she's still working on it. There are, however, more than seven novels and novellas with her name on them, including the multiple award-winning paranormal thriller, **The Skin Thief**. She lives in the San Francisco Bay Area with her cat, Onyx Calypso, in the Lower *Catswold* District of her apartment.

Please come see what she's up next to at
www.TEMacArthur.com

Made in the USA
Middletown, DE
22 April 2024

53307635R00163